Arthur the King AD517

ISBN 9798223437130

Aenghus Chisholme
Angus Peter Chisholm

Cover by Emily Bell

Also by Aenghus Chisholme

Merlin the Sorcerer AD491
Guinevere the Queen AD494
Sir Gawain and the Green Knight AD499
Arthur the King AD517
Murder on the Mary Celeste
Jack the Ripper: The Murder of Madam Athalia
The Monster of Matlock
Don't Delay Writing Your Book

This book is dedicated to everyone who uncovers secret meanings.

Chapter 1: North Gyrwe

Arthur raised his sword and pointed in the direction of the enemy. Even at this distance it had an effect upon them that could clearly be seen. The line of Angle warriors squirmed and looked at each other uneasily. Arthur commanded his Knights and foot soldiers with a single, shouted word.

"Advance!"

Arthur's Knights repeated the King's order and it could be heard across the entire front line that his forces offered. The irony of using a perfect Roman battle strategy was lost on Arthur. The line of shield-carrying foot soldiers advanced upon the enemy while behind them the archers remained at the ready. The moment they were in range they'd be called upon. But for now, they hid in relative safety behind the men before them.

Arthur and his equidistantly-dispersed Knights rode upon their mounts within the line of soldiers. All of them knew that there would soon be a rain of arrows from the Angle's archers to contend with. The men were seasoned soldiers, however, and were well-trained with Arthur's battle strategy for this conflict in mind. They would endure the first salvo of arrows from the Angles. They'd almost certainly be fired too soon in the battle and would therefore fall short. And that is what happened next. A cry from behind the Angle troops could be heard and then followed a sound of a hundred quivers being released within moments of each other. The arrows that were released en-masse even made a sound as they cut through the air and arced toward Arthur's attack force.

Not a single one found a victim. They landed about ten paces away harmlessly, impacting in the grass-covered meadow. The warriors from Caerleon marched onwards. A panicked order to re-arm could be heard from behind the Angle's unbroken line of shields. Soon Arthur's forces were treading upon the arrows that had so distantly missed their marks. This was the signal that the King and his Knights were waiting for. They now knew without a doubt that they were within range of the Angles.

Unlike the Angles, Arthurs' archers hadn't yet wasted a single arrow in the conflict. But now they were assured that they were in-range and they were ready to fire. The king's men released a fusillade of arrows toward their enemy. They could be heard impacting some of the shields, but more importantly there were four or five screams from behind the barrier.

"Gather!" ordered Arthur.

The archers huddled with the foot soldiers. They ceased their advance and angled their shields, awaiting the second volley from the Angles. It came in a matter of seconds. Arthur and his Knights grabbed the shields for their non-sword carrying arms, strategically placed foot soldiers on either side of the horses carrying two shields each for the task. One was then used to protect the carrier and huddled archer and the other was pushed up to protect the head and chest of the horses. Arrows hit the shields but not a single cry of pain or anguish was heard from Arthur's forces.

"Advance!" bellowed Arthur.

The force began to advance again. The archers had used the time huddled beneath the shields to place another arrow in their quivers. For the second volley of arrows from Arthur's men though, they were less randomly aimed at getting over the disjointed barrier in front of them. They were now close enough to take proper aim at any targets that presented themselves. In a fluid movement, the foot soldiers angled their shields sideways to allow the archers a direct line of sight to the enemy. They used the scant moments wisely and took aim and fired.

Again more screams of pain could be heard from behind the Angle shields and here and there shields were dropped due to injury or death. The next phase of the Caerleon's attack was upon them.

There would be one last huddle together to ensure the third round of arrows did as little damage to the men as possible.

"Gather!" commanded the King.

The men created the smallest possible target by bunching together behind their tightly-held shields. The hail of arrows from the Angles did little except for impacting on the shields. Some of the Angle's archers must have been panicked because their aim was off. This was a tactical waste of arrows and opportunity. Arthur observed it from behind his shield. The battle was going well already.

Another well-timed movement of Arthur's men allowed the archers access to the front-line. The result saw yet another shower of arrows from his side cause damage and despair in the Angle force. But this was the last time that he'd use the archers in this campaign.

"Swords!" Arthur shouted.

His archers threw their bows and arrows to the ground and drew their swords. All of them were trained in swordsmanship as well as archery. This is where the Angles differed in their fighting tactics from King Arthur's troops. They were specialised fighters, either archers or swordsmen. Spears didn't seem to be part of their repertoire, either. Arthur knew this and had allowed for it in his precisely orchestrated attack.

"Now!" he bellowed. This was the signal for the push forward to engage in man-to-man fighting. Arthur's men surged forward. The King's shield-carrying men raised their shields in the last few steps of the frantic run to meet their enemy head on. And when the shields impacted shields, they were used to push the Angles defences downward and out of the hands of the men bearing them. The manoeuvre worked with deadly consequence. Now all of Arthur's men were engaged in sword play. The former shield carriers having now battered down the Angle defences discarded their shields and used their swords to wreak havoc.

"Kill the archers!" was the next command from Arthur. His troops were now solely concerned with dispensing with the Angle archers. This was because the Angle archers could still do much damage at close range. They needed to be dispatched first. Wherever possible the front line of Angles would be pushed aside so that the Angle archers could be slashed and jabbed to death. Only then would the Caerleon force turn to fight more appropriately with their equals, the swordsmen of the Angle force.

Men were screaming and crying out in pain, fear, exhaustion and anger. Blood could be seen in patches on the ground. There were dead and wounded already. Arthur was busy wielding Excalibur and decimating any foolhardy enough to attack him. His magical sword effortlessly sliced through chainmail, wood, leather and iron.

From his vantage point on the highest part of the meadow, Merlin the magician was keeping tally of the fatalities that Arthur was inflicting upon the Angles. He could see the minutest detail with his old eyes and nodded in satisfaction at what he was witnessing.

Down at the fray, Arthur's Knights were making more kills than his foot soldiers. But that was to be expected. The Knights were more skilled and battle-worn than even the oldest and most experienced of the foot soldiers. Merlin predicted that the battle would not last much longer. The Angles were broken, their force in complete disarray. So sure was he of the result that the old Sorcerer even looked away and over the countryside that Arthur was successfully annexing. The Angles had held North Gyrwe for Arthur's entire reign as King. But today it would become part of Arthur's monarchy. The Angles would be driven to the lands of South Gyrwe and even to the West.

"This is a good victory" Merlin said to nobody. Then as if hearing his own words had taken him back to reality, he focused once more upon the battle. It was exactly what he expected to see: the few surviving Angles were either surrendering or on the run. Arthur's victory was complete. The land was now his.

***

Merlin had walked the long distance from his place high on the meadow to join Arthur and when the king saw him coming he dismounted his horse and handed the reins to a nearby soldier to tend.

"A resounding victory my old friend" began the King.

"Thine Kingdom is now larger than any native ruler hath ever held before," Merlin responded. There was glee in the old man's eyes and in his voice.

"Tell me then, Merlin; why do I not feel victorious? Nor does the reality of ruling such an expansive Kingdom bring me any joy?" Arthur's tone was difficult to interpret. He was not venomous with his critique of his feelings, but there was definitely no sign of maudlin acceptance of a situation that he did not wish to endure. Merlin however, had heard this grievance before. It had become more and more prevalent over the past year. Merlin did his best to quell the King's disquiet.

Motioning for Arthur to view the land that he'd only just added to his holdings, he waited for Arthur to join him before speaking.

"There was a time when the thought of adding Humbor to thine monarchy was considered a step in the right direction. Yet it was a small victory compared to thine battle to drive the Angles from their positions in Lyndsey. With this conquest all of this land from here to the border of Northumbria and west to the river Trent is now part of thine united land. That is what should make ye feel victorious." He finished and turned to face his King, putting a comforting arm on his shoulder.

Arthur almost made to argue but then simply bowed his head and nodded. Instead of arguing the point with his old friend, he changed the subject.

"I shall leave Sir Dynadane in charge of the local town to administer in mine place. He fought bravely today for one so young." If Arthur had wanted to distract Merlin then this ruse did exactly that. The old Sorcerer squinted his face at Arthur in apparent disapproval.

"Sir Dynadane is still a boy. How old is he? Nineteen or...?" Merlin was clearly ready to continue upon his diatribe about Arthur's choice for regent in his place but the king corrected him.

"I became King at seventeen Merlin. I think at the age of nineteen Sir Dynadane is more than capable of ruling this area in mine name."

That was the end of it as far as Arthur was concerned. Merlin nevertheless let out a snort of discontentment with the decision. They walked together toward the approaching band of Knights. Sir Garethe was the first to speak.

"Only seven fled the battle toward the end, mine King. Seven left out of a hundred to tell the tale of our triumph to the other Angles." Garethe finished his sentence with a broad but weary smile. Sir Lyonell took up the thought.

"That number is more than enough to spread the word throughout South Gyrwe that this land is no longer theirs and has returned to the rightful King of all Briton."

Sir Bors De Ganys and Sir Alynore spoke over the top of each other, something in agreement with Sir Lyonell's words. But Arthur and Merlin were not listening. There were other matters to attend to now that the battle was over, matters other than just gloating about the conquest.

"Rally the men to see to our injured and dispose of the dead." It sounded callous but was a necessary part of any battle. Arthur was just being pragmatic. It was all that the Knights needed to end their chest-beating and continue with the aftermath of the fight. Knights could be heard shouting orders at troops.

Through the crowd of people Arthur caught the eye of the newest and youngest of his Knights.

"Sir Dynadane!" he shouted and motioned with his hand that the Knight should join him. The young man had blood covering his right thigh. His chainmail seemed completely intact so the assumption was made that it belonged to a vanquished Angle.

"Aye, mine King" he said as he approached. The Knight almost made to kneel before Arthur but the King waved away the pleasantry. Sir Dynadane was prone to being somewhat overawed with the presence of the King. Something that Merlin and Arthur both knew would take him time to get over.

"I intend that ye should take half the soldiers and set up in the nearby township of Stamfyd. Ye will impose the laws and ideals that I stand for and rule with. Ye shall be the representative of mine ownership of North Gyrwe, the land, the villages and towns and the people." Arthur finished his summation of the duty that he was bestowing upon the surprised youth. At first the Knight could do nothing other than blink his wide green eyes at the King. Then looking to Merlin as if to confirm what he'd heard, he began to stumble through a speech of gratitude. Arthur and Merlin smiled wryly. They could see that the young man was clearly overjoyed with his new appointment and duty. Somehow his unbridled ebullience reminded them both of their younger days.

Through the mostly stammered speech of acceptance and assurance that he would do everything that he could to ensure his was a fair and just administration, there was a query at the end.

"When do I leave for Stamfyd Sire?"

Arthur looked around him to see how the progress of cleaning up was coming along.

"As soon as we have finished here we will split our numbers. Half shall return with me to Caerleon; half will follow ye to Stamfyd."

This gave the unsavoury job of cleaning up the battlefield a new impetus for the young Knight. He bowed and joyously gave another small speech of gratitude for the King's confidence in him before turning, and with renewed effort, began assisting in the efforts around him. Merlin looked at Arthur.

"Maybe it was a good idea to appoint the youth. He seems full of vigour." Merlin's compliment was his way of telling the King that he apologised for making such a fuss over the issue in the first place. Arthur could read the signals from his life-long friend better than anyone, except maybe Merlin's twin-Sister Ganieda. They once more looked over the newly acquired land.

"Now it does feel like a victory," Arthur said.

Chapter 2: Caerleon Castle

Arthur's half of the force rode through the front gates of Caerleon castle to much fanfare. Even as they approached they could see the usual scurrying of people upon the battlements watching them approach. There was the usual cheering and gaiety riding through Caerleon village, now more of a township. But it was always the greeting by the inhabitants of the Castle that the Knights and King looked forward to the most. All of the Knights' wives and children had gathered with Queen Gwenhwyvar and Prince Amhar in the main courtyard.

They broke out in a unified voice of loud cheer as they rode into the area. None of the men could help but smile at the display of genuine emotion. The Knights waited for the King to bring his horse to a halt and dismount before they did. Loved ones surged forward to embrace their returning heroes. Gwenhwyvar walked steadily up to Arthur and held him close.

"Mine love, returned safely once more." It had become the greeting of choice for the Queen for quite some years now. Arthur was never sure if he was supposed to answer or simply kiss his beautiful wife. But he always felt comforted when he heard the words. Amhar too gave his father a warm hug.

"Greetings, mine King," he said as he held his father. Arthur was still a little unsure of how this had come to pass. Amhar was a strikingly handsome man of twenty-five years. Since becoming a Knight in the service of Arthur's realm he had ceased to refer to Arthur as his 'father,' or even the more child-like 'Da'. Arthur missed being denoted as a parent should be, but did not insist upon it from Amhar. He felt that his son knew his own mind and used whatever expressions he thought were suitable.

"North Gyrwe is now part of Briton once more and no longer in the hands of the invaders" Even as Arthur reported his success to

Gwenhwyvar and Amhar he noticed that Amhar almost winced at the news.

"It is good to hath ye returned to us. There are matters of state that will need to be attended to." The mysterious inference from Gwenhwyvar brought a look from Arthur.

"Oh?"

"I bear sad news mine husband," she continued. "King Rhydderch Hael of North Rheged has died of old-age. Queen Ganieda was at his side and comforted him though his final days. His body was set adrift in the sea to find its way to Avalon. Eternal peace shall be his after a lifetime of fair and just rule. Ganieda now rules as regent in thine name."

Gwenhwyvar delivered the news in as dignified a manner as she could, befitting her position, and Arthur could see from a glace around that the people closest to the trio were waiting for a response from him. He turned to address those within earshot.

"King Rhydderch Hael will long be remembered as a true Briton that held the same vision as do we all, a united land for none other than ourselves."

This garnered a round of nodding and "Aye's" from those that had heard the announcement. Out of the corner of his eye Arthur managed to catch Amhar once more react as though he had been somehow injured by the words that he had spoken. Arthur wanted to ask him directly what was wrong, but held back. He would wait until the two of them could talk in private.

At that moment Mordrede made his way through the crowd to greet the King. Like Amhar, Mordrede had grown into a fine man. His flowing hair was a blonde version of Arthur's. Time had seen him grow to look much more like his mother now than when he was an infant. When they played together as children, Amhar and Mordrede were clearly brothers, or at least very similar looking half-brothers. But age had given Mordrede more of a look that assured that everyone knew that he was Morgan's progeny.

"I hope that there were no injuries that Merlin could not remedy mine King?" he asked as the two clasped each other's forearms in salute. Arthur smiled and shook his head.

"The Angles were predictable and easily defeated. Neither of ye missed much of a fight. The next time I free a part of Briton I will be sure to take both of ye with me." Arthur's response was designed to help them overlook the fact that he had left them here rather than joining them in the battle. Mordrede responded to the offer.

"It was an honour to be the Knight's chosen to guard Caerleon in thine absence Sire," he said. Then changing the subject he added, "I see that mine mother hath found the arms of her most favoured Knight."

Mordrede motioned toward his mother. The small crowd turned their attention in that direction. Morgan was embracing Sir Hemison. They had become quite an element of courtly gossip over the last few months.

"Thine mother hath chosen well Mordrede," said Gwenhwyvar. "Sir Hemison is a fine man and a skilled Knight."

"As ye say mine Queen," smiled Mordrede. He clearly had absolutely no objections to the pairing, but wanted to make light of it anyway. "Mine mother's happiness is long overdue; she devotes too much of her time toward aiding others and not enough time tending to her own needs."

Mordrede got no objections from any of the royals. They all knew how much time and effort Morgan put into curing the ill and in general casting spells that would assist the crops, the villagers and the inhabitants of the Castle.

"Come inside, ye must be hungry and thirsty after thine journey," Gwenhwyvar's offer was too tempting to refuse. He looked over to his mount to ensure that one of the stable hands was tending to the mare. Seeing that this was the case he agreed with an "Aye" and a weary smile. They all headed in the direction of the main doors and the comforts that waited inside.

***

A curious thing happened as they passed through the main entrance and turned toward the banquet hall. There was a large tapestry that was hanging to the left of the main doors that they walked past. It had been there some five years now and depicted in life-size all of Arthur's Knights that were with him when the tapestry was made. There were twenty at that time and all of them were handsomely represented by the skill of the tapestry weavers that created the artwork. King Arthur was depicted at the centre with ten Knights to his left and ten to his right. Except that there were eleven Knights to Arthur's right.

If any of the passers-by had noticed and taken a closer look, it could be seen that the additional figure was not even dressed as the other Knights were. He was a tall man with a long thin face. His expression was menacing. His dark eyes followed Arthur as he walked past.

Subliminally alerted to something or maybe because he had part-inherited his mother's other-worldly abilities, Mordrede glanced backwards as he passed the tapestry. However, nothing out of the ordinary caught his attention. The mysterious figure was gone.

Chapter 3: The Round Table

Arthur was walking around the Round Table. There was nothing on it. The chairs were all at the side of the room. He looked at it as though he were seeing something though. A man appeared at the door and stood unsure if he was supposed to enter. Too afraid to speak, he waited for the King to notice that he was there.

Arthur looked up impatiently, waiting for the man that he'd summoned, and found him standing at the door.

"Excellent, come in," he said with a 'come here' gesture of his right hand. The man walked quickly across the floor and then bowed deeply. He was still a little too intimidated to actually say anything so he simply rose from his bow and gave the King a look as if to ask, *what is it?*

"It is said that ye hath travelled the length and breadth of this land, selling your clay pots and statues carved from wood and stone," Arthur said. "Your skill is in great demand. I am fortunate to hath ye in Caerleon Castle at this time."

Arthur's small speech gave nothing away and forced the man to respond, although he didn' know exactly what he was responding too.

"Mine thanks, King Arthur. I am humbled to be in thine presence." Then he asked, "Is there something that I can carve in stone or wood for ye?"

"Clay," replied Arthur.

"Surely" said the artist," There is plenty of it in the ground to the east of the Castle. What is it that ye would like me to mould mine King; a likeness of thine regal head?" guessed the man.

"A map of Briton, covering the Round Table" he said, whilst motioning to the large structure. The man was immediately intrigued. He looked more closely at the table. It was large. Certainly large enough to seat all of Arthur's twenty-four Knights around it and still leave room for the Queen and the two Caerleon magicians. This was quite an undertaking, one that filled the man with anticipation.

"A wondrous idea, Sire. I do not know of the like anywhere in Briton, 'twill be unique in the land." He was clearly relishing the idea of the new commission.

"Then ye will do it?" asked the King. In the sculptor's mind there was no-doubt.

"Aye, mine King, of course I will!"

"Excellent, ye shall have access to mine library of maps, the finest in the land to reference during the..." Arthur hesitated for an appropriate word to finish his sentence, "...construction. I wish it to be as accurate as possible and reflective of the current borders of mine Kingdom. How long do ye think 'twill take to complete?"

He waited eagerly for the man to reply. The clay-worker furrowed his brow and rubbed one cheek whilst he contemplated the size of the task. Arthur interjected in the hope of influencing his estimate.

"Ye shall have access to as many assistants from mine Castle, and Village as ye needs."

This gave the commission a new angle of intrigue. He could avail himself of a small workforce to dig up the clay and have it prepared for him. This would save him from doing it himself. Access to the King's maps meant that he wouldn't have to try and remember all of his journeys without visual assistance. He could even have a couple of understudies engaged on the more tedious aspects of the build whilst he crafted the more intricate parts of the map. He estimated exactly how long it would take and then added a week just to be sure that he didn't understate the timeframe he'd require.

"Three weeks, mine King." He said with a confident air.

"Excellent, ye can begin at once. See mine head of Kitchen and tell him of my desires, he will gather for you the people and materials that ye need."

The audience was at an end. With a satisfied final look at the soon to be transformed table, the artist bowed and hurried in the direction of the kitchen, eager to begin work on his new piece.

***

Later that day Arthur was sitting in his study by the window. He'd sent for Amhar, mainly because he hadn't had the chance to talk with him in private since returning from Gyrwe the previous day as there was so much that needed doing. Amhar arrived with a recognisable knock at the door. Arthur looked up from reading a scroll and bade him 'enter.'

"Amhar; good, come forth and sit with me," he said.

The young Prince closed the door behind him and collected a stool which he carried over and placed near to his father. He sat and looked expectantly at the King. Arthur paused briefly considering his words before he spoke again.

"Amhar, I can sense that there's something that troubles ye. Speak to me as a son to a father and not as a Knight to his King; tell me what bothers thine thoughts."

Amhar was a little taken aback at the thought of bringing his private grievance to his father so abruptly. But he garnered his bravery, took a breath and expressed himself as best as he could with his words.

"For many years thine ambition hath been to unite our land and drive out the invaders. This one goal hath occupied thine entire Kingship for these past twenty nine years. But consider how the land and the people hath changed over these almost three decades. Since ye set out on this quest, the Angles, Saxons and Jutes hath become entrenched in the land, tilling it for food, working as artisans in their villages and townships." Amhar paused briefly, contemplating his next polemic invective.

"Marriages occur, children are born and they grow up with parents, not Saxons, or Angles or anyone that they think of as invaders. They are just families like any other. In the coming decade these children that hath matured here in our land, will in turn find wives and begin families as well. What are we to think of these offspring? Do they hold true the ways observed in the old lands from which their grandparents originated?"

Amhar looked as if he was expecting a response, even though to Arthur it seemed toned as a rhetorical question. Arthur wasn't sure whether to answer or wait for Amhar to continue speaking. He gently furrowed his brow and almost imperceptibly shook his head. This was interpreted by Amhar as agreement with his thinking rather than a sign of not-quite understanding it.

"Excellent! Father I am relieved that ye can see mine point of view." Amhar let out a visible sigh at the end of his statement. Arthur for his part was more perplexed than he was before Amhar had started talking.

"I feel sure that when those Grandparents that ye speak of are driven from Briton then they will surely take their offspring with them." Arthur stated what he thought may be the point that Amhar was trying to make. It clearly was not from the expression of horror on Amhar's face.

"No!" he shouted at his father. "That is not what I mean to say! Ye hath not heard a single word that I hath uttered!"

Amhar was very annoyed. Arthur was stunned at the reaction from his son. The raised voice served to pique Arthur's temper. He slapped the scroll that he'd been holding down in his lap noisily, and with a firm and loud voice demanded to know exactly what was the cause of Amhar's concern.

"What do ye mean then? Are ye not telling me that the longer we wait to evict the invaders the more of them we shall hath to deal with!?" He leant forward looking directly into Amhar's eyes and waited for confirmation that he had indeed correctly interpreted what his son was saying.

"No Father!" he shouted. "Time hath past ye by! We hath no invaders in the land anymore! There are only Britons!"

This infuriated Arthur and he jumped to his feet as though Amhar had struck him across the face. The accusation that he had allowed time to pass him by as if it were something that he could have prevented made no sense to him at all. And the further criticism that the land no longer held any people that could be considered invaders was absolutely absurd.

"Of course they are invaders! They come from the homelands of the Jutes, the Angles and the Saxons. Their place is across the sea and not on this land with us! The very thought that they may hath taken Britons for wives or husbands only means that there are those from within our borders that betray everything for which I hath devoted my entire office to remedy. They should be sent far from here, they hath no rights to be counted as Britons loyal to our land and our ways!"

Amhar made to interject but Arthur was in no mood to be interrupted whilst he was admonishing his son for this idiotic viewpoint.

"What if the Romans hath never abandoned our land willingly; wouldst thee say that after so long a time they are now Britons and not Romans!?" the king continued. "They hold only their allegiance to the Emperor in Rome. They do not integrate or become a part of the people that they conquer. The Saxons and the rest are no better. They seek to subvert and occupy our land. If they do that by taking Britons into their bed, then it is only because they are insidious and need now more than ever to be stopped. Mine thanks Amhar for opening mine eyes to the real problem that we face. I shall prescribe a more urgent focus upon removing all of them from our land as soon as it can be accomplished."

Amhar stood up and faced his father just a clenched fist's length away from his face.

"Ye are wrong father! There are no invaders....." Amhar was clearly about to restate his outlandish point of view and Arthur was in no mood for it. But nor was he in any mood to continue a shouting match with his son. He thought quickly of a way to end the conflict. He interrupted Amahr.

"I hath need of thine services to travel to North Rheged and pay a visit to Ganieda," Arthur said with a narrowed eye. "Ye will be mine representative on a mission of diplomacy."

The ruse to divert Amhar's attention from the current argument worked. He was taken off-guard at the offer of an ambassadorial mission to the north. He had not seen Ganieda for at least five years. During his boyhood she'd become a regular visitor to Caerleon. He had grown very fond of Merlin's twin sister. She was a wise and kindly old woman who always had a way of making him smile.

"North Rheged?" was all that Amhar could think of to say in reply to the offer. Arthur could see the calming effect that the assignment was having so he pressed his advantage.

"As Regent, ruling North Rheged in mine place without King Rhydderch, Ganieda will be requiring more assistance from us than was needed in the past. In time when she passes over to the otherworld, I shall need to place one of mine Knights in the Castle to administer in her place. Thine mission will be to lend any assistance that Ganieda requires and learn more of the nuisances of the ruling the land and people of North Rheged. This shall yield valuable information for us to use in the coming years. Do ye understand what is required of ye?" Arthur tilted his head waiting for confirmation that his orders had indeed been understood. Amhar had some questions racing through his mind but did not want to seem hesitant in the face of such a prestigious undertaking. Instead he chose only the most urgent question from his silently thought list.

"How long shall I stay with Ganieda before returning with mine findings?"

The question pleased Arthur immensely and it showed in his tone and on his face. "One month should be sufficient. Return to me then and report thine findings" he responded. Then anticipating what Arthur hoped would be Amhar's final question he finished off with, "Leave tomorrow and take one of the other Knights with thee; to let Ganieda know that we value her allegiance to us."

There was a moment's silence. The only thing that could be heard was the rain that had started to fall outside. Amhar took a step backwards and bowed to his father.

"Mine thanks, King Arthur. Thine trust in me is not misplaced."

With his thoughts still full of questions, Amhar turned and walked to the door. As he opened it he looked back at his father who smiled at him. He opened the door to find Gwenhwyvar standing there.

"Mother?" he said and stepped aside to allow her to enter the room.

"Amhar was just leaving," Arthur said to his wife. Amhar needed no further cajoling, he left closing the door gently behind him. Arthur looked at Gwenhwyvar.

"Listening at the door?" he said with mock accusation. She smiled and responded.

"It would hath been hard to not hear ye even down stairs in the main hall" she said exaggerating the volume of the shouting that she had been privy to. Arthur threw his arms in the air in exasperation.

"What ails the boy? Where does this madness come from? Saxons to be considered as Britons? Never!" he finished his summation of the problem for his wife. Then he motioned at her.

"Did ye know of this bizarre point of view?" she looked sheepish and he knew instantly that she did.

"He hath grown into a man that hath his own opinions on everything, Arthur. It is to be expected that he does not share every though and belief that ye hold dear. That is the way of things."

She hoped that her words would somehow explain Amhar's passionate viewpoint and make Arthur more receptive to it, or at least less offended by it, but Arthur just groaned and rolled his eyes. Gwenhwyvar knew that she had been unsuccessful in moderating his demeanour toward Amhar.

"Why can he not leave the burden of rule to me and simply follow all of mine commands?" it was definitely a rhetorical question but Gwenhwyvar answered nevertheless.

"Perhaps he did not express himself properly," She offered as consolation. "Try to have the same conversation with him again when he returns from visiting Ganieda."

Arthur raised an eyebrow at the hearing abilities of his wife through the thick oak door. She had even managed to overhear the parts of the conversation that were not shouted. The look on her face told Arthur that she was genuinely looking for a happy medium for the two men to reach. Unable to resist the wiles of his wife even after these many years he nodded his acceptance of the proposition.

"Aye, perhaps the time away from Caerleon will do him good. I shall undertake to discover the meaning behind his...unusual opinion upon his return." He looked to Gwenhwyvar hoping to see a pleased look upon her face and was rewarded with just that.

"Now," she said, changing the subject, "what is happening at the Round Table? There is a flurry of activity from various servants around it, and I do not seem to know why. What shall I tell the ladies of the court? That the kitchen staff know more than their Queen...how can this be?"

Gwenhwyvar was just a little put out and being left in the dark, but Arthur was jolted. He'd forgotten to tell anyone but the sculptor about his plan for a new type of map of the land.

"The Round Table? Aye of course. Let me tell ye exactly what I hath planned"

He began to tell his wife of the commission that he had given to the artist.

***

Unnoticed by either of them, one of the tapestries hanging on the wall was watching and listening to them. The thin-faced man was now a part of the wedding scene that was depicted. The man's dour expression was in stark contrast to the happy faces that were skilfully woven and portrayed in Arthur and Gwenhwyvar's wedding scene. He had a look of menace upon his evil face. He listened to every word that had taken place in the room since the entrance of Amhar. With each passing day he amassed more and more information about King Arthur and his court.

Chapter 4: The Township of Stamfyd in North Gyrwe

Sir Dynadane had been less than enthusiastically welcomed by the people of the largest town in the area of North Gyrwe. They were a mix of Britons and Angles that had married into Briton families. Mostly there were just women, children and men too old to have participated in the battle against Arthur's annexation of the land. Clearly there were now quite a number of women that had become widows when their husbands died during the conflict. They were the most vocal in their derision of the Knight and his force when they marched into town.

It was a difficult mission for such a young Knight, but one that Sir Dynadane was eager to carry out to the best of his ability. He wished to prove to King Arthur that his faith had not been misplaced in him. Finding the person that could be best considered to be the town elder he wisely moved to make peace with him first of all and assure him that the bloodshed was over and that life beneath Arthur's rule would be fair and just. Also, and most importantly of all, safe from further conflict; Arthur had yet to lose any of his lands to a challenger.

He had eventually won-over the old man and even moved in with him so that the townspeople could see that the elder had accepted him as the new administrator. The foot soldiers were scattered around the township to find their lodgings where they could. They were to remain visible, rise early and patrol the township assisting the locals where they could and in general making themselves useful.

The strategy had taken time, but it had eventually worked. Life in Stamfyd began to settle into a happy routine. The mourning widow's lamentations had eased. Trade with the neighbouring villages had re-started. Replacements for the roles that the deceased men had held were for the most part taken over by the foot soldiers. Where this was not possible, Sir Dynadane and the town elder had negotiated for replacements from other towns, or promoted the apprentices to their master's roles.

***

It was about three weeks into his role as overseer when Sir Dynadane noticed a man in the main street of the township. He saw him from afar and tried to get a better look at him through the crowd. The Knight was certain that he'd not seen this particular man before. He stood out because he was of the age of someone that would have most surely been conscripted into the battle to defend the area from Arthur's advance.

He was squinting to get a better look at the man when someone interrupted him with a question about some iron-work that was left undone by the now deceased Ironmonger. He turned his attention to the local that was questioning him.

"Fear not, the new Ironmonger arrives this week to take-over the work that hath been left fallow. It will take some time for him to get through the backlog of commissions, but if it is not complicated then perhaps the apprentice can do it for ye?"

"Simple nails Sir Dynadane. We hath been waiting for them since before the battle. How are we to finish building our new inn without them?" The old builder was clearly irate. But now Sir Dynadane understood the exact details of the grievance.

"Nails should be one of the first things that an apprentice is taught in his trade. I am sure that the young boy will be able to produce them for ye. He simply lacks organisational skills. I shall direct him that building materials such as nails and hinges are to take precedence over the cooking utensils that he is currently working on. Will that be acceptable?" he asked, hoping that his diplomacy was once again going to save him from yet another complainant. He was correct. The old builder was pleased that his nails would now receive the priority that he thought that they deserved.

"Aye, Sir Knight. That would be acceptable. Mine thanks." He gave a small bow of his head and walked away satisfied that his supply problem would soon be relieved. Sir Dynadane looked around for the man that had previously garnered his attention but he was nowhere to be seen. At that moment one of the foot soldiers walked past him. The Knight beckoned him over. The soldier hurried forward and asked a simple query.

"Aye Sir Dynadane"

"There is a man that I hath seen. He looks quite Saxon in appearance. Perhaps twenty-five years of age. He wears a dark brown cloak, hath shoulder-length hair that is very light-brown in colour. Pass the word amongst the other soldiers to watch for this man. If they see him, bring him to me. Do ye understand?'

"Aye" said the soldier.

"Go" instructed the Knight. With all of his men engaged in the search for the stranger, it would surely not be long before he is identified. Sir Dynadane had a feeling that he should detail and question this man. Satisfied that he had done what he was able to for the time being he set off toward his lodgings.

***

Sir Dynadane answered a knock at the door. He opened it and found two of his men holding a struggling man between them. It was the stranger that he had seen only a few short hours earlier.

"When did ye find him?" asked the Knight.

"Hiding in the stables Sir Dynadane" answered the Caerleon foot soldier. Sir Dynadane looked at the man. He was angry.

"Bring him in," he ordered the soldiers. It would be best to conduct the interrogation away from the prying eyes of the townsfolk. The soldiers practically dragged the squirming man inside the stone hut. The Knight closed and latched the door affording them privacy.

"What is thine name?" asked the Knight. The man responded by simply glaring malevolently back at him.

"From whence do ye come?" Dynadane continued. He was met with the same silent stare of hatred. Sir Dynadane advanced upon him menacingly. The man did not flinch or try to shirk away. Leaning in toward his face the young Knight tried to be as imposing as he could.

"Why stay silent unless ye are a spy from those filthy Saxons?" He accused the man. It was a calculated guess. The man could just as easily have been a spy from the Angles or Jutes, but Sir Dynadane was following his gut-instinct. And by adding an insult about the Saxons in general, he was hoping to illicit a reaction from the stranger. He was more successful that he had expected. The man twisted his face and angrily spat directly into the Knights face.

Sir Dynadane turned his face away in reaction and wiped the spittle from his forehead. One of the soldiers punched the man in the face in retaliation for his show of disrespect to a Knight of King Arthur's Round Table. He shouted as much to the man after doing so.

The stranger was left with a bloody nose and with an even more defiant look upon his face. The soldier that had punched the man made to do so again but the Knight held up his hand.

"No. I hath a better way of extracting the information from him," said the Knight ominously. He turned away and waked over to the fire. There was a small cast-iron pot with water near to the hearth of the fire. He swung the pot out by the swivel arm that held it in place. Inside the pot, water had been heating. The Knight drew out a wooden mug worth of it. He rummaged through some of the belongings on the nearby bench and came across what he was looking for.

A small package wrapped in a rough material. It was about the length of his thumb and twice as thick. He undid the contents and exposed them for all to see. It was a solid mass of black something, which he dropped into the hot water. Then finding a wooden spoon he stirred the mug vigorously. The two soldiers and the captive man watched. The soldiers were curious to the goings-on the man was worried but tried to not let it show. Were they planning to threaten him with poison he thought.

The Knight returned to the trio.

"Hold his nose," he ordered. The man's nose, still dripping blood was grabbed by one of the soldiers. It must have been painful because the man let out a stifled cry of anguish.

"Open his mouth," ordered the Knight next. The other soldier dug his nails into the lower lip of the man and dragged his protesting mouth open. Sir Dynadane poured about half of the liquid into his mouth. With a nod and before the man could spit it out his mouth was forced shut and lips painfully held together tightly. The man coughed and gagged but swallowed the hot foul tasting liquid. The process was repeated with the remainder of the brew.

After he had been forced to swallow the second half, Sir Dynadane signalled for the men to release his mouth and nose. The man greedily gulped air and coughed trying his best to compose himself under the circumstances. He gave the Knight a look of pure malice. He had no idea what he had just been forced to swallow, and not knowing was somehow worse than knowing exactly what it was.

"It will not take long to work, perhaps half of an hour. Find a quiet place where he can lay his head to rest, and tie him to the bed. Let me know when he is asleep." The Knight waved the two soldiers away. He unlatched the door allowing them to exit.

***

The soldiers had found a hut nearby that was abandoned by the man that had once lived there. He was one of the victims of the battle against Arthur's troops and had no wife and no other relatives so the hut was not in use by anyone. It was a simple round cob walled dwelling with a thatched roof a stone chimney and only one window. The man was tied to the bed protesting for a lot of it, but more sluggish than he had been. The fight seemed to have gone out of him.

Sir Dynadane was summoned when the man was peacefully sleeping. The Knight entered the hut. It was almost sundown by this point. He produced a memory stone from within his robes and with a length of material bound it to the head of the man so that it rested in the very centre of his forehead. He was watched in wonderment by the two men that had accompanied him this far.

"What are ye doing, Sir Knight?" asked one of the soldiers, unable to contain his curiosity any longer.

"The brew was a simple mixture from Merlin to aide in sleep and to bring back the memories that one wishes to hide the most. And this," he indicated to the stone, "will capture the memories so that we may see them for ourselves."

The men could scarcely believe what they were hearing. But they did not know that these devices were now widely distributed amongst the Knights of the Round Table. It was part of a directive from Arthur that the Knights be given the means to extract information from any potential spies caught in his realm. Merlin had prepared memory stones for the Knights and the sleep/memory brew. He had instructed them upon their correct use. And even how to view the contents of a freshly populated memory stone.

"Post guards to watch him all night. And most importantly remove the stone before sunrise and bring it to mine quarters. Do ye understand?" he looked at one then the other.

"Aye," replied one.

"Aye Sir Dynadane," responded the other. Satisfied that his orders would be carried out, the Knight left and made his way back to his quarters. His work was done for the day, he could now enjoy an evening meal with the town elder and retire for the night.

Chapter 5: The Contents of the Memory Stone

Sir Dynadane was awoken before sunrise by a loud knocking at the door. He jumped out of bed. He was wearing only a white tunic. He opened the door. It was a foot soldier. Even in the dim light he could see the look of satisfaction on the man's face. He was delivering the memory stone to the Knight as instructed. Sir Dynadane reached out and took it from the man.

"Mine thanks," he said and closed the door on the soldier without a further word. He walked over to the fireplace and drew out a long thin candle and lit the end in the still-smouldering embers. Taking the newly-ignited flame, he lit a lamp near to the fireplace, then looked over his shoulder. The village elder, Mynwhyss, whom he had taken lodgings with, watched him from his bed. He'd been disturbed from his slumber by the loud knocking at the door.

"Go back to sleep, Mynwhyss," instructed Sir Dynadane. He didn't offer any further explanation. Taking the stone, the young Knight studied it in the light of the lamp. It emanated a small glow from within. This was a good sign. It meant that it was full of memories. This was exactly what he'd hoped for. All of the secrets that the captured, and still not yet convicted 'spy', was holding within his thoughts were now contained within this stone. Sir Dynadane had everything that he needed in order to now make a proper judgement about the incarcerated stranger.

Sunrise was still at least an hour away. The farmers would already be up and milking the cows. But Sir Dynadane snuffed out the flickering candle and retired to his bed. Clasping the stone tightly in his hand he first lifted it to his head and touched his forehead. Then he held it tightly and allowed the gentleness of sleep to overcome him. Soon he was fast asleep.

***

Sir Dynadane was in an assembly of people. It was large, there were more than he could readily count. He surveyed them. These were surely Saxons, but more than that. The blonde, striking features of the Saxons were interspersed with those that he could have sworn were Angles and Jutes as well.

"Mine friends," someone was shouting whilst banging on a table. This was the largest hall that he had ever seen. It eclipsed the largest all in Caerleon. He wondered where it was. And yet, somehow he knew exactly where it was located. This was Sussex and the Castle of the former King Aelle, now long since dead of natural causes.

"We are agreed then!" continued shouting the man that was trying to garner everybody's attention.

"The threat of King Arthur to our sovereign borders can no longer be tolerated. We must take action to ensure that our lands and our villages and peoples are safe from his incessant incursions." There was a lull in the overall din that was the murmuring of the large crowd. The man speaking was somehow known to Sir Dynadane even though he had never seen him before. This was Cymen one of the three sons of Aelle, former King of Sussex.

"I say that we unite and hold fast against King Arthur," he was still speaking when someone in the crowd challenged his idea.

"Arthur is powerful; he has a skilled force and two magicians to assist him. What chance would we stand against him?" With this observation the crowd noise once again rose to a shouting between people. Again Cymen had to try and restore order.

"If not a direct confrontation by any one of our outposts, then what?" he posed the question to the crowd. There was more shouting of ideas, but none substantial enough to draw the attention of the host of this gathering. Instead he offered a solution of his own.

"No direct conflict with Arthur then. But what about this?" his words brought an almost-silence to the large hall. Cymen continued.

"Let us therefore agree to unite in battle against Arthur should he threaten any one of us. As a unified army of Jutes, Angles and Saxons, not even Rome itself could stand against us! Arthur will surely not take us all on at once!?" His idea gave rise to some healthy debate. There were shouts of 'how can we depend upon...each other," emanating from the attendees. Again Cymen had to wait for the noise to subside before he gave more detail about his idea.

"We will sign a covenant that should King Arthur try to engage any one of our peoples in battle then the others will rally behind them as one. Not even Arthur and his Knights and Magicians can hope to stand against the combined might of all of our peoples?" the overall idea found favour with the crowd. There was the sound of acceptance of the onlookers. Cymen looked for the representatives that were appointed as the spokesmen for the Angles and the Jutes, but they'd disappeared into the crowd at some time during the debate. But now satisfied that they had the agreement of the people that they represented, they made their way back to the place where Cymen was standing with his two brothers.

There was a clasping of forearms between the three men and a fierce nodding of the acceptance and belief that the agreement was exactly what they needed to assure their continuance in the land. It was done. The three of then turned to face the assembly. Cymen spoke.

"We are united against Arthur the aggressor. He will not drive us from our homes!" a cheer louder than anything that Sir Dynadane had ever heard before erupted from the men. It awoke him from his dreaming.

***

Sir Dynadane sat upright in his bed. It was morning and Mynwhyss was busy preparing some food over by the now fully stoked fire. At first he was a little disoriented. He was unsure of how 'real' the dream had been. Unclasping the memory stone he looked at it and recalled everything that he'd seen in his vision. The spy that he'd captured must have been looking for support for the plan that Cymen and the other leaders of the Jutes and Angles had agreed upon. Both that and spreading the word within their borders, he knew.

Mynwhyss spoke, jarring the young Knights from his thoughts.

"Did ye manage to sleep after our early morning disturbance?" he asked.

"Aye," came Dynadane's one word response.

"I hath made some broth to begin the new day with – come and join me," offered the kindly old man. Sir Dynadane pushed the blankets off him and looked around for his sandals. He pushed his feet into them and made his way over to join his friend for the first meal of the day.

"What chores await ye today young Knight?" asked Mynwhyss. The Knight looked at the curious old man and answered.

"I must return to Caerleon for a short time. But fear not, Mynwhyss, I shall come back to Stamfyd as soon as I am able. Mine work here is not yet done."

This made one of the grey eyebrows of the old man rise. He wanted to ask more details from the Knight but could see that the man was preoccupied with other thoughts. He decided to wait until after the meal to see if he could find out any more details from him. They ate their food in comfortable silence.

Chapter 6: A New Type of Map

Arthur was more impressed than he thought that he would be. The sculptor had made a beautiful representation of the entire country on the surface of the Round Table. The mountains were there as were the valleys and rivers. The clay had been unable to be fired into a hard glaze, but somehow the sculptor had managed to colour it nonetheless. The rivers were a beautiful shade of blue, the valleys green, and the highest mountains were covered in white, a fair depiction of how how they were often topped with snow in real life.

Arthur waked around the circumference of the table again and again. Each time he managed to see a new piece of incredible detail that he'd somehow missed the first time around. He leaned forward and then stood back trying to take it all in. It was difficult, as the map was unlike anything he'd ever seen before. Even when he was originally describing it to the artist, he had no way of knowing how beautiful and utterly beguiling the outcome would be.

All of his lands were shown in the map. The southern area of Dumnonii where he was born now had its new border expanded from Hengests Dun all the way to the river Isca. All of the major townships and largest of the villages were shown on the map. All of Arthur's various castles were also indicated. When viewed in their totality even Arthur was taken aback at the amount of land that was now united beneath his rule.

The artist stood back, watching Arthur move around and around the table. He watched as the king leaned in to view some minute detail that he'd added and then stand back to try and take in the whole scene. He was nervously awaiting the king's critique of his work. It had taken exactly as long as he had predicted. Thankfully he had added a week to the overall timetable because every one of the seven days was used to make the final finishing-off touches to the artwork.

Eventually though he could not contain himself any longer and asked the king for his reaction to the work.

"Is it what ye expected, Sire?" he queried the monarch. Arthur did not verbally reply at first but nodded as he continued to circle the Round Table. At some point something must have triggered the need in Arthur to verbalise what he was thinking.

"This is beyond what I hath imagined, mine good man. Ye hath mine gratitude and any fee that ye think is reasonable for such an inspirational piece of work!"

The words fell upon the artist as soft and warm as a spring day's sunlight. The King still did not look at his as he spoke, so entranced was he with the map he was viewing. This new map made all of the intricately hand-drawn maps in his study seem inconsequential by comparison. It was as if he would never need another map drawn upon parchment again. All of his plans would henceforth be made by referencing this map. It was the centre of his entire monarchy.

"It was a pleasure to work for thee, King Arthur," the artist said, although it was in doubt as to whether or not Arthur had heard the complement. He was still very much engaged at looking at the incredible detail of the landscape before him. Feeling that he may have been outstaying his welcome and sure that he was not going to receive any more praise from the king, the man bowed deeply, unnoticed by Arthur, and left the room. He would present his fee for services to the head of the kitchen staff who had acted as liaison for between him and the Caerleon servants for the duration of the build.

As he pulled the door closed behind him, Arthur looked up and realised that he was now alone with the work of art. The depiction gave him a great sense of pride and achievement...but somehow the middle sections of the map scorned him. He hadn't noticed it until now, but there is was.

There were three large sections that were not part of his monarchy. They were the lands still very much in the clasp of the

Juts, Angles and Saxons. Arthur's expression dimmed. He looked up at the beams high above him as if looking for inspiration. Something had to be done about ridding the land of the remaining invaders and finally unifying Briton beneath his rule. He began to formulate a plan.

Chapter 7: Warwick Forest

Sir Dynadane had provisioned his mount and departed Stamfyd on the day that he had seen the contents of the memory stone. He'd left Mynwhyss in charge of the soldiers. This was a politically tactful move that was sure to garner even more support from the villagers for the Caerleon men now 'occupying' the town. He wanted to give the impression that as Arthur's representative in Stamfyd, he saw Mynwhyss as the next in charge, and equally capable of characterising the values that living within King Arthur's kingdom brought.

It was clear thinking in difficult circumstances. His primary goal at this point was to get the information about the Saxon, Angle, Jute alliance to the King as quickly as possible. He'd ridden his horse hard for the day, giving it as little rest as he dared during that time, and made excellent time as a result, although he was fatigued. As night fell he had reached the outskirts of Warwick Forest. This marked the half-way point between Stamfyd and Caerleon. All of this was Middle Angle territory and he was taking a risk by riding through it rather than around it as Arthur and his returning force would have done. But he would shave three days off the journey this way. He felt it was worth the risk.

He dismounted and walked his horse up to the edge of the forest that he now had to traverse if he was to get to Caerleon by tomorrow evening. There was the river Avon to cross as well. He'd have to choose the narrowest and shallowest point to do so. All of this weighed on his mind. He spoke to his horse whilst giving her a stroke down her long nose.

"We shall take refuge in the forest for the night. There is less chance of Angles seeing us there. Every moment that we are in the open we risk detection. And mine mission is too critical to fail." He looked at the horse as if expecting a response. The mare simply blinked at him. The young Knight smiled. What else was he expecting?

Soon enough they had entered the forest. The thick canopy of the trees cut down what little light was left in the day. The evening birds were out in force already. They tooted and chirped all around him. It was strange, no matter how hard he tried to actually catch sight of any one of them, he was unable to. They continued to be disembodied cries in the trees all around him.

***

He set up camp in a small clearing. There was a felled tree that bordered one side of the mostly circular area and short ground-dwelling ferns had sprouted all around. The earth was covered in moss that was soft but not damp. He'd managed to find enough dry twigs to start a fire and contained it in a small circle of stones. Taking out some of his provisions he sat before the fire and began to eat and drink some wine from a bladder.

For just a moment he could have sworn that he was being watched. He turned around. There was nothing there. He returned to his meal admonishing himself for being so nervous. There was nothing in the forest that could hurt him, a Knight of the Round Table.

Out of nowhere a voice cut through the twilight. "I am hungry."

Sir Dynadane jumped up in fright and spun around reaching for his sword all in one quick and smooth move. Standing a few paces away from his was a beautiful young woman. He was stunned.

"Where did ye come from?" he asked a little too aggressively and loudly. She did not react to his gruffness. Instead she simply repeated her first words.

"I am hungry."

Sir Dynadane looked about him for any sign of others, or a hint as to which direction she may have come from. He could not reconcile either query.

"Will ye not feed a wayward lady?" she asked and looked innocently at him.

The Knight was still confused about her sudden appearance.

"How did ye get so close to me without making any noise?" He asked. There was no response.

"Do ye live here in the forest?" again nothing from the woman. She looked down at the provisions that the Knight had staked up near to the fire. The Knight began to feel a little inappropriate in his behaviour. Perhaps if he offered her some nourishment she'd be more disposed to tell him what he wanted to know. He gathered himself and presented his best chivalrous nature.

"Please forgive mine ill manners dear Lady. Join me for some food and wine. Take comfort here by the fire that I hath lit." He indicated that she should sit near to him. The woman walked forward and took the position that he'd pointed to. She moved gracefully, almost too effortlessly, and now revealed by the light of the fire, her features could be seen more clearly. He was correct that she was beautiful, but it was more than that; she was an absolute vision of splendour!

It took a moment for Dynadane to realise that he was staring. He shook his head and unpacked some bread, cheese, and salted dried meat for the woman. Handing her the portions she nibbled at them demurely. He waited for her to say something. His body language gave away that he was eager to hear her speak once more. He was leaning forward when she rewarded him with a single word from her exquisite mouth.

"Epona," she said somewhat mysteriously.

Dynadane had no idea what this meant. Was it another language that he was unfamiliar with? He tilted his head and gave her an expression of not understanding.

"Mine name is Epona," she revealed. Dynadane breathed an 'Oh' and nodded his understanding.

"Welcome to mine humble camp, dear Lady Epona," he said and smiled as he did so. "What brings ye to the depths of Warwick forest? Are ye lost and in need of assistance?" he offered hoping that she would illuminate the situation of her presence.

She looked at him and let out a small laugh. It was impossible to not smile along with her. Seeing her amused gave Dynadane a warm feeling.

"I search for ye," she said. The answer made absolutely no sense. Dynadane felt obliged to point out the fact.

"But dear Lady; I did not know that I would be here until this very morning. I only left mine township then. How could anyone else know that I am here and send ye to seek me out?" hoping that his logic was not too abrasive he then thought of the most obvious flaw in what Epona was saying.

"And Lady Epona; ye do not know mine name? How could ye be seeking me? Perhaps it is another that ye expected to find here and hath come across me instead?" It somehow felt wrong to point out the inconsistencies with Epona's words.

"Sir Dynadane of Caerleon, it is ye that I seek," she said.

The Knight was amazed at the same time as being elated. The very thought that this vision of loveliness had somehow sought him out gave him a feeling of pure joy. He did not know what to say next.

Epona stood up and he felt obliged to do the same. Then bending her arms and bringing both hands to her shoulders she somehow loosened the white and blue and grey silken robes that she was wearing. They fell to the ground. She stood there in naked splendour.

All of Dynadane's self-control and instincts to be chivalrous abandoned him in an instant of time. His breathing became laboured. His penis filled with blood giving him an erection so hard that it hurt. Without even realising it his hands moved up to clasp her perfectly formed breasts. She stepped toward him. He grabbed Epona by the waist and pulled her body against his. He almost savagely kissed her.

When then separated it was only so that Dynadane could grab at his tunic and wrench it from his body. There would be damage to it but nothing like that entered his mind. He had become lust. Every breath he took he wanted nothing more than to penetrate her.

And he did. Her vagina was smooth and wet. The head and shaft of his penis rammed their way deep into her. She groaned with pleasure. He grunted with animal-like pants as he held her by her magnificent behind so that he could get better leverage pushing his way into her.

Over and over it went on. They stood there in the middle of their small clearing their naked bodies entwined in zealous love-making. Lit by the flickering flames of the diminishing fire they did not notice a set of eyes watching them from afar.

It was impossible for Dynadane to tell how long he had been making love to Epona. His climax was so severe that he arched his back and almost howled to the sky like a dog. The semen leaving his body felt like it was a surging river. He could feel his satisfaction at ejaculating begin to envelope him. It simultaneously spread from his loins upwards through is body and from his head downwards to his torso and stomach. Where the two feelings met and merged he felt warmth he had never encountered before.

With the last few jerks of his body ensuring that every precious drop of his seed entered Epona he let out a gasp for air. He slumped to the ground, his legs unable to support the weight of his body. He floated away into a slumber deeper than any he had taken before. There was nothing; complete blackness.

***

Slowly he began to come around. There were sounds: the fire; someone moving near to him. As if he was climbing out of the darkest pit he forced his eyes to open. Epona as tending to the fire; she was still a vision of perfect nakedness. More of Dynadane's provisions had been set out. She looked over and saw that his eyes were open.

"Ye hath slept for three hours, young Knight. Come, take refreshment," she offered.

It was difficult at first to move but he pushed himself up to a seated position. Epona handed him the bladder of wine. He drank from it. It tasted much better than he had recalled from earlier in the evening.

"Eat," she said in her seductive voice. He ate some of the dried salted meat. It was the most scrumptious food that he had ever tasted. Likewise the bread and cheese, he gobbled it down finding that the more he ate and drank the more energy he had.

Soon he had finished off the amounts of food that Epona had set out for him.

"Are ye recovered?" she asked. He nodded, now energised.

"Good," she said "Now lie back, I shall rub this lavender oil upon ye"

He did not need to be told twice. The very thought of Epona rubbing her hands over his body began to give him another erection. She produced a small vile of oil from somewhere, and spread it upon her hands.

Leaning over him she massaged it into his youthful and muscular chest. After she had finished tending to his pectorals, she turned her attention to his shoulders and down his biceps and triceps. It felt wonderful. He allowed himself to be submerged in the feeling of bliss.

Unexpectedly, she straddled him. His penis was already fully erect by this stage and she positioned it so that he could insert it into her. Without warning she descended her form upon his erection. Epona began to rhythmically move up and down sending shudders of ecstasy through every part of Dynadane. For the second time that night he was completely lost in the feeling of making love to this beautiful stranger.

Nothing else mattered except the union that they felt when they were joined in this way. Somehow, with incredible muscular control, Epona began to manipulate her vagina in a way to squeeze Dynadane's manhood as she ascended it to its swollen head. Then she loosened her inner muscles upon the reverse manoeuvre. Again and again she did this; it was incredible. He lost his sense of time and self. He could no longer tell where he was. Nothing but Epona existed in his entire world. She was all that he needed, not food nor wine, nor even air to breathe, only Epona mattered; she was his entire reality.

It was impossible to tell how much time had passed when Dynadane reached his excruciating climax. A guttural moan came from deep within his thorax marking the exact moment. It made a sound that he had never made before. With his eyes rolling back into his head the world of Epona came to an orgasmic conclusion. He was unconscious with satisfaction.

***

There were sounds in the distance. But they were far away and did not matter. Dynadane drifted in the void between the waking world and the sleeping one. Someone was calling his name. He tried to concentrate upon the words that he was hearing but it was difficult. He preferred to lose himself in the peace of sleep. Again and again his name was called. It had a jarring effect upon him. He could no longer reach the bliss that was sleep. He was waking up.

"Dynadane; eat; drink! Replenish thine strength" it was Epona's voice that beckoned him from his slumber. His eyes opened but his vision was blurry at first. Bit by bit he managed to focus his sight upon the woman calling him to alertness. She leant forward with the bladder of wine and poured some into his mouth. He swallowed the velvet-like liquid. It tasted good. Epona leaned forward with some more food and placed a chunk of it in his mouth. He automatically began to chew upon it. The salted meat mixed with the saliva in his mouth and the remnants of the wine. Unbelievable flavours erupted in his mouth. He groaned with pleasure at the taste of the food.

"Ye hath slept for over three hours, young Knight. Soon 'twill be morning."

Even has Epona spoke the words Dynadane knew that there was something that he had to do in the morning. Something important, but he could not quite remember what it was. He looked at her. Epona was still naked. The fire had once more been rekindled. It was lighting the small clearing that they occupied. The light danced over her perfect body. He looked at her the entire time that she fed him. Twice now he had been completely intimate with her, and yet still he desired her.

He had eaten and drank his fill when she stood up and waked over to the fallen tree. She set her hands upon the trunk bending over in the process. It was more than Dynadane could take. He leapt to his feet, blood surging once more into his manhood. She spread her legs and wiggled her hips seductively. It was all of the encouragement that the young man needed. With his erection once again at full bloom he raced over to her and entered her from behind. She moaned in pleasure. This in turn made him begin to pound her perfect bottom with his loins. The sound of skin slapping on skin echoed off the surrounding trees.

From a distance the same eyes that had watched the first two encounters between the two attractive people, observed this one with more intensity.

Sir Dynadane had abandoned any notions of gallant behaviour. His forehead and torso were covered with perspiration. He rammed his penis deeply into Epona's vagina again and again. Each moan of acceptance and pleasure from her, only served to heighten his enjoyment and the ferocity at which he was performing. As he approached climax for the third time that night he encountered a feeling of absolute fatigue moments before he ejaculated once more. Then there was nothing. He did not register falling backwards onto the soft ground oblivious to the world around him.

***

This time the young knight woke with a fright. It was morning. The sunlight was prevalent but not overly bright. The sun must have surely risen above the horizon by this time, but not by very much. He was astounded that he had slept so long and so deeply. He remembered that he wanted to wake before sunrise so that he could continue his journey. Somehow that had not happened.

The events of the night then came flooding back to him. He remembered the appearance of the mysterious Epona and the three frantic sessions of love-making. He felt embarrassed that he had behaved in such a way. He looked around him. Epona was nowhere to be seen. He scrambled to his feet. Looking around for his clothes he saw that they were spread in two areas surrounding the campfire, or what was left of it.

He was just leaning down to pick up the first part of his clothing when he heard an all-to-familiar voice behind him.

"Do not dress" it was Epona. He spun around. She was wearing her multi-coloured silken robes and was carrying the bladder of wine that she had emptied into his mouth during various points during the night.

"I hath fetched water from a nearby stream. It will replenish ye," she said. It was impossible to not believe every word that came from her perfect mouth. He would not normally think of drinking water unless it was absolutely necessary. But when Epona said it, he could think of nothing else that he would rather have to quench his thirst.

"Come; try it," she offered. She walked up to him and offered the bladder. He took it from her and sampled the water. It was invigorating, clean, cool, and tastier than any water he had ever drunk before.

"Mine thanks Epona," he said, smiling at her. She looked even more beautiful in the soft morning light then she did in the flickering light of the fire. He began to be lost in the vision of her magnificence again. But there was something niggling at the back of his mind. Then it hit him.

"I must go, mine mission is not yet complete!" he said. She looked at him as if he had just injured her with his words.

"Do not leave me yet young Knight!" she pleaded. "There is much left of this day, surely thine mission can wait a few more hours. Time that could be spend with..." she left the idea unfinished. 'Ye,' he thought. 'Surely he could spend a few more hours with this beguiling woman.'

Satisfied that he had taken his fill of the water, she again loosened her robes and they fell in a graceful mess upon the ground. Again, the sight of her impeccable form completely captivated him. But this time he managed to somehow recover his senses. There was a memory stone hidden in his tunic that he needed to get to King Arthur. This had precedence over everything else that he was doing. But Epona's body was an absolute vision to behold.

He vacillated between lustful instincts and his need to fulfil his objective and reveal to King Arthur the threat that now faced him and his monarchy. He was torn between the two feelings. On the one hand, he had never before encountered such a captivating woman as Epona. On the other, the entire reign of Arthur was threatened by the newly formed alliance between the invaders. Something had to be done about it as soon as possible.

The anguish of the decision must have shown on Dynadane's face because it elicited a response from the watcher in the woods.

"Epona!" shouted a man's voice from off to Dynadane's right side. They both turned to see who was there.

Standing about ten paces away was a man. He was tall, taller than Dynadane. His dark hair and emerald green eyes marked strong features. He was surely from the Pictish tribes of the very north of the country. But he was not dressed in animal skins and roughly weaved material. Instead he was draped in very similar multi-coloured and shimmering clothing much like Epona's. If he had to use a word to describe it, Dynadane would have used 'Roman'. He seemed regal somehow.

"Ye hath taken thine fill of this helpless young man. Now go!" he signalled with his hand that Epona should leave them. His tone suggested that he was not going to take no for an answer.

"He is mine, Amaetheon! Go away!" she practically shrieked at him in a most unbecoming way. This made Dynadane look upon her in a slightly different light. Somehow, now she seemed less attractive and more threatening. He was amazed that he hadn't noticed it before.

The man marched forward clearly in no mood to entertain objections from Epona.

"Ye heard me; be gone before I smite thee with mine powers!" He continued to advance intimidatingly upon them both. Epona was losing her demure nature with each advancing step. She began to breathe in and out like a caged animal. Her panting made Dynadane step back instinctively.

"*Coolwhyth ness lethe byworgh nah ellis path bar!*" the man shouted.

They were words that Dynadane had not heard before. He could not tell which language it was of the many that he spoke and were spoken throughout the land. Whatever the meaning of the words they had a dramatic effect upon Epona. She screamed as if someone had just doused her with boiling oil. The ferocity of her wailing made Dynadane retreat in haste even further from her; suddenly he wanted to put as much distance between them as he could. Again the man spoke the words.

Epona and her clothing shot into the air; straight up and through the canopy of the trees. She screamed as she did so. It was terrifying. She disappeared from sight but the remnants of her cry of despair were still echoing through Dynadane's head. He was shaking when the stranger came over to him and clasped his shoulder in a reassuring way.

"Be calm, young Knight of King Arthur," he said. "Gather thine clothes and dress. Then I shall tell ye what hath transpired here this night." It was a clear instruction and one that Sir Dynadane was happy to enable. It was easier than trying to wonder what had just happened. He struggled to pull on his torn tunic and pants. Somewhere he found his boots, and pulled them on. Readying himself and trying to dust himself off and make himself as presentable as the situation allowed he stood before the man awaiting the promised explanation.

"Mine name is Amaetheon. I am a faerie of sorts. Not the kind that King Arthur has had dealings with over these years, but it serves as best an explanation that I can give ye." His words were warm, his tone comforting. Yet the words that he spoke should have given Dynadane cause for concern. This was a faerie; the first that he had ever encountered. He had heard so many stories from the other

Knights about them. And here now, before him, within touching distance was one right now.

Sir Dynadane was amazed; unsure of what to say or do next. He elected to simply nod his belief of the explanation that the man had given him.

"Come, sit with me, this story could take quite some time to tell," he offered. Dynadane and Amaetheon sat in the clearing. Sir Dynadane's head was beginning to fill with questions. As if guessing the most urgent of them Amaetheon spoke.

"Epona is a faerie that seeks to extend her existence. She and I are a different type of faerie to the ones that King Arthur hath thus far encountered. Unlike them we live much longer lifespans and have greater magical powers. There are very few of us and we live apart from the other faeries, preferring our own solitary company to living in their so-called civilized society. Much in the same way that faeries are considered myth with the normal folk of the land, we are considered to be a story that few in the faerie social order truly believe exist. And that is good, we prefer it that way." He continued his mesmerising explanation of his people.

"We do share the same problem that faces all faeries throughout the land however, we are slowly but surely being driven from our lands." The revelation that such a mystical being could be threatened in any way absolutely amazed Dynadane.

"How?" he asked softly

"The people that you call Christians; the ones that believe in a God that they cannot see; they are inadvertently driving us from our traditional lands. To us these Christians feel as if they too should be magical beings, we can sense it of them, and yet they are incapable of practicing magic at all. It is a puzzle that we cannot reconcile. Whenever they are near we must flee. There is something about them that prevents us from taking on the shape of animals, the most fundamental of faerie powers." He shifted in his sitting position to make himself more comfortable, then continued his story. "

"One of the faeries in the north of our land, living near the township of Pen Rhionydd met and fell in love with a human; a Christian. By becoming betrothed to him not only could she no longer perform any magical spells at all, she began to age in the same way that humans do; quickly." He looked at Dynadane as if he had just made a point of major significance. But the Knight was so taken aback with all of the information that he was receiving he was unable to react in the way that Amaetheon may have expected.

"Ye said that Epona was trying to extend her life. How?" he queried.

"Epona thinks that by stockpiling a man's seed she can use it to weave a spell that will give her a faerie child, just like herself. It is her way to propagate her own life. But she is deluded. I hath consulted with the greatest of our number, a Faerie Queen that hath lived longer than any other. She assures me that there is no respite from these Christians except fleeing from them. No magic that will help us fight them. No solution to our inability to conceive children. I hath tried to tell Epona these things but she is frantic to bear a child and will not listen."

He looked around him as if gathering his thoughts. The daylight was filtering through the treetops. It was a fine morning.

"Perhaps ye should gather thine belongings and complete thine mission to King Arthur." Even as Amaetheon said the words Dynadane touched the memory stone that he had carefully stitched into his clothing before leaving Stamfyd.

"How do ye know of mine mission? Who I am? Where I am from?" asked Dynadane.

Amaetheon laughed. "One of the main differences between us and the other faeries, is that we can read minds. Epona read thine mind and found all of the qualities that ye want in a woman, she then took on those traits and presented herself to ye. That is not as she truly appears."

The young man was shocked.

"How does she truly appear then?" he asked, and then thinking of the logical follow-on question added; "And ye, is this how ye look or do ye present a false image too?" Even though it was not meant to be insulting, it somehow came across as such. Amaetheon looked a little hurt by the query.

"Mine appearance is true young Knight, rest assured of that. Now enough questions, there is valuable information in that memory stone that must be presented to King Arthur. Go now!" As he finished his goading he stood up as if to punctuate the urgency of the situation. But Dynadane could not help ask more questions. He stood up and said.

"Why did ye help me? And why do ye care of King Arthur and the threat that hangs over his Kingdom?"

Once again the questions had an unintentional abrasive edge to them. Amaetheon however answered as if they did not.

"The Faerie Queen cares for King Arthur and his rein. And as a Knight of his I felt an obligation to assist ye. But now young Knight, I must go. I am leaving this land too before the spread of these Christians threatens mine powers and mine very life." This time the dramatic point had an impact on the Knight. He asked with genuine concern and sympathy in his voice.

"Where will ye go?"

"Magna Frisia, or Gaul. Somewhere that hath not been touched by these unusual people. I wish to continue mine solitary existence, undisturbed." He said winking at Dynadane as if he was actually wanting the complete opposite to what he had just said.

At that point Dynadane's horse snorted in an agitated way. It was long after sun-up and the horse was still tied to a low branch some way off. By this time of day the stable-hand would have fed and watered the beast. These thoughts were going through Dynadane's mind as he looked over and then back.

But when his eyes returned to where Amaetheon should have been standing there was nobody there. Dynadane looked around him in every direction, even upwards. Amaetheon was nowhere to be seen.

He walked over to his horse and began to untie the reigns.

"Come along" he said "We hath a long journey to reach Caerleon before sunset."

Chapter 8: Caerleon Castle at Sunset

There was the usual fanfare when Sir Dynadane was spotted by the lookouts. The young Knight had carefully managed his arduous journey throughout the day, resting his horse when he could, but saving the beast's energy for a final frantic ride through Caerleon Village and up the hill to the Castle. It was not meant to be a dramatic entrance but it did have all of the markings of one.

Alerted by his Knights Arthur had come out to the main courtyard to greet the young Regent, and he'd guessed that it must have been urgent news indeed to get him to abandon his posting at Stamfyd and return to Caerleon.

As Dynadane came through the main gates he immediately recognised the figure of Arthur standing just outside the main doors leading to the Great Staircase. He veered his horse in the direction of the King and dismounted at the same time as bringing the horse to a stop.

"Mine King, I hath grave news of a plot by the Angles, Jutes and Saxons to form an alliance against ye!" he spoke even as he approached the king and knelt before him. Rising he could see the effect that the news had had on the King.

Merlin appeared at the doorway just as Arthur grabbed the arm of Sir Dynadane and began to lead him inside.

"Merlin; with me!" was all that Arthur said.

Merlin dutifully stepped aside to allow the duo entry and then followed them in without a further word.

***

Merlin had the memory stone held to the centre of his head. The visions that he was witnessing he was sharing with Arthur, Dynadane and Morgan. She had sensed that something was wrong and had sought out Arthur, finding him in the King's study. Now the four of them were in communion, sharing the intricate details of the gathering that had resulted in the newly formed alliance between all of Arthur's enemies.

Morgan was distracted though. She could not understand why at first. She was immersed in the ongoing vision from the memory stone, but every now and again she would come back into the study and find herself looking about as if a servant was bothering her about something trivial. Finding nothing she concentrated upon Merlin's thoughts and re-joined the collected vision. This pseudo-interruption happened three times before a realisation struck her.

There were too many people represented in the tapestry that was on the side wall of Arthur's study. She tried to not look directly at it. Sensing somehow that to do so would be wrong. Instead she repositioned herself so that she could clearly see the hanging and then placed her hands over her eyes as if concentrating fiercely upon the images that Merlin was projecting into their minds. However, she was surreptitiously scanning the images on the tapestry. She had worked upon this tapestry along with the court ladies and knew everything there was to know about it.

Looking carefully at each of the images woven into the material, she identified the one that should not be there. It was a man, dressed inappropriately for the wedding scene in which he was standing. He was tall, thin-faced and looked menacing. How could this be? Was it a vision within a vision? Was she experiencing some event that was yet to occur?

Even as she was wondering Merlin's sudden ending of the projection of the memory stone jolted her out of her musings.

"Arrogance!" he shouted angrily and threw the memory stone across the room. Unaccustomed to such outbursts of anger from the old Sorcerer, the other three were hesitant to try and calm him.

"How dare they conspire against the rightful King of the land! We should..." His voice trailed off, unsure of what they actually should do under these bizarre circumstances.

"This is unheard of," quipped in Arthur. "The Angles hath no love of the Jutes who hath no allegiances to the Saxons. How came they to find security in the arms of each other?"

"Clearly Brother, it is thee that hath driven them to this desperate act." Offered Morgan. "They are wary of thine support, unsure of who will be next to hath their lands annexed and added to thine Kingdom. It is an act of desperation."

Morgan's words rang true, but it did not make the situation any more palpable for any of them.

"What can we do to dissolve this cowardly partnership?" asked Arthur of his two magicians. His question was insightful. He had not immediately asked how to overthrow his adversaries, because he was smart enough to know that fighting them all at once would be untenable. Instead he wanted to know how to drive them apart once more so that they could be chipped away at, as he had been doing all of these years. That was the immediate objective as far as Arthur was concerned.

Merlin was impressed with the direction of Arthur's thinking.

"Aye Arthur; that should be our goal, but how to achieve it, that is the trick."

Morgan began to walk around in a circle as she addressed them all.

"We should not be hasty to decide upon a course of action immediately. There is much to consider in this instance. How strong is the bond between them? Can we wait for it to dissolve on its own? What actions from us would it take to enable their new-found alliance and bring about a simultaneous defensive attack from them?" she stopped and looked at the tapestry depicting Arthur's wedding. There was incompleteness to her summation as if someone had disturbed her.

Morgan was looking intently at the tapestry. The strange figure that she had spied there was gone. Any further musings were interrupted by Arthur.

"Call all of mine Knights to the Round Table!" she spun around to face him thinking that he had given her the command. It was only then that she realised that Arthur was speaking to Sir Dynadane. He hurriedly bowed and left the room. Arthur held out both of his hands as if to gather Morgan and Merlin to him. They responded by moving closer to him.

"We will discuss what is to be done with all of the available Knights and decide upon a course of action. And we will not leave the Round Table until we hath come up with a viable plan to overcome this threat." He was speaking passionately. Both of his magical advisors gave their consent to the idea.

***

Night had fallen and the evening meal was being prepared, but that did not concern Arthur right now. He had his mind upon greater things and he wanted his Knights to share the burden of producing something that could aide him in this desperate hour. All of the Knights that were in Caerleon Castle were at the Round Table when Arthur entered. They had all previously seen the new extraordinary map-sculpture covering the table, but it was such a fine piece of work that even now it held the attention of more than half of them when Arthur made his entrance.

"Sir Dynadane hath brought us news of an alliance between the Jutes, Angles and Saxons. They will rally to the aide of each other depending upon whose encampments I next try to bring into mine Kingdom." He let the words sink in to the crowd.

There was a moment of silence, then calamity. Never before had Arthur heard so many of them shouting so loudly about 'conceit', 'overconfident dogs', 'savages', and the like. He was not in a mood for letting the Knights have their say about how haughty the very thought of such an alliance was, instead he raised both his hands to quell the noise.

"Everything that ye say, I agree with. We all do!" he said with a sweeping gesture of his arms. "That is not what we need right now. What is required is a response to this threat." He indicated the map on the table.

"See the borders of mine land. They hath been extended over the years of mine rule and yet these areas are still in the hands of the Saxons." He indicated the southern lands of Wessex.

"These are still in the clutches of the Angles," he indicated the areas of Mercia and South Gyrwe.

"And this is where the Jutes call home," he pointed to Kent. All of the Knights followed his display and then looked up at him.

"What are we to do in order to win back these lands without bringing the combined wrath of all three invader nations upon us?" the problem was laid bare for all of his Knights to see. It was quite a conundrum. How could they further expand the Kingdom without risking all-out war with the allied invaders? There was silence. Somebody made to speak and then thought the better of it and stifled his utterances. This happened a further three more times before Arthur began to show his impatience and banged his fist upon the table where there was no part of the country-map sculpture to damage. It made a less than dramatic sound now that the table was mostly covered with the heavy, clay-painted model.

"Think! There must be way?" he shouted at them. Sir Dagonet spoke.

"We could disguise ourselves as marauding Gael and attack the Jutes from the sea. The Saxons and Angles would hath no reason to come to the Jutes assistance all the way down in Kent." He delivered his plan to the group and looked around for support for it.

"Then what Dagonet?" asked Sir Bors De Ganys. "Even if we completely annex Kent and bring it into the Kingdom how would we hold it? It is too removed from our current borders to adequately defend from the Saxons to the west and the Angles to the north."

Sir Dagonet made to rebuke the criticism but realised that Sir Bors De Ganys was completely correct. It made no sense to even try for Kent at this stage, it was too far away from Arthur's current borders.

"The plan has merit though," quipped in Sir Ectorde Maris. "Instead of Kent let us move next to push the border of Dumnonii further east to the town of Sherborne. Disguised as raiders of course." He added nodding to Sir Dagonet.

"They will see through such a rudimentary ruse with ease and unite to defend themselves," criticised Sir Brumean. "Nobody will believe that Gael raiders would come that far south." This assertion brought more of the Knights into the fray and the discussion quickly became heated and descended into a cacophony of people all trying to talk over each other to express their viewpoints about the plan.

"Enough of this!" shouted Arthur over the top of them all. "What other ideas are there?" Again Knights all looked at each other for inspiration. Sir Pellus was brave enough to offer his own idea.

"Sire, if they fear ye so much as to form an alliance then they may be desperate enough to accept a solution that does not involve fighting." This intrigued everyone present.

"Meet in secret with the leader of the nearest land holding to thine southern border. Deorham and the surrounds all the way up to the River Usk. Offer him an assurance that he and his lands will find peace if they willingly accede to thine rule and distance themselves from the other Angles bordering their holdings." It seemed a perfectly reasonable idea to most of those present. The war lord that claimed these forested lands would hand over his rule to Arthur in return for abandoning his alliance with his fellow Angles in return for the benevolent rule of King Arthur. Arthur's reaction however took Sir Pellus completely by surprise.

"NEVER!" he screamed in a volume and with a naked temper that none of the Knights had before witnessed. Even Merlin and Morgan who were standing to each side of him were shocked.

"I will not hath these vermin in the land at all. They are all to be driven out! Do ye understand Pellus!? There will be no more talk of concession to these dogs nor trying to deal with them in a civilised manner. None!" He dramatically swiped the air with his right forearm to punctuate his point. This brought complete silence to the Round Table.

The discussion had reached an impasse. Arthur would not entertain anything other than removing the invaders from their lands and to do so would bring down the wrath of all of them upon him. They could not fight without being drawn into a battle the likes of which they had never before seen. They could not rid themselves of the invaders without fighting them off their lands. Sir Garethe was the only one brave enough to speak next.

"If we fight, and all of them unite as they say that they would. Can we win such a battle? If we are prepared for it and call upon all of the forces that are available to us; would we be in a position to win the battle and claim all of the errant lands into the Kingdom" he too pointed at the objectives to highlight his question to them all. This invoked a small amount of murmuring from all of them. It was a radical idea indeed. Risk a war, the size of which none in the land had seen before in their lifetimes. A number of the Knights looked over to Merlin. Realising that Arthur too had looked his way he felt obliged to speak his mind.

"Arthur, such a war should not be entered into lightly. We must consider the consequences of both victory and loss should we undertake such a battle. Sir Dagonet mentioned the Gael earlier. What of our northern lands? Galloway and North Rheged would be open to attack without our forces stationed permanently there." He stroked his beard and added more thoughts to his reasoning.

"Should we win, the survivors of thine force may not be enough to adequately maintain thine rule throughout the land. Should we lose then we will hath lost everything that thine father King Uther started and you Arthur, have continued. Are ye prepared to risk everything for such a bloody battle? Is the price of complete unity throughout the land worth what ye will be required to pay?" He finished his questions.

Arthur considered carefully before speaking. He wanted to slam his fist upon the table once more and say 'Aye - it is all worth the risk because we will be victorious.' But deep-down he did not know that. In fact the more that he thought about it, the more he did not like the idea at all. Galloway and North Rheged at the mercy of the Gael and Scotti raiders from Hibernia; no he would not risk it. The silence was awkward. Arthur drew a breath and tried to take all of the emotion out of his voice.

"No, Merlin. We cannot risk it, as ye say, the outcome is too uncertain. And yet I will not leave this table until we hath a definite plan to take some action that does not result in the alliance of the invaders moving against us." Again he reaffirmed his resolve.

Morgan again found herself a little distracted throughout the proceedings. It should have been the most riveting meeting of the Knights that she had ever attended. But instead her attention was again drawn to one of the tapestries on the far wall. In an instant she realised that she must be experiencing the same thing that had happened in Arthur's study. She scanned the scenes trying her best to look as if she as thinking and not really looking intently at the tapestries. It was more difficult to do so here than in the Arthur's study. The walls were further away from where she was standing.

There was no light available from the windows to help her. All that she had was the flickering of the torches and the fireplace to light the woven scenes that were hanging around the walls.

Nevertheless she persevered and was rewarded. It was a tapestry depicting a hunting scene. This was the one that she and the other ladies of the court had been working on when Ganieda first came to visit at Caerleon. There standing near the Stag that had been slain in the hunt was the thin-faced man again. He was once more looking out of the tapestry at the proceedings. She guessed that he too must be a magician of some sort and that he was using his abilities to spy upon them in this way. Was he a faerie or a human with other-worldly abilities like herself and Merlin? There were many questions that needed to be answered.

But right now they needed to stop these discussions from being overheard by this mysterious sorcerer or faerie or whatever he was. Morgan looked at Arthur, he was in no mood to be interrupted. Thinking quickly she ambled behind the King and over to Merlin as if she was walking and thinking at the same time. She gently placed her hand upon Merlin's shoulder and spoke to him directly into his thoughts.

"Merlin, there is a magical person watching us from the tapestry hanging to the right of the fireplace. I hath seen him before. He was watching us from within the tapestry in Arthur's study shortly before coming to the Round Table. He is surely a Sorcerer or faerie or some other magical being. He is spying on us Merlin. We must find a way of preventing the King from giving away any battle strategy that is thought of in this discussion until we can learn more of this infiltrator." Morgan delivered the news in a far shorter timeframe than it would have taken to actually say the words.

Merlin's reaction was immediate. She could feel and hear the speed of his multiple thoughts of *who could it be?*, *what is this new threat?*, *how can I stop Arthur from saying anymore in this Round*

Table conference?' Then there followed a blur of thoughts so rapid that Morgan could not keep up with any of them. Merlin spoke, cutting off the king in mid-sentence.

"The solution is simple, Arthur. Ye must find a way to fight the Saxons and Angles without actually seeming like ye are fighting them. Then choose those that are at the fringe of the borders. Those that are in dispute even now. Do not try to annex an entire land-holding from a war lord, instead push gently so that it will not mean provocation of a unified retaliation." Merlin hoped that his semi-solution would both find favour with the Monarch as well as stop him from discussing this critical conversation any longer.

Arthur looked as if he was far away, considering the proposal. Merlin chanced a glance toward the tapestry that Morgan had told him about. Sure enough, there he was. A tall thin-faced man wearing flowing robes. He had not doubted Morgan for an instant, but he could not resist the most casual of viewings to see the object of their fear for himself. Arthur had reached a decision.

"Aye, Merlin; ye speak true words." Unknown to all of them Arthur was recalling his conversation with Amhar a month ago; talking about Saxon and Angle families that hath taken up residence within his borders by marrying Britons. Joining together the observations from Amhar with the proposed strategy from Merlin Arthur resulted in his own plan of attack.

"We shall fight within mine borders!" he proclaimed. The shocked look of all surrounded him. Either oblivious to it, or ignoring it pertinently he continued.

"There are Saxons and Angles that hath taken Britons into their beds and think that they can live beneath mine Monarchy. No! They will be dealt with as all invaders shall be dealt with, by leaving of their own free will or leaving this life at the end of our swords!" The gathered Knights did not quite know how to react to the news.

"We shall wage war upon all of the border townships that lie within mine Kingdom and drive out or slay any intruders that we find. That will be how I reaffirm mine commitment to driving out all of the invaders over time. When they run back to their war lords, what can they say? That Arthur hath driven them out of his own lands. Do I not hath a perfect right to do so? Fear will be mine new campaign. Fear of reprisals from me will drive the last of them from mine Kingdom." Arthur was clearly set upon his newly devised plan. The Knights obediently followed his commands and began to cheer, a little at first then it gathered momentum and became a rousing song.

Merlin and Morgan looked at each other. The information that this spy would take from here could be of no possible use to whoever he worked for, or represented. They were relieved that the proceedings would now come to a close. Coincidentally the call to the evening meal could be heard throughout the room as the cheering for Arthur's plan died down.

"Come, Knights of the Round Table, let us feast this evening in the knowledge that we are set upon the course to fulfil our destiny!" Arthur was swept up in his own exhilaration. He brazenly signalled that all should follow him to the banquet hall. They rallied behind their King and noisily marched away from the Round Table.

'Morgan and Merlin were left behind. Merlin leaned in to speak softly to Morgan.

"See, the tapestry. Our mysterious figure is gone." Morgan looked over to where she had previously seen the stranger. He was indeed now gone.

"I want ye to sleep with that tapestry in thine chambers tonight. I will order it taken down and delivered to thine room. I shall take the one in Arthur's study. Together through our dreams I hope to uncover more about this...*person*" Morgan nodded her understanding of the plan.

Morgan spoke her summation of Merlin's plan in acknowledgement of her understanding of it. "It is thine hope that close proximity to the tapestries in which he hath been seen will assist us in having dream-visions of him?"

"Aye" he replied. They nonchalantly made to follow the others to the evening meal. There was much to do afterwards in the nether land of their dreams.

Chapter 9: Dreaming

Morgan and Merlin were noticeably non-conversant during the evening meal. Any attempt at engaging them met with failure. Eventually people stopped trying. The meal ended and they made their excuses to retire for the evening. Queen Gwenhwyvar had seen the servants taking down the tapestry near the Round Table and when she inquired why, she was informed that it was under Merlin's orders. She did not ask for more clarification. Whatever he was doing must be part of the reason that he and Morgan were so quiet during the meal.

In Morgan's chambers the tapestry was waiting. It was unfurled across the floor to the right of her bed. She regarded it cautiously as she entered. There was no mysterious additional figure in the scene now, but nevertheless she was wary of it. She prepared herself for sleep regularly looking down at the tapestry to ensure that it was still as it should be.

When at last she did climb into her bed she settled herself and blew out the candles. For a moment she thought that she may be too ill at ease to fall to sleep easily; but the softness of sleep gradually overtook her and soon she was peacefully in the arms of slumber.

***

Merlin too entered his room with a little trepidation. He saw the tapestry. The servants had slung it over his scroll shelves and must have weighed it down on top of the structures to ensure that it stayed in-place. He looked at it in the candlelight. He was very familiar with the scene having seen it many times before, but now instead of showing the happiness of Arthur's wedding, it intimidated him a little. He hadn't been able to make himself appear in the tapestries of others, he thought. If he had, then he would have most surely used such a power to spy upon the adversaries that he and Uther and now Arthur had encountered over the decades.

Not realising that he was mimicking Morgan only moments before, he readied himself for bed, looking towards the hanging over and over again as he did so. Then like Morgan he snuffed out the candles providing light to the room and closed his eyes to await sleep.

***

"Ivorwulf!" called a brutish voice.

Merlin turned to look who had called out. He was in a longhouse of sorts. The architecture was most assuredly Jute. He must be somewhere in Kent. The man that he'd seen earlier that evening as a figure in the tapestry was there. He was instantly recognisable in the crowded noisy room. He walked toward Merlin and straight past him. Merlin turned to follow his movements. The man pushed his way through the crowd to the one that had called out 'Ivorwulf'. That must be his name. Already this vision was providing valuable information.

Merlin moved through the crowd to take up a position close to them. He was safe in the knowledge that he was in a dream and nobody here could see or hear him. But just as if he were dealing with another magical being, he tried to be as inconspicuous as possible. Even as he neared he ensured that he was sheltered from view behind a large warrior eating a charred leg of something that was still on the bone.

Ivorwulf stood to the side of the man that had called for him; they were in conversation. The man seated in what looked to be an ornate chair was more than likely the local warlord and this was his residence. All around were his men with their women typically feeding in the almost barbaric way that the Jutes would have been doing since their civilisation began across the sea.

"What conjuring hath ye done today to increase mine wealth and the number of women in mine bed!" he said as he slapped Ivorwulf on the back and laughed loudly. Ivorwulf replied.

"Karal, I hath been busy trying to negotiate the proposed alliance between our peoples so that we may fight off the further advances of King Arthur. No conjuring hath been done this day other than *conjuring* up words that will massage the vanity of the Saxons and the Angles."

Ivorwulf's answer clearly amused Karal because he laughed and banged the arms of his chair with his fists in mirth.

"I swear Ivorwulf ye are the most useful one of mine warriors and ye hath never laid hands upon a sword, nor fired an arrow nor thrown a spear," he complimented his sage.

"Words can be more powerful than all of the swords, arrows and spears in the country; provided they are spoken to the correct people and hath the effect for which they are meant," smiled Ivorwulf. It was hard to tell if his reply was some sort of gratuity for the compliment he had just received or a snide retort. It had the edge of both. Karal was clearly a little vexed at the retort but did not quite know how to react or respond. He instead chose to alter the direction of his questioning.

"Will they be talked into this alliance?" he inquired.

"Aye, Karal; it is in their best interests to do so. When we meet in one month's time at Anderitum in the Castle of Wlencing there will be much chest beating, but common sense will prevail. The alliance will be formed and we'll be safe from King Arthur and his Knights."

"So be it then!" said Karal. "When this is done I expect thee to return to conjuring up wealth for me and mine land" He stood and reached over for a tankard of wine on a nearby table. "Drink, Ivorwulf, drink to our success. Safety from the wretched King Arthur and his belligerent Knights."

He lifted his tankard high. Ivorwulf was caught unawares and looked around him for a suitable vessel in order to honour the request from Karal. He saw a tankard close by and reached out for it. Its owner reacted angrily until he realised who it was that was taking possession of it, and then almost fearfully waved him his permission.

Karal and Ivorwulf clashed their tankards loudly and drank to their forthcoming diplomatic victory.

***

The loud hooting of an owl interrupted Merlin's sleep. He shook himself awake and looked over to the source of the noise. A barn owl had taken up position on the ledge of his window. He groaned and looked around for something to throw at it. Finding nothing he raised himself from his bed and made to shoo it away. Feeling threatened the owl took flight before he'd managed to completely disentangle himself from his blanket.

Merlin groaned. He was gathering such important information during that dream, he thought. He wasn' happy at his slumber being so rudely disturbed by a common owl. The moonlight was steaming through the open wooden shutters. In order to prevent a reoccurrence of this, Merlin decided it was best to cross the cold stone floor and close them. Just before he did so he looked at the tapestry. It was exactly as it should be; there was no additional figure in the depiction. Merlin closed the shutters and returned gruffly to his bed.

Chapter 10: The Kentish Sorcerer, Ivorwulf

Merlin had a broken night's sleep for the rest of the night. He never fully made it to a deep restful sleep, nor did he have any additional visions about Ivorwulf. Frustrated he had arisen early and was committing everything that he had seen to a memory stone, so that it could easily be relayed to Arthur and anyone else that needed to know about this mysterious Sorcerer from Kent.

Somehow, he had become distracted within his scrolls and managed to lose track of time until he heard the call to the morning meal.

"Excellent" he said to nobody, and packed away the scrolls that he had been studying and made his way downstairs to the banquet hall.

***

Morgan was already seated when he arrived. He took a seat next to her so that they could converse about the events of the previous night. When Morgan saw him enter the room she told him with a look that she had something very important to relay. However, when he took his seat, out of respect for the aged Sorcerer she allowed him to begin the briefing.

"Mine vision was of the past; the sorcerer in a warlord's house in Kent mediating for the warlord the pact between the three disparate peoples. His name is Ivorwulf. I can estimate that the time was about two months ago maybe a little more. There was talk of the forthcoming meeting to ratify the agreement at Rumon's castle in Anderidae." He summarised his newfound information succinctly and clearly for Morgan.

Morgan nodded her understanding.

"Mine vision too was from the past. But the actual meeting at *Wlencing's* castle in Anderitum" she said correcting Merlin's mistake of identifying Rumon's former castle before he was overthrown twenty-six years before. He vaguely acknowledged his mistaken naming of the castle's current occupier and waited for her to continue.

"The agreement was ratified. Ivorwulf was there too. It is clear that he is a skilled negotiator as well as a powerful Sorcerer. How are we to fight this magical being?"

Merlin shook his head.

"The question should be, 'what does he want from us?' Is he trying to ascertain if Arthur plans to attack...and where? Or is he spying on us for another reason?" Merlin opened his eyes wider at the completion of his question. Morgan had not even considered that Ivorwulf could have any other motive than trying to find out Arthur's movements.

"What other reason could he have for surreptitiously listening in on our conversations?" she asked. And with that, she looked around at all of the tapestries in turn whilst awaiting a response from Merlin. Merlin saw what she was doing and joined in the scanning of the images hanging on all of the walls. Their behaviour drew a few curious looks from those closest to them.

Arthur entered the room with Gwenhwyvar. They sat down at their usual positions at the table, whilst offering their good morning greetings to those around them. The Servants began to bring in the morning meal offerings. Arthur leant over past Gwenhwyvar and spoke to Merlin and Morgan.

"What are ye discussing this morning? Our strategy decided upon last night no doubt?" His question gave the answer that he was expecting. Rather than let Arthur know that anything was wrong they both gave a small laugh and gesture of agreement.

"Good, we should decide upon the first of our villages to drive the invaders from?" he said before Gwenhwyvar spoke.

"I hear rumours that in the village of Exeshulme the Saxons that used to live across the river Exe in Aelle's old territories hath taken up residence. It is an insult to thine rule Arthur."

Gwenhwyvar hit a nerve with Arthur. Even though long since dead, the very mention of Aelle provoked the worst from Arthur. The king slammed his fist upon the table in front of Gwenhwyvar, bringing silence to the banquet hall.

"Then it is settled. Our first fight will be to clean out the vermin from mine village of Exeshulme!" he stated his intentions in a tone that did not offer any scope for discussion. Merlin and Morgan looked nervously around them at the tapestries hoping that Ivorwulf was nowhere to be seen. Their apparent distraction from his directive annoyed Arthur.

"What ails ye both this morning!?" he said angrily. Merlin and Morgan looked at each other for inspiration as to how to explain their skittish behaviour. Morgan spoke.

"Dear Brother" she always used 'Brother' if she wanted to coax him into doing something, "there are finer points to discuss in this instance; magical points that cannot be spoken of openly."

Her mysterious proclamation intrigued Arthur and Gwenhwyvar. But before either could ask her to elaborate a servant interrupted them by depositing a plate of some cold meats on the table before the King and Queen. They waited for the serving girl to go away before querying Gwenhwyvar on her statement.

"Are ye planning a magical intervention to aid the battle?" asked Gwenhwyvar.

"Aye; is that it?" asked Arthur. This only served to provoke another round of looking at each other for inspiration. This time Merlin tried to salvage the situation. It was vital that they let him know about Ivorwulf, but not here in the presence of so many tapestries within which he could be hiding, watching, listening.

"We shall ride out to the shores of the River Usk this morning, Arthur, immediately after the morning meal. Bring the three brothers," he said, referring to Sirs Galahallt, Garethe and Guaen. "Then we shall reveal what we are thinking."

He gave Arthur a look as if he had supplied and answer that would overcome any further questioning from the Royal duo. Recognising the non-verbal queue from the old Sorcerer, they did not ask any follow-up questions. Instead they elected to eat the morning meal with some haste so that the *ride* could begin as soon as possible so that all would be revealed.

Chapter 11: The River Usk

The river surged before them. Merlin and Morgan hadn't made any effort to speak to Arthur for the entire journey to the shore of the river, something that made the journey to the body of water that separated this part of Arthur's Kingdom from the south Angles seem longer.

Merlin and Morgan had ridden a little ahead and were waiting for Arthur and the three Knights to join them. They remained on horseback. The party managed to manoeuvre their horses close enough together so as to speak without raising their voices.

It was not a particularly bright day. Clouds hung overhead threatening rain. The wind was cold and unrelenting. Merlin gave them the disturbing news.

"We hath seen a spy within the walls of Caerleon. He is a Sorcerer that watches and listens to us, hidden from within the tapestries that cover the walls. We know only that his name is Ivorwulf and that he's in the employ of a Jute warlord in Kent by the name of Karal." Merlin let the significance of what he'd said sink into the men.

Their shocked expressions told him that it had had the desired effect. Morgan took over the explanation.

"Ivorwulf is the man that brokered the agreement between the Jutes, Angles and Saxons to unite against thee should any one of them be threatened. So Karal hath in his employ a skilled diplomat as well as a powerful Sorcerer. This constitutes a threat to us in a way that we hath never before encountered." Morgan's words were true. King Arthur had not faced any enemy with a magical sage in their employ. Although Hellekin, former king of the faerie people had allied himself with Aelle in order to defeat Arthur, they'd learned that it was for selfish motives rather than any direct malice against the reign of Arthur. The Minotaur that Queen Gwenhwyvar had battled to recover Excalibur was not interested in Arthur's lands or expansion, only in appropriating more magical beings that he could drain of their power. And finally, the Green Knight that'd been resurrected in order to destroy Arthur and his Knights one by one, was really nothing more than an attempt to take revenge upon Merlin and Morgan for meddling in Hellekin's malicious plans.

This was different. Karal, like Arthur, had a powerful Sorcerer at his side. A very human warlord with all of the typical human desires of a Jute invader and also access to a magical being, one that was described by Morgan as 'powerful'; a reference not lost on Arthur. He looked at Galahallt who shrugged and offered the obvious question.

"What do we do about this?" he looked to his brothers. Guaen was more concerned with the reasons behind Karal employing a Sorcerer.

"What binds this magician to Karal? Can he be tempted away to instead serve King Arthur?" he looked over at the King as he spoke. Garethe like Guaen was more interested in the logistics of how the relationship between them worked.

"What rewards does this Sorcerer hope to attain in the service of a Jute warlord, one that I hath never before heard spoken of?"

Merlin was unwilling to enter into conjecture at this point.

"That is all that we know. There are still many unanswered questions. Morgan and I hath tried to uncover, through vision, all that we can. It was yesterday that he was seen for the first time in thine study, Arthur; then again at the Round Table meeting. We sought to find out more information so that we would hath something to tell ye other than the fact that we're being spied upon." Merlin finished his rebuff of the three brother's pointless questions.

Arthur listened and considered what he'd just heard. Merlin and Morgan had only recently confirmed that they were now dealing with a magical intruder in the Castle.

"Can he be kept out of Caerleon?" he asked, being particularly pragmatic rather than just pointlessly concerned.

"Perhaps all of the tapestries can be removed?" offered Morgan "If he has nowhere to hide then he cannot infiltrate our walls."

"See to it when we return to Caerleon," ordered Arthur, pleased with the thought of cutting off the scouts secret way into the castle.

"We hath no way of knowing if he is capable of other means of surveillance. Removing the tapestries may not stop him," warned Merlin.

"Until ye know otherwise, we shall do what we can to mitigate any further loss of our secret information," advised Arthur. "However, preventing him from working for Karal should be our goal now. It takes precedence over all others. Do ye understand?"

He looked for confirmation of understanding from all present. It took only a few seconds for Merlin to present a possible solution.

"We can disguise ourselves as Angle traders and infiltrate the house of Karal, taking Ivorwulf by force and returning to Caerleon," he said, clearly pleased with his proposed solution.

"How can we take by force a man that will most certainly not want to be removed from the house of his employer?" asked Sir Garethe.

"If his is so powerful, then we can use that power, combined with ours to cast the spell of instantaneous travel. We can take him right out from under the noses of the Jutes and return to Caerleon in a moment of time." Now that he was forced to come up with more detail, Merlin's mind was racing, and as usual, coming up with creative solutions. It was Morgan however, that chipped in.

"We can bind him with faerie silk ropes – I hath some – for they effectively bind magical creatures, and he will be no different."

Morgan's offering to the newly hatched plan brought a resounding 'Aye' from Merlin. That was all that they needed. Unknown to Arthur or the three Knight Brothers, a moment of unsaid communication occurred between Merlin and Morgan. Morgan began.

"Do ye think that together with Ivorwulf we will be capable of travelling back to Caerleon?" Merlin replied.

"We must assume that Ivorwulf's power along with our own will be enough. Otherwise ye may hath to steal his power and use it for our escape. Either way we'll prevail."

They had a silent agreement that the most critical phase of their plan, their escape, hinged upon being able to force Ivorwulf to use his powers to open a portal back to Caerleon and almost certain imprisonment. Either that, or Morgan being able to remove a section of Ivorwulf's powers, just as she had twice before stolen the Minotaur's and used them for their magical escape. It was a good plan; there was no need to bother Arthur or the brothers with their own uncertainties.

Arthur was impressed with the turn of events. From being spied upon by a Wizard from Kent to producing a plan to end his association with the Jute warlord by taking him from the land in an instant. He slapped his thighs in delight and his mount took this as a signal to move and began to rear up. Realising his mistake, Arthur had to quickly settle the beast.

"I swear, Merlin, it's genius like this that will finally win us what we have sought for so long!" He commended his sage before pointing off down the road. "Let us ride back to Caerleon and outfit thine party ready for thine journey to Kent. How shall ye infiltrate, via South Gyrwe?"

Merlin shook his head. "We shall go to Humbor and take a boat disguised as an Angle trader. We shall arrive at their main port and begin our search for Karal and Ivorwulf."

As Merlin finished the final detail of their plan it all made perfect sense. It was settled: Arthur, Morgan, Sir Guaen, Sir Galahallt and Sir Garethe would travel to Humbor and disguise a long boat as an Angle trader. Enter the main Jute port in Kent, seek, locate and retrieve Ivorwulf, the Kentish Sorcerer.

Chapter 12: Humbor

Having the stable hands outfit the mission to Humbor was problematic. They weren't told where the party was going, nor how many days they'd be gone. Morgan also took charge of instructing the provisioning of the journey, much to the surprise of the servants. Enough provisions were made for a journey to one of Arthur's closest other castles. They had left Caerleon along with Sir Dynadane and travelled with him for most of the way, but at some point he had to make his way back to North Gyrwe, whilst the raiding party moved onwards to Humbor.

They arrived at Arthur's post in Humbor, which had been surrendered to him by the then-king some seventeen years before. Here Arthur had stationed Sir Kay for the past year to act as his regent and he was delighted to see the arrival of Merlin, Morgan and the three Brother Knights. He fussed over them like they were visiting dignitaries. The small castle and surrounding village was abuzz with the 'important' visitors from Caerleon. As it was located on the coast, it had a port with a number of long boats moored. It was here that Garethe had taken Sir Kay to choose the appropriate boat for their journey. Still quite in the dark about their reasons for being there, Sir Kay was not quite sure what to offer Garethe.

"The three largest long boats would be good for an extended journey over the sea to...Magna Frisia?" he said, fishing for further information from his fellow Knight. Garethe gave him a look as if to say 'nice try', and pointed out the boats next down in size to those.

"These three here are mid-sized boats. It looks as if they would not be used to travel such a long distance, Aye?" Garethe asked for confirmation of his assessment of the boats that he was indicating.

"Aye, Sir Garethe, they would not look as if they had travelled a long distance at all."

"This one in particular," pointed out Garethe," seems to have a look about it that is...foreign," he said. Indeed he was correct. Sir Kay gave him the exact information that he was hoping to hear.

"Aye, it was captured from a battle with the Angles to the south some three years ago. The sail should hath been changed to colours more befitting a boat of Briton but..." He did not get to finish his explanation.

"It is perfect for our requirements Sir Kay, requisition it and fit it out for a journey south of no more than two days. Sir Kay acknowledged that he would do as instructed.

***

"Our journey will be made in the forms that we are now," Informed Merlin to his raiding crew. "But before we dock at the main Jute port of Londinium, Morgan and I shall transform us into the likenesses of Angles." He looked over to Morgan to finish the briefing of the Knights.

"Merlin and I hath stored the likenesses of some Angles that we hath seen over the years or in visions. These images will be used as the basis for our new bodies and faces."

Sirs Garethe, Galahallt and Guaen were being told the finer details of the plan by Merlin and Morgan in the former king's throne room, which was now the administration hall. All of the nonessential personnel had been cleared from the room. They were alone; not even Sir Kay had been allowed to attend this final meeting before the sea journey from Humbor to Kent.

"Will it hurt; the transformation?" asked Sir Galahallt. He could see immediately from the reactions of both Merlin and Morgan that it would.

"Aye," answered Merlin in his own good time, "but it's for a greater good. And it won't hurt once done, only during the process," he assured them. The brothers were less than comforted at the good news that the old Sorcerer was offering them.

"What if we encounter an Angle boat at sea that challenges us?" queried Sir Guaen. His brother answered that concern.

"The boat being readied was formerly an Angle boat. It looks like one that they would use because it was one of theirs. So we should be able to pass by other Angle boats and wave as if we are friends, on our way to trade in Kent."

"When we arrive at Londinium, how do we find the house of Karal and therefore Ivorwulf?" It was Sir Guaen again. There was no hesitation before Merlin answered.

"He is a significant Jute in Kent. We shall simply ask other traders where we are to find him as we hath swords and spears to offer his armoury." It was a logical extension of their masquerade. Other traders would be the source of their information once they arrived in Kent.

"What if Ivorwulf is away at another meeting...?" began Galahallt but Morgan cut him off.

"Merlin and I will be able to hath visions of him before we make port. If we find that he is not in Kent, we shall turn back and return to Humbor." It was not quite a lie, but it was very uncertain that they would have visions of Ivorwulf once closer in proximity to the Sorcerer. The Knights did not need to know that however.

Everyone seemed satisfied that the plan was achievable in its current form.

"When do we leave?" asked Sir Galahallt.

"Immediately" said Merlin.

***

The journey down the coast and past the East Angle-occupied shoreline was uneventful. There were occasional sightings of other boats but always they were too far away to see in any detail. This helped ease the mood of the party on the boat. They were without their usual oarsmen and other servants, so they all had to rely upon any knowledge that skills of sea-going travels that they had each accumulated over the years.

Eventually though they had left the lands of the East Saxons behind and were entering the mouth of the Thames. Now there were more boats around them, but dressed as they were in plain robes, nobody gave them a second look. They felt somehow strangely cocooned in the midst of the other traders coming and going up and down the river. They were in effect hidden by the great number of other traders. The plan was working, even at this early stage. It was a comforting feeling for them all.

When the time came for the transformation it had to be done as quietly as possible and without raising the attention of any of their fellow boats. So Morgan and Merlin worked in a way that they had not done before. Merlin casting the spell of transformation upon the first Knight, basing his new Angle face and body upon a man of similar age and height that he'd witnessed at some time in his travels; Morgan using her powers to supress as best she could the pain associated with taking on a new form.

One by one they brothers were transformed into very ordinary looking men. Morgan elected to transform herself whilst Merlin did his best to mitigate her pain and then finally Merlin turned his powers upon himself while Morgan did her best to quell his discomfort. It was done. The party was unrecognisable form the one that had left Humbor barely one and a half days prior.

Merlin was pointing to the docks of Londinium now ahead of them.

"Use one of the less crowded areas to moor the boat," he directed Garethe who was at the rudder. They made their way to a smaller set of docks that were way from the main cluster. It was a wise decision. Hardly a person looked at them as they made port and tied up their boat. Once they had disembarked they moved through the crowd and the stench toward the main street of the old city. Merlin grabbed the arm of a similarly aged man passing by and asked him for directions to Karal's house. He was annoyed at being disturbed and pointed angrily with his finger.

"It is the largest house down the second largest street yonder." He said, and did not wait for thanks before stomping away. The party huddled together for a quick conference. Morgan spoke

"Our luck could not be any better. Karal is situated here in Londinium. That will save us much time." Merlin joined in her delight at the turn of events.

"Take only what we need in order to present ourselves as Traders to the house of Karal. No other provisions will be necessary."

"What of the boat, should we leave one to guard it?" inquired Garethe

"No. It can be abandoned. Taking Ivorwulf by force all the way back here to pick up one of our number will be infeasible," stated Merlin. "We all go together, capture Ivorwulf and together escape to Caerleon. If all goes well we shall be back at the Castle within the hour."

Merlin's tempting offer to complete their mission and retreat to the safety of Caerleon Castle hundreds of miles away in that very hour was all of the encouragement that the group needed to proceed with all haste. They made their way in the direction of Karal's house as quickly as they dared without wanting to look as if they were hurrying.

***

Karal's house looked familiar to Merlin, and although he'd only seen it from the inside, the outside reflected his memory of it perfectly. The proportions, the angle of the roof, the overall size...it was all as he had seen in his vision. There were guards at the main entrance questioning everyone that entered. The group were in close conference once more.

"Hath ye seen any visions of Ivorwulf? Is he inside?" asked Sir Garethe, looking from Merlin to Morgan.

"There is no need. I can feel his presence inside," comforted Merlin. Morgan agreed.

"Aye, it's a very definite feeling of a magician; singular and most assuredly a Sorcerer of great power." Morgan's words were somehow less comforting. Now there was knowledge that the man that they had to capture was thought of as 'powerful' by Morgan, who herself was a force to be reckoned with. Although now somewhat ill at ease the three brothers were too proud to show it. Garethe spoke for them.

"We continue as planned," he said, and waited for all of the others to acknowledge. When he received it he brazenly turned and led the way to the main doorway.

The two burley guards had to deal with an old woman who had reached them slightly ahead of the disguised Caerleon raiding party. She was complaining loudly about not receiving her due payment for cleaning the Lord's room. The guards were having none of it. It was not their concern but that of the man who divvied out the wages for the many staff that were in the employ of Karal.

"Go inside and speak to Ganautas," one of the guards said in the hope of dismissing the ugly and quite smelly old woman as quickly as possible. He was successful. She hobbled past the men. They then brought their suspicious faces to bear on the party of five before them.

"What do ye want here?" challenged the tallest and widest of the two. Galahallt answered whilst bringing out a sheathed sword to show the duo.

"We are traders from Edmans; purveyors of weapons for Karal's armoury. See what we hath to offer." He handed the sword to the guard who accepted it and drew it out to inspect it more closely. The group could tell from the expression on his face that he was enamoured with the blade. Guaen took up the story.

"All made by the finest craftsmen in our artisan town. Swords, arrows and quivers; these are our speciality. Ye will find none finer." He said embellishing the original cover story that they'd practiced on the boat journey here.

"Nor more expensive, I'll wager," replied the guard in a somewhat snide tone.

"Of course," said Merlin, "Karal could content himself with inferior weaponry for a cheaper price, we can always sell our wares to Wlencing of Anderidae." This clearly struck a nerve with both of the guards.

"Karal will be eager to see what ye offer," said the other guard, quiet up until then. The first guard gave his compatriot a displeased look but begrudgingly agreed. He slammed the sword back into its sheath and handed it back to Galahallt.

"Go to the end of the main room and ask for Ivorwulf – he's in charge of purchasing weapons for Karal."

The group couldn't believe their luck. The very man that they were here to capture was the man that their cover-story had serendipitously led them too. One or two of the group nodded in thanks to the guards as they walked past and through the large double wooden doors.

Inside the main hall was almost pandemonium. It was exactly as Merlin had seen it in his vision. They had all eventually witnessed Merlin's dream through the memory stone that he had made of it. So the surroundings were familiar to all of them. There were people everywhere, either talking or arguing or bartering with what looked to be Karal's men. There was a similarity about the way that many of them were dressed. The leather arm bands that they had seen on the two outside guards were present on many of the men inside. This must have been some sort of uniform for Karal's men. But there was no time to think of such details now. They had to find their objective and make off with him.

Easing their way through the crowd and noise, they moved so as to not push or shove anyone. They wanted to remain as inconspicuous as possible. Just as with the journey down the coast and up the river Thames, nobody gave them a second look. Feeling safe behind their disguised bodies, they were also becoming emboldened by their success so far.

"There!" said Morgan, alerting them all and indicating with her gaze a small doorway at the other end of the main room. Standing outside of it was Ivorwulf. He seemed to be finishing up some business with someone. Their timing couldn't have been better. He'd finished whatever deal or business he was conducting by the time the party reached him and the three brothers were ahead of Merlin and Morgan. They began by bidding Ivorwulf greetings and took him through the prepared story that they'd used to get this far.

It didn't seem to have the same effect upon him, though. He even ignored the sword that Galahallt offered him to view. Instead he seemed focussed upon Merlin and Morgan. A look of curiosity and almost befuddlement covered his face. Merlin and Morgan guessed immediately that Ivorwulf must be sensing their magical prowess just as they could feel his.

"You two," said Ivorwulf whilst pointing out the magical twosome. "Come forward."

With their hearts in their throats they complied. Ivorwulf leaned forward almost as if to sniff the air around them both. He squinted his eyes and wrinkled up his nose.

"Christians?" he asked.

Morgan and Merlin looked at each other. This was the perfect way to explain the feeling that Ivorwulf was experiencing. He too must have experienced the way that Christians feel to magical beings.

And he too must have been perplexed that they were completely incapable of actually practicing any magic at all.

"Aye," said Merlin.

"Aye," mimicked Morgan, "how did ye know?" She tried best to look vexed and amazed at Ivorwulf's identification of their religious leanings. For his part Ivorwulf looked disgusted and waved them away without any further explanation. He instead turned his attention back to the three brothers.

"Weapons ye say?" he said. indicating that they should show him what they had to offer. Galahallt, Garethe and Guaen all took out their still-sheathed swords to allow Ivorwulf to see them more closely. Guaen partially drew his out so that the fine work on the blade could be seen. Just like the guards outside, Ivorwulf looked impressed. He took the one from Guaen and studied it more closely.

"How many and how much?" he asked somewhat gruffly.

"Forty swords of similar ilk; forty bows made from seasoned birch, flexible but strong, and two hundred of the straightest arrows that ye will hath ever seen in thine lifetime." The confidence in Galahallt's voice was apparent.

"No doubt," said Ivorwulf. Although it was now impossible to tell if he was being sarcastic or accepting of the boast because of what he could see of the workmanship being presented to him.

"Come inside, we will discuss price," he said and turned to open the doorway behind him. He impatiently waved all of them inside. "Quickly, quickly!" he bullied. One by one they moved past Ivorwulf and into the hall that lay behind the door. They stood aside and allowed Ivorwulf to close the door and then take the lead. Flickering torches lit the way and there were a number of doors off to each side. They were in a central corridor that must have led to a number of other small chambers that made up the rest of the long house.

He led them to an ornate doorway and produced a key to unlock the door. Inside there were racks of swords, shelves of bows and arrows, spears and shields. They gathered just inside the doorway and waited for Ivorwulf to close the door behind them. His tone sounded a little less gruff.

"These will make a fine addition to Karal's armoury. How long before ye can deliver all of the number that ye hath available?" the silence that greeted him was a little awkward. He looked from one to the other waiting for a response. Morgan broke the silence.

"There is one more weapon that ye hath not yet seen," she said rather mysteriously, tempting him with the unknown. From her robes she produced the faerie silken rope and began to unfurl it. Ivorwulf was disappointed.

"Rope?" he said disbelievingly. "We hath rope my dear, there is no need for more." He was dismissive of the offer. But Morgan insisted.

"But this rope cannot be easily cut. In fact, it cannot be cut at all." She gave him a look of mischievousness and once again Ivorwulf's curiosity was aroused.

"What?" he said "I hath never heard of such a thing. Show me!"

"With pleasure," Morgan replied to his demand, and flicked the rope out towards him. It curled itself around his body almost as if by its own accord. Ivorwulf was alarmed and made to cry out but all three swords were hastily drawn and each shoved toward his open mouth.

"Shout and 'twill be the last thing that ye ever say," warned Guaen. Ivorwulf's eyes narrowed at the threat.

"Do ye know who I am?" he said and without waiting for a response he completed his sentence "I am the Sorcerer of Kent. I shall cause thine bodies to become engulfed in flame. Thine death will be excruciating."

"Proceed," challenged Merlin. His tone was mocking. This drew an immediate response from Ivorwulf. Mumbling beneath his breath he spoke the spell of fire. Morgan and Merlin knew it well enough.

Even the three Knights had heard it often enough to recognise some of the ancient words. Then as he concluded the spell...nothing.

Ivorwulf was alarmed. It had not worked. Why? All of this could be seen going through his head. Morgan took it upon herself to explain the mystery to him.

"Magical ropes to capture a magical man," she said rather smugly.

"Now hear these words Ivorwulf, Sorcerer of Kent. Consider thee a prisoner of King Arthur of Caerleon. His eyes widened. He looked more carefully at Morgan and then at Merlin. The realisation of who they really were dawned upon him.

"Merlin Ambrosias," he said looking at the body that Merlin had assumed.

"Morgan Le Fay," he said, identifying the woman that he didn't recognise but was standing before him, holding him captive with her magical rope. There was an air of awe in his tone. It pleased both Merlin and Morgan considerably.

"What do ye want of me?" he said, somewhat panicked.

"All in good time," said Merlin, failing to allay any fears that Ivorwulf was having. "For now ye should consider what we want of thee, and not King Arthur."

This changed the situation a little. Could it be that Merlin and Morgan had set out to capture him for their own ends rather than those of King Arthur?

"What is it that ye would hath me do?" he queried.

"Join with us to cast a spell, here and now," instructed Merlin. Ivorwulf considered the demand for only a second before dismissing it with logic.

"How odd Sorcerer, for I am bound by magical ropes that prevent me from performing magic." The absurdity of the offer from Merlin was making Ivorwulf even more irritable than he already was.

"We shall remove the ropes, but only if ye agree to join with us to cast a spell the likes of which ye hath never before seen." Merlin leant forward pointing to Ivorwulf as he spoke so as to give his offer a small dash of drama. This quietened the Kentish Sorcerer. They could see that he was pondering the proposition.

"What spell is it that we should cast together?" he asked, clearly intrigued.

"The spell of instantaneous travel" replied Merlin. This however did not resonate with Ivorwulf at all.

"What? I hath never before heard of such a spell. What does it do?"

"As it says, Ivorwulf," explained Morgan, "travel to anywhere that ye desire in an instant of time." This was clearly more absorbing for the Wizard than even the fine weapons that they had shown him prior. He looked from Morgan to Merlin and back again.

"Surely not?" he said, but there was a note of hope in his voice almost as if to say please don't be joking with me, I want to believe this. Merlin and Morgan knew that they had his full attention. It was time to appeal to his magical curiosities and make a bargain with him. Merlin stood before him and tempted Ivorwulf with something that he knew would be valued higher than any precious metal or currency that he could otherwise have offered.

"A bargain, Ivorwulf; accompany us back to Caerleon. I give mine word that ye will be treated well, and Morgan and I will show ye the spell of which we speak." He finished his simple agreement and waited for the response. Even now Morgan and Merlin were guessing that Ivorwulf would agree to the pact thinking that once learned he could similarly use the spell to escape. Little did he know how much power it took to create the wondrous door? Unless both Caerleon magicians had greatly underestimated his power, he would be unable to do it alone. Or even if he could, it would not take him very far and he could be recaptured.

"Ye promise that I will be treated well and not as a Jute prisoner thrown into a cell bound by these....magical ropes?" He looked for confirmation of the outcome of accepting their accord. Merlin closed his eyes and nodded deeply indicating that he would be a man of his word. Ivorwulf took a few more moments to consider.

"The offer is too tempting to refuse, Merlin. I must learn this spell of which ye speak. Unbind me; I shall go with ye willingly." The enthusiasm in his voice was unmistakable. They had judged the situation and the man well. He would do exactly what they needed to complete their plan in return for what he desired, assist them all to escape from Londinium.

Morgan removed the faerie silk ropes. He looked much more carefully at them as she did so.

"Amazing, magical inhibiting ropes. Ye must show me how they were made?" the change in his demeanour was amazing. He seemed like an old friend that was enthusiastically exchanging ideas with a member of his inner circle. Morgan took up her place to one side of Ivorwulf and Merlin to the other. He looked expectantly at them.

"Hold our hands," instructed Merlin. Ivorwulf took Merlin's left and hand and Morgan's right. This left Merlin's right hand and Morgan's left free to trace the outline of their escape portal in the air in front of them.

"Send thine power into our bodies as we trace the air with our hands," said Morgan. They could feel that Ivorwulf was complying. The surge in their power was astounding. Together they felt that there would be nothing that they couldn't achieve. It was intoxicating. Concentrating now as one, the three magicians thought of Caerleon castle. Even though he'd never before seen it, the image of it was alive in Merlin and Morgan's joined mind. Ivorwulf was a part of that now; he could see the king's study.

"That is where we shall travel to," said Merlin. With those words, the portal appeared before them, like an impossibly detailed tapestry. The King's study was there on the other side of the opening.

Torchlight lit the room and the fireplace had a roaring fire going; it must have only recently been stoked, for it looked inviting.

"Step through," commanded Merlin to the three Knights. Dutifully they did so, one at a time.

"Now ye Ivorwulf," bade Morgan.

Releasing their hands, he walked up to the shimmering doorway and reached out as if to touch it. But it was as if he was touching only air. He could feel the warmth of the room beyond. It was more cosy that the one in which he stood. Watching his foot as it stepped over the edge of the doorway and landed securely on the flagstone floor beyond. He turned around to watch the progress of his other leg as he repeated the movement.

"I am standing in King Arthur's study, three day's hard ride from here by horse! Incredible!" he was positively beaming with delight. Merlin and Morgan stepped through the doorway. They both turned to look at the room that they had just left. The doorway shimmered and faded away. Ivorwulf watched this too, with absorbed attention.

"Let King Arthur know that we hath returned," instructed Merlin to Sir Galahallt. The Knight made to follow his order from Merlin when a curious thing happened. A voice from above them somewhere countermanded the order.

"Do not waste thine time Sir Galahallt" said the disembodied voice. It was a very familiar voice to Merlin and Morgan.

"Nimue?" questioned Morgan, addressing the room around them. The faerie Queen was nowhere to be seen. Then just like the portal that had made good their escape from Londinium, the walls of the King's study began to shimmer and break apart into small silver fragments that dissipated into nothing; like vapour coming from a hot pot of stew. Soon it was gone. They were not in the King's study at all. It looked to be a cave of some description. There were stalagmites and stalactites of rock coming up from the floor of the cave and hanging down from the ceiling. It was a huge cavern.

Light filled it from oversized torches coming out of the rock walls surrounding them.

Nimue was standing to the right of the surprised sextet of people, partially hidden by a huge outcrop of rock. She stepped forward. Alerted by their peripheral vision they all turned in unison to look at her.

"Ye are now our prisoners!" she said rather coldly. Before anyone had a chance to question any part of what she had just announced, two other figures stepped forward flanking her.

"There is no escape" added Nimue. With that she gave a signal. Faerie silken ropes appeared out of nowhere flung by unseen assailants. They wrapped themselves around Merlin, Morgan and Ivorwulf and the three Knights. They were now powerless to even use the spell of instantaneous travel to escape, much less any other of their abilities. Nimue was correct, they were all prisoners.

Chapter 13: The Ultimatum

"What are ye doing Nimue? How dare ye capture us!" roared Merlin, not quite knowing where to begin with his verbal tirade against the Queen.

"Why Nimue, Why?" was all that Morgan could say under the circumstances. For her part Nimue held up her hands to stop any further objections.

"We hath taken this action out of desperation. It is not thine captivity that we desire Merlin, Morgan. We seek to make a bargain with Ivorwulf." The captured party all turned to look at Ivorwulf. He was perplexed. Nimue and her two cohorts moved so that they were standing directly in front of Ivorwulf. The three brother Knights were wise enough to not struggle against the strange looking ropes binding them. There were magical forces at work and they knew without Morgan and Merlin's aide, they would be no match for them.

"I am Aine, Queen of the faerie people of Gaul," stated the woman on one side of Nimue. Her tone was regal.

"I am Kendrik, King of the faerie people of Magna Frisia," said the man on Nimue's other side.

"I am Nimue, Queen of the faerie people of Briton. Ivorwulf, we wish to employ thee to cast us a spell." Nimue reached out and held Ivorwulf's shoulders.

"Will ye hear us out?" she pleaded. Ivorwulf nodded in silence.

"Release him," commanded Nimue. The guard that was holding the faerie rope that had entwined Ivorwulf gave it a flick and it disengaged itself and returned to a neat pile resting in the guard's hands. Ivorwulf watched all of these proceedings with wide eyes.

"Faeries?" he said "From here and other lands?" Ivorwulf looked around the cavern. Now that he did so he could see a great number of guards had appeared as if from nowhere. There seemed to be three distinct types. Some were dressed in the style that King Kendrik was, although nowhere near as ornate clothing. Similarly there where those whose clothing had a passing resemblance to that worn by Queen Aine. And lastly the remaining third seemed to come from Nimue's tailors. Their clothing was strange though, all of it shimmered as if it was silk, but it looked more like leather.

The guards were stone-faced and clearly not to be trifled with, and their leaders seemed to be similarly disposed. All three converged upon Ivorwulf each had their turn in speaking to him. Kendrik was first.

"Thine prowess as a powerful Sorcerer is apparent Ivorwulf, what we ask should be easily accomplished by ye." Aine was next.

"One spell with various ingredients that need to be mixed and warmed all ready and waiting for ye." Nimue concluded the brief information session.

"Speak the spell of fertility for our combined faerie peoples, Ivorwulf, so that we may once more bear children of our own." The held his gaze. As if to answer Ivorwulf's unasked question, Nimue produced a scroll and handed it to Ivorwulf. He accepted it and unfurled it gently. There upon its surface were the words to the fertility spell. He brought it up to his face more closely and studied the words carefully. There was an agonising silence whilst he judged the spell against his own magical ability.

"The ingredients are already.....available?" he asked when it became obvious what they were, and from whom they needed to be resourced.

"A former ruler of Briton, now making himself useful to us all," said Aine in a rather snide and mocking way.

Merlin and Morgan were watching the proceedings with growing alarm. This was not a situation that they could with clear conscious allow to continue. They signalled to each other to move closer so that they may have a 'private' conversation with each other.

Without looking like they were trying to struggle against their captor's ropes, they pretended to be interested in what was on the scroll that Ivorwulf was reading. Craning their necks and tilting their bodies they managed to close the small distance between them without raising the suspicion of the guards holding them. Eventually their shoulders touched and they were free to converse without being overheard.

"Merlin, we cannot allow this to happen. Matrona was very clear about us not casting the spell of fertility for the faeries."

"I agree, Morgan, but what can we do? If Ivorwulf could be convinced to join powers with us again, then I am certain that we could either open another portal or at the very least fight these faeries. But if not, then we are no match for three faerie rulers. Ivorwulf is the key to this; we must get him on our side if we are to prevail."

"Then Merlin, we must await a suitable opportunity."

With their brief exchange over they re-joined the conversation happening in front of them.

"What is it that ye are offering me in exchange for this work?" asked Ivorwulf.

"We know that gold and money do not tempt ye," stated Aine. "So we hath arranged a payment greater than any other paid to a mortal man." There was a brief pause. The small group collectively wondered what such a payment could possibly be. King Kendrik told them what they wanted to know.

"Access to the faerie library of spells, here in Briton, in Gaul and in Magna Frisia," he said indicating the ruler of each as he spoke. "Limited access of course; we would not give ye unbridled use of every faerie spell discovered, forged and written by our peoples throughout our history. But there would be more spells than any other man hath ever before seen. More magic available to ye than any other Sorcerer that hath lived before, Ivorwulf. Think of it!?" he said.

Merlin and Morgan looked worriedly at Ivorwulf. The expression on his face said it all. He was absolutely captivated with the thought of gaining so many spells. Merlin quickly interjected to see if he could make the offer somehow seem less appealing.

"What if Ivorwulf refuses; what then?" he challenged the faerie rulers with his inappropriate question. This brought Ivorwulf's attention back to the present. He did not look as if he was going to refuse and yet he did not dismiss Merlin's question outright. The faerie monarchs were displeased with Merlin's outburst.

"Silence him Nimue or I shall take matters into mine own hands!" bellowed Aine, her tone dripping with malice. Merlin actually took a step back he was so intimidated by the threat. Wanting to support Merlin's initiative Morgan took up the line of questioning.

"Will ye try and force Ivorwulf to do thine bidding if he does refuse?" asked Morgan trying to look as innocent as she could under the circumstances. This time King Kendrik shouted down the objection.

"Silence witch or I shall see thee flogged for thine insolence." He was clearly not to be antagonised. In a small way the tactic had an effect upon Ivorwulf. He looked at the three faeries before him and could be seen wondering 'what if I *do* refuse?' Accurately reading the situation Nimue sought to stave-off any further inquiries about the consequences of refusing the offer put before him.

"Ivorwulf is being offered a prize greater than any Sorcerer or even any single faerie ruler hath ever before been offered. Let there be no more talk of refusal. Think only of the mysteries that ye will be able to uncover, the magical powers that ye will accumulate from such a collected book of knowledge." Nimue let the temptation sit in the air before Ivorwulf.

The moments dragged by slowly. Ivorwulf turned around and looked down at the floor and then up at the cavernous ceiling far above him. He turned to face the rulers once more. Considering his words he drew a long breath before he spoke.

"Aye, the offer is indeed too tempting to refuse" he said brining looks of satisfaction from the monarchs.

"However, what if I were to refuse thine most generous offer? Would I be free to leave?" the follow up question came unexpectedly from the cunning Sorcerer. Nimue looked worriedly at her counterparts. For their part, Aine looked as if she were about to run Ivorwulf through with a sword, had she been holding one. Kendrik summed up the consequences for the trio of captive magicians.

"Free...Aye" he said simply and firmly. "I shall grant ye the freedom of...death!" he looked poignantly at Ivorwulf as he spat the final word of his threat at the Kentish resident. Merlin, Morgan and Ivorwulf unknowingly and unwittingly all drew in their breaths simultaneously. There was a moment's silence, broken by Merlin.

"Liar!' he said pointing an accusatory finger at Kendrik. "Nimue would not allow ye..."He did not get the chance to finish his sentence. Kendrik stepped forward and struck Merlin across the face, the brute force of the blow both shocking and stupefying the old Sorcerer. He stumbled beneath the ruler's hand. Morgan let out and unintentional scream of horror. Ivorwulf too was stunned at the show of anger.

"We are desperate old man," hissed Kendrik, "and with no other Sorcerer of Ivorwulf's abilities to be found in any of our lands we will hath the three of ye face the same extinction that we do rather than see Ivorwulf refuse our most generous offer!" He shouted so loudly that it echoed again and again in the cavern.

Nimue pushed past Kendrik and offered Merlin a steadying hand. She looked him directly in the eyes.

"King Kendrik is correct, Merlin. We *are* desperate. There hath been no births in any of our lands now for more than a decade. What other choice is there?" The way that Nimue presented the plight of the faeries was more inclined to garner sympathy from the magicians. Merlin and Morgan however knew that they were fulfilling the wishes of Matrona, the Lady of the Lake by not assisting the faeries. It was by her expressed wish that they would not. Ivorwulf was not under any such onus though.

In an act of immediate conciliatory diplomacy Ivorwulf spoke up.

"Then let us not speak of refusal. Instead let us set a time and day for the faerie people from all thine lands to gather so that the spell may be spoken."

This pleased the three faerie rulers immensely. They nodded in unison and smiled at the acceptance from their newly employed Sorcerer. Merlin was not going to be so easily silenced. He trusted the Lady of the Lake. She must have had reasons for not wanting to see the continuance of the faerie people. He objected strongly.

"No Ivorwulf. Ye should not help the faeries..." His tirade was cut short by Queen Aine with her shrill and malevolent voice.

"Gag him; gag them both, so that their objections will be silenced!" she ordered some of her nearby guards. The two that responded to their Queen's command produced faerie silk cloths of some description from within their garments. Merlin and Morgan looked worriedly at the two guards then at each other and then at Nimue. Seeing their concern she moved to quell their fears.

"Faerie silk, it will stop ye from talking but still allow ye to breathe." The comforting explanation did little to ease the nerves of the duo. Ivorwulf took this moment to begin his employment and moved to allow the two approaching guards easier access to Merlin and Morgan. He reached out and grabbed both their arms and pushed them in the direction of the guards. Time stopped.

Chapter 14: Nowhere

Merlin and Morgan looked around them.

"Where are we?" asked Morgan. Merlin was at a complete loss to explain; he'd never seen a place like this before.

"This is every place and no place," came the nonsensical explanation from a familiar voice behind them. They both spun around to see Ivorwulf standing there.

A fog covered the ground and occasionally billowed up like a roman column and then formed a ceiling of fog above them. Then the reverse happened, the fog floating eerily above them occasionally formed a column which funnelled more fog to the ground below. The earth felt soft, not like rock; more like wet soil but with the absence of squelching when pushing down into it. The horizon was unclear. Sometimes it seemed to be quite close to them and other times far away, much further than either of them had ever seen before. The sky was occasionally dark and other times all of the colours of the most brilliant sunset. There was no sun, no Galeach, no stars and no clouds other than the fog that swelled around them. There were no birds in the sky and no trees, no rocks, nor the sound of any beast of the wilderness.

"Ivorwulf?" said Morgan, completely at a loss. "Hath ye rescued us from the faeries?"

"No," he said, "we are still there. At this moment I'm pushing ye towards Queen Aine's guards to be gagged lest ye try to further convince me to not aide the faeries."

Merlin had the feeling that this had happened before. In a way it had during the battle with the Minotaur and Hellekin on Skellig Mhor. Matrona had taken Merlin out of his body and spoken with him at her lake. Although their conversation had seemed to take a long time, it had in fact occurred in a moment of time.

"Ye hath taken us all out of our bodies so that we may converse freely over any length of time before returning us to the cavern" stated Merlin confidently. Ivorwulf was impressed.

"Merlin, ye are living up to thine reputation as a wise sage. Aye, that is exactly that I hath done. We may converse for as long as necessary and only a second of time will hath passed in the real world."

Ivorwulf looked to Morgan for her reaction. She too was impressed. And although she tried hard to not show it, it was such an amazing show of magical ability her feelings could not be hidden very successfully.

"Why Ivorwulf? And where is this place? And no ambiguous answers either!" she warned, thinking back upon his first explanation of their surroundings.

"This place I hath created for the three of us," he answered. "It does not exist in our world nor the otherworld, but instead between them. A land of my own making between life and death that has no affiliation with either. We are here to sort out our current predicament. And when done we shall return." His words did little to clarify the situation.

"When we return to the cavern, what then, Ivorwulf?" Merlin asked. "We are to be gagged and will ye enter the employ of these untrustworthy creatures?"

"I will not," he said sternly, raising the eyebrows of both Morgan and Merlin.

"I lied to the faeries. Like ye, I believe that they're mischievous and untrustworthy. But the thought of death at their hands is not one that I wish to entertain." Ivorwulf's words were more welcome to Morgan and Merlin than the heartiest of meals.

"Then there is hope that ye will join with us to battle them and escape?" asked Morgan.

"Ye are not tempted by the faerie's offer?" queried Merlin. Ivorwulf turned to Morgan first to answer her question, then to Merlin.

"Aye and No," he stated firmly, "but how do we extricate ourselves from this situation without inciting a merciless retaliation, upon us all?" the reality of their situation weighed heavily upon the three magicians. They each looked at each other at a loss for ideas. This was an impossible situation one that would have consequences no matter what action they took.

"We need to exploit their weaknesses," said Morgan, pondering what those weaknesses were. Merlin thought with staggering speed for an old man and spoke his thoughts on what to do next.

"We must fight." Merlin waited for a reaction from his audience of two.

"Go on," prompted Ivorwulf.

"Before we are gagged in the cavern, the three of us shall combine our powers and speak the spell of faerie expulsion. Together we'll be a force to be reckoned with, even against three faerie rulers. Ye are indeed a powerful Sorcerer, Ivorwulf; think of what our combined powers hath already achieved. Now imagine the effect that we would hath expelling the faeries from the cavern?" Ivorwulf pondered and nodded seeing the sense in the plan.

"We shall need to act quickly," he pointed out. "And then when the faeries are fleeing, we shall again open a portal and travel, back to Kent." It was a perfectly reasonable request from Ivorwulf. Without him they could not hope to battle the amount of powerful faeries that they were facing. But to have achieved their goal and taken Ivorwulf from Kent and not return with him to Caerleon was not appealing to either Merlin or Morgan. Morgan tried to salvage the situation.

"Ivorwulf, ye would be alone in Kent and once again at the mercy of the faeries should they wish to mount an attack and reclaim ye.

But together in Caerleon the three of us can find a way to ensure thine safety." Morgan's ploy had the desired effect upon Ivorwulf. They could see that he did not relish the thought of being alone in Karal's longhouse. He spoke his thoughts.

"At least in Caerleon there would be the three of us, we would hath the safety of numbers." Ivorwulf's observation pleased the Caerleon magicians.

"Exactly," said Merlin hoping to seal the deal with Ivorwulf.

"Then so be it!" shouted Ivorwulf.

"Ye know the spell of faerie expulsion?" Morgan wanted to make certain their plan was going to succeed. Ivorwulf spoke the first line of the spell. Morgan and Merlin indicated that it was indeed the same spell that they were all going to be using.

"Then I see no point in delaying any further. Let us rid ourselves of these troublesome faeries," Ivorwulf said with a clap of his hands.

Chapter 15: The Battle

Ivorwulf finished pushing Merlin and Morgan toward the approaching guards. They were back in their bodies, restored. Only an instant of time had passed in the cavern, however, and the two guards that were to gag Merlin and Morgan were upon them. Coincidentally, Merlin was now closest to Kendrik, Morgan to Aine and Ivorwulf to Nimue.

The guards grabbed hold of Morgan and Merlin.

"Now!" shouted Merlin. In perfect unison they began to recite the spell of faerie expulsion. Even the first few words of the spell had an immediate effect upon the faeries closest to the magical trio. The guards stopped dead in their tracks almost as if stiff with fear. Then as each of the old Galatian language words spewed forth from the magicians the faeries began to react. It felt to them as if the very air that surrounded them had become impossibly heavy and was now crushing them. At the same time the air in their lungs felt as if it had become ignited and burned them from within. Their eyes felt like a hundred tiny fingernails were scratching at them, and closing their eyelids as tightly as they could did nothing to alleviate the pain they suffered. The combined agony was a torture more than any of them could bear.

Everywhere faeries screamed in torment. They would do anything to escape from the suffering that they were suddenly enduring. The magical trio began the final sentence of the spell, which was the nexus of the spell. Had a faerie not taken flight by now, the final words would have ensured that any faerie nearby would abandon their greatest desire in order to escape; love, loyalty, duty, all would mean nothing a few short words from now.

The guards, all fiercely loyal to faerie monarchs, had borne the anguish up to this point, but as the final three words rolled out of the mouths of the magical humans their distress became unimaginable.

Everywhere faeries screamed and took on the form of bats and birds of every description in order to take flight from the cavern as fast as their wings would take them.

The mismatched flock of birds scrambled and fluttered and flapped in multiple directions. Ivorwulf, Morgan and Merlin had to duck in order to not be hit in the head by any of them. Some flew so closely to them that they could feel the downdraft of wind that the wings were making as they lifted the birds up and away. A line of sorts seemed to form and many of the birds fell into it. The humans each correctly were guessing that the birds were making for the nearest exit to the caverns.

The three Knights seized upon the opportunity presented to them and struggled successfully against the ropes binding them. They freed themselves without too much bother as there were no longer any faeries around. Soon the cavern was silent. Merlin and Morgan too took the opportunity to disentangle themselves from the faerie ropes. The faeries were gone...except for Nimue, Aine and Kendrik.

The three humans looked worriedly at each other and then at the three faerie rulers that hadn't taken flight with their guards. There was a look of absolute murderous rage upon the faces of Aine and Kendrik while Nimue wore an expression of disappointment. It was difficult to tell if she was disappointed in Merlin, Morgan, Ivorwulf, or a combination thereof, or in the fact that their faerie plan to employ Ivorwulf had failed.

Shaking with rage, Aine spoke in a voice so icy that it made the three magicians shudder.

"The faerie spell of expulsion does not work on faerie rulers, insidious creatures!" Realising that the numbers were much more even for a fight, even if their adversaries were magical, the three brother knights all drew their swords. King Kendrick spoke next.

"If ye will not aide us then DIE!"

He lifted both of his hands and used a magnification spell to punch Merlin with both of his hands, and even though his hands did not physically connect with Merlin's body, the result threw Merlin across the cavern hitting the far wall with a thud that knocked the breath out of his body. He felt something break as he slid down the wall, it was most probably a rib. The pain tore through him. The rock face that he slid down scraped away skin from his back and feet. He hit the ground a let out a winded cry of shock and soreness.

Galahallt, Guaen and Garethe were the next to suffer at the hands of Kendrik. Again he punched the air with his hands and the impact scattered the three brothers in three different directions. They were similarly thrown across the cavern and way out the way of being able to offer assistance to anyone. They were incapable of helping themselves under the circumstances, much less anybody else. Guaen fell to the ground. Garethe impacted a stalagmite and cried out in agony as bones were broken by the rock. Galahallt was less fortunate than his brothers he had been lifted off the ground with such force that he speared his shoulder on a particularly slender and sharp looking stalagmite. The force of the levitation caused the rock icicle to pierce his trapezoid muscle and he bellowed as it pushed into it and the surrounding sinew. Then the weight of his body reversed the spearing and he fell to the ground in a heap. Without the rock holding back the flow of blood it was free to gush out of him like a red waterfall.

Queen Aine had somehow produced a faerie rope and entangled it around Morgan's neck pulling it tight. Morgan could not breathe; her fingers clutched and tried to grasp the rope that was choking her. But she could not get a grip on the silky rope.

Ivorwulf looked at the scenes surrounding him with horror. The Knights were all incapacitated. Merlin was most certainly mortally wounded and Morgan was close to death. He turned on Nimue who was similarly looking at the happenings around her with alarm; but she made no aggressive move toward Ivorwulf. He looked at her as if to either challenge her to begin attacking him or do otherwise. It was then that he noticed the distress upon her face. She looked at Morgan wilting beneath the onslaught of Queen Aine and moved as if to offer assistance but then thought the better of it and did not. She was conflicted, he could see that now. She wanted to assist Morgan and Merlin. She was looking from one to the other. Ivorwulf took the initiative and stepped toward her.

She looked alarmed but he held up his hands in a gesture of surrender and he offered her his hand. She looked down at it as if she were expecting a fireball to erupt from his fingers at her. But nothing happened. He offered her his hand again, more urgently this time. She instinctively reached out and took hold of it.

***

Garethe suddenly awoke. He was lying in a crumpled mess on the cavern floor. Something had happened, he felt different – alive, invigorated, no even more than that...fortified, rejuvenated and exhilarated. There was nothing that he could not do.

He jumped to his feet and surveyed the scene before him. Morgan was being strangled by a rope at least twenty paces away from him. He reacted; he threw his sword at her attacker, the Queen faerie. It flew through the air with unbelievable force and precision and stuck into the spine of the vicious faerie from Gaul. She squealed in a shriek more insidious than he had ever before heard. Dropping the ropes she turned to face her attacker. To her surprise it was one of the Knights. He had seemingly attacked her with his sword from an amazing distance for a human. Without caring to think how he had achieved this miracle she ran toward him howling like a wounded feral cat.

Morgan tore the faerie rope from her throat and gulped in the precious air that she had been denied. She was disorientated but managed to see in her haze of greedily inhaling the life-giving air that Garethe was about to be attacked by Aine. Somehow the Queen had reached around and grasped the sword protruding from her back by its handle and pulled it from her injured body. Now she was going to run the human through with his own weapon. He was only a second or two from death. Morgan could see he was looking about him for inspiration or anything that he could use to defend himself. There was nothing. He would have to fight hand to sword.

Morgan levitated the faerie rope that had been used to nearly end her life and with a flick of her wrists it snaked through the air and wrapped itself around Aine in the last step before she reached him. She had actually raised the sword to slash him from head through to his stomach when the magical rope entwined itself around her causing her to fall flat onto the hard rock. Once more she screamed a wail of such anger and hatred it would surely stay with them all the rest of their lives.

Kendrik turned his malevolence to Morgan.

"Wretched thing!" he called out as he jumped from where he was over to just in front of Morgan, surely levitating himself as the distance that he jumped was impossible to contemplate for a non-magical being. He landed with an angry thump only an arm's length from Morgan. Reacting with the only thing that she could think of to do Morgan cast a ball of fire at the faerie ruler in the hope of incinerating him. He knocked the fireball away from him with the back of his hand with contempt.

"Insignificant worm!" he cried as he repaid her in kind by producing his own fireball, this one of a much greater size. He hurled it at her. There was nothing that Morgan could think of to do. If she tried to deflect it as he did, her hand would be consumed by the fire. But instincts took over and that is exactly what she did. She would have to sacrifice her hand in order to save the rest of her body.

Instead of searing her flesh, the red fireball was perfectly deflected from its collision course with Morgan and it flew aside hitting a stalagmite and exploded. Kendrick was surprised and alarmed at the show of magical prowess from the Sorceress. Morgan could see on his face *'hath I underestimated her?*

She took the initiative and bluffed.

"Aye, Kendrick, ye hath indeed underestimated mine abilities. I am more than a match for a simple faerie ruler. Now feel my wrath as I squash ye like a bug beneath mine foot!" she shouted the final few words of the threat. King Kendrick was at best a practical faerie that wanted to preserve his own well-being or at the very least a coward more accustomed to his guards fighting his battles, because he took flight. Scared by the show of strength by Morgan he transformed himself into a falcon and flapped away and out of the range of this newfound enemy. Having been effectively deserted, Queen Aine called after him.

"Coward! Come back here and kill them! Kill them all!" she screamed from her bound position on the cavern floor. Morgan looked around; Ivorwulf and Nimue were nowhere to be seen. She rushed over to Galahallt as he seemed to be the one most in need of assistance. Pressing her hand over the wound, she invoked as much of the spell of healing as she could under the circumstances. Her heart was pounding; she was still gulping air at too fast a rate.

Garethe still feeling unbelievably alive and energetic ran to join his wounded brother and the Caerleon Sorceress. He pondered his amazing throw of his sword at the evil faerie Queen; the incredible distance that it had travelled and the amazingly accurate finding of its target. But when he saw how much blood had left Galahallt's body it pushed all other thoughts away.

"Galahallt?' he said as he bent down to offer what assistance he could.

"I hath stopped the bleeding," said Morgan. "I will tend to him, go and find Merlin and Guaen."

Garethe dutifully stood up and looked around the enormous cavern. He could see Merlin lying against a far rock-face wall. Guaen was at least an equal distance away in another direction, but he was on his feet and looking dazed and confused. At least he was standing; Garethe headed in the direction of Merlin.

Morgan had stopped the bleeding and was now in the process of closing the wound and repairing the muscle and skin. To her own amazement she was much more successful at a faster rate than she would normally have been. The wound was gone. She could see through his skin that the muscle was repaired. She looked over the Knight for further signs of damage. He had a broken ankle. She moved her hands to cover it. Remarkably the ankle was cured in hardly any time and with very little effort from her; at least it felt that way. She did not stop to wonder about her newfound amplified powers of healing. Instead she looked for all of the other bruises and other minor scrapes and gashes and cured them all.

Galahallt's eyes sprang open. He looked up at Morgan kneeling over him.

"What happened?" he asked.

"Ye are safe, and mended. King Kendrick caused ye a great injury, but he hath fled the cavern." Her explanation was welcome news to the Knight.

"Garethe? Guaen?" he further inquired.

"Garethe is assisting Merlin, Guaen is making his way toward us as we speak" she indicated to where she could see Guaen traversing the uneven rock floor of the cavern to re-join them.

"Ivorwulf?" he asked. Morgan looked all around. She could not see any sign of him. There was no sign of Nimue either. She stood up in order to get a better view of the uneven surroundings. Perhaps they were both obscured from sight by a rock formation. She shook her head.

"I cannot see Ivorwulf," she stated. A terrible thought occurred to Morgan at that very second. She was no longer in control of the faerie rope that had captured Queen Aine. Her heart pounded in her chest with the advent of the realisation. But there was nothing to be afraid of. Fixing her eyes upon the fallen faerie she could see that somehow the rope still had Aine ensnared. Morgan could not understand why. But then she felt something. She was still manipulating the rope using the power of levitation. She had been using it all along since she first flung the rope around the murderous Queen. That was why Aine was still imprisoned in the magical twine.

Morgan's own prowess at the spell astonished her. She had somehow managed to continue to bind the Queen ensuring that she was powerless whilst administering healing to Sir Galahallt. Morgan was amazed. Had she underestimated her own powers? And then another thought occurred to her. She had flung a fireball away from her without any damage to her skin. This was not something that she had learned from Merlin. How had she managed to do that? Morgan was perplexed.

Meanwhile, Sir Guaen had reached the Sorceress and his brother.

"We were victorious" he stated as he approached. This interrupted Morgan's trail of thought. She responded.

"Aye, although I am not entirely sure how we came to be so." The caveat on the victory was of little interest to Sir Guaen, all that mattered was that their enemies were vanquished.

Sir Garethe had now reached Merlin. He could see that the old man was in a bad way.

"I shall use the power of healing upon him" said Ivorwulf. Garethe almost jumped out of his skin. Ivorwulf had appeared behind him from nowhere.

"Where did ye come from!?" shouted the startled Sir Garethe. Ivorwulf either chose to ignore the question or could not be bothered to answer it because he motioned for the Knight to get out of his way.

"Stand aside so that I may offer assistance to Merlin" Ivorwulf was firm, his words carried the weight of truth. Without realising what he was doing, the Knight stood aside to allow the Kentish Sorcerer to work his healing magic upon the old Caerleon Sorcerer. Ivorwulf bent down and assessed Merlin's injuries. They were extensive. It would take time for him to heal the old man properly, so he called over to the trio at the other side of the cavern.

"Morgan! I am in need of assistance to help heal Merlin's wounds!"

The words echoed through the cave. Morgan, Guaen and Galahallt looked over to where Ivorwulf and Garethe were with Merlin.

"Where did he come from?" asked Guaen perplexed at the sudden appearance of their former captive. Morgan and Galahallt may have shared the wonderment but did not put it into words.

"Quickly!" beckoned Morgan, alluding to their helping Ivorwulf with Merlin's healing. The three of them managed to traverse the uneven cavern floor in a reasonable time given the rough terrain. When they reached the other three Ivorwulf, kneeling beside Merlin, looked at Morgan and gave her his assessment of the old Sorcerers injuries.

"Broken rib; broken leg, fractured arm, and many cuts and bruises; but most concerning is his heart, it's not beating properly, in a natural rhythm."

The news from Ivorwulf was dire. The group allowed Morgan to join Ivorwulf kneeling beside the critically-injured Merlin.

"We must first see to his heart, lest it spasm and kill him!" advised Morgan urgently.

"Together we can save him," said Ivorwulf with such conviction that nobody believed otherwise. He took her right hand in his left. Then they began to act as one. They both touched him on his chest over his ailing heart and bowed their heads in deep concentration. The Knights could actually feel the energy flowing from the duo into Merlin. It felt good, restful and restorative all at the same time. They could not tell exactly how long it took, but it was very obvious when they'd succeeded. Merlin's eyes sprang open as if he was startled from his slumbers. He did not say anything but looked at Morgan and Ivorwulf. There was an understanding of what they were trying to achieve and Merlin did his best to aide them in his weakened condition.

Together they healed his broken bones and one by one, his contusions and bruises as well. It took well over half of an hour to accomplish everything. Occasionally Morgan would look over to where Queen Aine was still imprisoned in the faerie ropes that the Caerleon Sorceress was still controlling from afar. The embittered faerie had stopped shouting hollow threats of violence to the sextet. Instead her silence was bellowing her brooding hatred of them and at her incarceration at their hands.

Merlin made to get to his feet. He was assisted by Garethe and Guaen. He stood up and stretched as if he'd just woken from a restful sleep. It looked very much like he was alert and happy and as if he'd been completely rejuvenated.

"Excellent work Morgan, Ivorwulf; I hath not felt so alive for a long time." He gave his companions a broad smile confirming his general demeanour.

"It is time that we left this dismal place and returned to Caerleon," he added. The party, including Ivorwulf, all agreed vigorously.

"Together then," instructed the old Sorcerer. The three magicians once more combined their powers and opened up a travel portal ahead of them. This time it was the main entrance to the main hall of Caerleon. A servant was staring in disbelief back through the floating doorway. Any suspicions that they had about once more being duped were put to rest by the amazed expression upon the servants face. Without any further prompting they stepped through the doorway one by one to the safety of Caerleon Castle.

Strangely, Morgan insisted on going through the portal last of them all. She did not know why she wanted to be the last to leave the cavern all she knew was that it was what she wanted. After a minor kerfuffle with Sir Galahallt that insisted that she go first, a steady stare saw to it that he capitulated; she was alone in the cavern.

She walked bravely forward and through the portal. Nimue remained behind as if she had previously occupied the same space as Morgan and when Morgan walked forward she did not. Morgan was completely unaware that she had just shed Nimue as if she was a second skin. None of the sextet bothered to look back through the doorway to where they had just come from. If they had, they would have seen Nimue standing there looking at them. Now, however, it was too late, the doorway blistered and shimmered, broke into a million pieces and was no more.

Chapter 16: Even Odds

King Arthur was absolutely perplexed with what he was hearing from Ivorwulf. After they'd magically appeared in the castle he'd come to find them and see if their mission to Londinium was successful. Indeed it was. They had returned with the very prize that they'd set out to claim. The Kentish Sorcerer was with them. It seemed as if he'd willingly accompanied them to Caerleon and the main power-base of King Arthur's rule over a large portion of the land. Ivorwulf had submitted to questioning and was at the Round Table with all of the available Knights in attendance. Queen Gwenhwyvar, Merlin and Morgan were present too.

"Ye seek the spread of Christianity throughout all of the Saxon, Jute and Angle held lands...why?" Arthur could not believe what Ivorwulf had just told him.

"Because, King Arthur, Merlin Ambrosias and Lady Morgan Le Fay, it is well known everywhere that ye hath two powerful magicians at thine disposal to assist ye in any battle that is fought. The Saxon, Angle and Jute rulers seek to even the odds should they need to face ye in battle. The...*effect*, that Christians hath upon magical people is known to them. They would see Merlin and Morgan incapacitated in this way so that they'd only need to face thee and thine Knights without the aid magic to assist ye." Ivorwulf's answer only served to confuse matters further for Arthur. The Knights were busy interrupting with their murmuring and objections raised at every point making progress with the questioning difficult. Arthur was beginning to regret including his Knights in this questioning session.

"But Ivorwulf," he said, shouting down the ruckus from the Knights. "Surely Karal realises that thine own powers would also be useless in such a situation?"

Ivorwulf nodded. "Aye, King Arthur, he does. What is one Sorcerer against two? So better that there be no chance of magical intervention in any future battles from any of us at all; rather than leaving ye with such a powerful resource to use." He waited for any follow-on questions on the subject.

Scratching his head and also trying to listen to some of the comments that the Knights had yet again erupted with, Arthur pondered his next question.

"Tell me this, Ivorwulf; the agreement between the rulers, is it specifically aimed to rally against me in attack?"

He leant forward in anticipation of the answer. Ivorwulf shook his head.

"No, no no no." he said "It could not be because they simply do not trust each other enough to take up that burden. It took me almost a year of negotiations with the various rulers to come up with this simple agreement to come to each other's defence. The complexities involved in organising them to form a unified attack upon thine borders would be too much for them to consider. Which of thine castles should they attack? How much of thine land should they attempt to annex? How many of their own men would they be prepared to lose in such an assault? Would any of the other rulers try to take advantage of one of the others should one suffer heavy losses? The questions surrounding such a thought were complex and difficult. No, King Arthur, rest assured that thine position is indeed safe...providing ye do not spread any further with thine...unification." Ivorwulf's final sentence brought yet another loud and clambering tirade from the Knights. Arthur was not listening to them by this time, however. He was focused upon his own thoughts.

Merlin added his own thoughts to the summation that Ivorwulf had just finished.

"It is clear that the rulers of the foreign-held lands see ye as a formidable threat Arthur, but it is equally clear that they do not pose a threat should ye remain within thine current borders. This talk of nullifying the powers of magicians with the Christians bothers me though. What of thineself, Ivorwulf, what would ye do in such a circumstance? Live amongst them, powerless, stripped of thine abilities?" He challenged the veracity of Ivorwulf's commitment to the overall plan from the other rulers. Ivorwulf was circumspect about the consequences though.

"Merlin, would ye seek to stop the sun from rising tomorrow? How much of thine energies would ye put into such an endeavour? And yet it would be fruitless. In the same way, I cannot see that there is an escape from the spread of this unusual religion. I had hoped to have lived a full and happy life by the time Christianity finally rules the entire land. By then, I'd be a happy recluse in a secluded place far from prying eyes and bizarre religions, content with mine own company and dabbling in magic to pass my time." He concluded his plans for retirement with a far-away look in his eyes. Merlin had no reason to doubt the honesty of Ivorwulf's answer. Indeed he'd made it seem a somewhat attractive alternative to trying to stop the growth of something that there was really no hope in stopping.

The Knights were, as usual, loudly vocal in their opinions about everything that had so far transpired. Merlin looked to Arthur for further direction on the questioning of Ivorwulf. He saw that Arthur was deep in thought. Looking around him he tried to remember how long this session had gone on for. It did seem to be quite some time.

"Perhaps a recess to contemplate everything that hath been learned," suggested Merlin. Arthur did not hear. Gwenhwyvar gently knocked on the table in front of her husband bringing him back to the present.

"Aye?" he queried his wife.

"A recess Arthur, to ponder these matters further," she said, paraphrasing Merlin.

"Aye, aye," he said, rising and bringing the current debate from the Knights to an abrupt end.

"Enough of this for one day, it's late and the evening shall soon be upon us. We shall reconvene after the morning meal tomorrow. Until then, Ivorwulf is a guest in Caerleon and shall be treated as such." He made clear that the Kentish Sorcerer was to be extended every courtesy in the meantime. Gwenhwyvar stood up and took Arthur's hand and they left the room together. Morgan and Merlin stood from their chairs and moved to be with Ivorwulf. The Knights began to dissipate slowly, nodding their respect to the visiting Sorcerer as they passed by.

"Tired?" questioned Morgan.

"Aye, I feel drained. Although it could be the use of that interesting spell of instantaneous travel that ye hath taught me." He looked from one to the other for confirmation of his suspicions.

"Indeed, it will take its toll and can only ever be used sparingly," confirmed Morgan. They were about to engage in further conversation about magical things when one of the nearby servants interrupted them. Addressing Morgan he said.

"Prince Amhar and Sir Mordrede hath returned from North Rheged, mine Lady." This was welcome news. Morgan unwittingly let out a sigh of relief. Mordrede and Amhar had been with Queen Ganieda for much longer than was originally planned. She'd tried to not worry, but could not help fretting a little. Even though she knew that Amhar and Mordrede were in the heart of Arthur's territories and that they could more than look after themselves, she was after all a mother and subject to such worrisome thoughts.

"Please excuse me," she said, taking leave of both Ivorwulf and Merlin. Any further discussions about magic could wait until she had greeted her son and assured herself that he was well. She hurried out of the room.

***

Prince Amhar and Sir Mordrede were dismounting when Morgan arrived in the main courtyard. She waited at the main entrance for them to approach. They handed their reins to stable hands who led their horses away. Together they approached the doorway, blocked by Morgan.

"Lady Morgan 'tis good to see ye" said Amhar.

"And ye Amhar; how is Queen Ganieda and North Rheged?"

"Troubled by many minor political intrigues and upheavals, which is why we hath taken so long to return. There was much to do in order to ensure that the land would not succumb to unrest. But we are sure that Ganieda is now on a firm footing and will carry out Arthur's interests to the best of her abilities." His summation was mercifully brief. It was really Mordrede that she wanted to talk to.

"Queen Gwenhwyvar and King Arthur are in his study; they will want to see ye," she prompted, hoping to end any further talk of their mission. He bowed and took his leave of her. Mordrede smiled knowing exactly the reasons behind his mother's gentle cajoling.

"Greetings Mother," he said simply. The words were music to Morgan's ears.

"Mine beautiful son, come here and give ye old mother a hug," she said. He did so.

"I hath missed ye terribly Mordrede. It does mine heart good to know that ye are safely returned to us here in Caerleon." She said looking lovingly at her son. He asked her,

"What hath been happening here in our absence; anything of interest?" although an innocent question, it did require more than just a cursory reply.

"Perhaps ye hath best come inside, there is much to tell," she said, "we have a visiting Sorcerer from Kent. His eyes widened at the unexpected news. She put her arm around him and together they moved inside the main entrance."

Chapter 17: Sir Hemison

Morgan opened the door to her chambers. It was late; the evening meal had gone on for much longer than normal. Ivorwulf turned out to be the life of the gathering after he had imbued a few mugs of wine. Far from talking about the divide between the Jute held land of Kent and King Arthur's kingdom, conversation revolved around the best way to grow spelt and oats and many other things that seemed quite normal. It served to show how much the inhabitants of the far south east had in common with everyone else in the land, invader or not.

Adding to the lengthened mealtime were the stories of North Rheged that Prince Amhar and Sir Mordrede had brought back with them from their mission. They had many to share given the length of time that they'd been away from Caerleon.

She walked into her room. Sir Hemison was there waiting for her. He was standing by the window looking out at the gathering rain clouds in the sky. He was completely naked. As he turned his head to look at her, Morgan couldn't help but ponder that he had the most striking physique that she'd seen on a man, anywhere. He was perfect of body and beautiful of person as well. It was no wonder that they had become lovers shortly after he had joined the ranks of Arthur's Knights.

Morgan finished closing and latching the door. She walked up to him slowly still admiring his form. Although they'd been lovers for over two years now, and not secretly so, she still got a thrill from looking at him in the nude. As she came into range of his muscular arms he enveloped her waist and shoulders with them, bringing her into a close embrace. They kissed as lovers do, with fervour.

She could feel him untying the laces to her garments. Skilfully he achieved this in a very short period of time and her clothes fell to the floor. Then he bent down and lifted her off the flagstone floor. Her shoes fell of as he did so. He carried her to the bed and gently laid her down on her back. He positioned himself over her supporting himself with his arms and they continued kissing.

***

Morgan was glowing with satisfaction of perfect love-making with a man that was completely in-tune with her body and her desires. Similarly, Morgan knew all of the pressure points and erogenous zones on Hemison's body. Together they satisfied each other in a way that none of their previous lovers ever had. Not encased in his warm body they were talking about recent events.

"What do ye think Arthur will do now that he knows that expansion is no longer an option, without facing formidable opposition?" asked Hemison.

"I think that he will continue with his plan to push any strays out of his current borders; there seems little else that he can do at this time. Maybe if he waits long enough the alliance between the warlords will crumble. Then 'twill no longer be holding him back."

"Hmmm. Arthur is patient. He hath achieved so much during his rule. Surely the remainder of the land falling to his monarchy is only a matter of time."

Morgan snuggled further into the warm embrace of her lover.

"Mordrede will not be happy with the thought of any attack within our own borders; nor will Amhar," she observed.

"But he will obey his father's wishes surely?" he asked. Morgan was silent. She was not sure if Amhar would fall into line and do something that he has expressed dire opposition in the past. She felt that too long a pause had eventuated before answering Hemison's question.

"I'm certain of this; whatever Prince Amhar sets his mind to, he will do. And should he oppose his father, I fear that Mordrede will support him. They have the same feelings on this subject." Morgan's worried tone in turn caused Hemison to be concerned. He tried to console her.

"Perhaps it will not come to that. Maybe with the advent of tomorrow's further questioning of Ivorwulf, some other strategy will be born."

His words did offer comfort to Morgan. Perhaps if they'd been spoken by anyone else, she may have refuted them or argued with a worst-case scenario. But there was something believable about everything that Hemison said. He had an air of being intrinsically trustworthy.

"Aye," she said, agreeing with his solace. Morgan turned her head as much as she was able to in the tight embrace so as to look at him.

"Promise that ye will always watch over Mordrede and Amhar, for me. I would feel better knowing that ye watchful eyes were upon them."

"Ye know that I will, mine love, aye," he responded.

The words flooded over Morgan like warm sunlight. She could feel herself giving way to restful sleep. Soon it overtook them both and they were fast asleep.

Chapter 18: The Decision

The next day's further questioning of Ivorwulf was a waste of time. There was a sense that they'd extracted all the information from him that they could as he gave them no news that had not been discussed the day before. The questioning had only gone on for a couple of hours after the morning meal and then he was given leave to depart. Merlin and Morgan went with him. This was the first chance that they'd had to talk to him about how he was spying on them from within the very tapestries that hung on the walls of Caerleon. They were fascinated with the magic involved so they retired to Merlin's chambers to talk of magical spells, potions and devices.

Arthur in the meantime took charge of the discussions with his Knights.

"Enough debate, the time for talk is through. We need to impress upon everyone that we're not defeated by this new alliance between the warlords." He waited for the cries of *Aye* to die down before continuing.

"The township of Exeshulme on the River Exe borders Dumnonii and the Saxon held lands to its east. There are Saxons freely living in the township. Tomorrow we ride there to expel them once and for all time. Should they not go they'll die upon our swords!" the order was given with such conviction that almost all of the Knights jumped to their feet to shout in agreement. The Round Table room was a cacophony of cheering and shouts of support for the plan. But amidst all of that there could be heard a single dissenting voice. Eventually it became too out of place to ignore.

"No Father! This is WRONG!" shouted Prince Amhar. "These *Saxons* as ye call them are no longer to be considered so. They marry Britons, raise children in Briton. Stop this dividing of the land between what ye think are the un-rightful land owners and us! It does nothing but cause hatred and now it incites ye to battle when it's not called for!" Prince Amhar's words silenced the other Knights. They'd seen disagreements between the heir to the throne and the King before but not so vehemently and publically displayed. Their confused silence only served to highlight the vitriol in Arthur's voice when he replied.

"Nonsense! What do ye know of these matters, ye are still a boy!" he said belittling his own son before his fellow Knights. "A Kingdom with invaders is not secure. The Saxons will fester like a sore and cause damage to us all. They need to be excised like a boil from a limb. Then we can be sure to live in peace with our own kind!" Arthur was clearly not abiding anything of Amhar's point of view. This inflamed the situation even more. Amhar jumped up from his chair and slammed his fist down upon the table.

"That is an arcane analogy and unworthy of the King of so many people!" Amhar's insult to his father caused a shocked *Ohhh* from his fellow Knights. Perhaps because of the reaction that his words had caused or perhaps that he realised that he had gone too far with his rebuttal, Amhar became silent. He waited with trepidation for the response from his father.

Arthur very poignantly left his place and began to walk around the table to the far side where Amhar traditionally sat. Not even the sound of people breathing could be heard in the large room. The expectation was that Arthur was going to admonish his petulant son very angrily. The King's steps echoed in the room. He stopped in front of Amhar, who'd turned to face him, although the expression on the young Knight's face said that he'd rather be anywhere else at that moment.

"Thine presence will not be required at tomorrow's battle. Ye will take the duty of guarding Caerleon in mine absence." The royal command was not said with any love at all, but neither was it shouted or spat into the Prince's face. There was a collective sigh of relief. Amhar had insulted the King and got off with a very light retort.

Amhar knew that this was true and backed down completely. He bowed his head and said the usual "By thine leave" response that a Knight would say after receiving an order from his King. Arthur turned to face the Knights.

"Make ready for tomorrow. We leave at first light!" Without any further words he left the room.

The Knights began to follow him, some giving Prince Amhar a scornful look for being so disrespectful to the King as they passed him by. Soon only Sirs Mordrede and Hemison were left and Amhar looked at them both. He'd expected to see the support from Mordrede but not from Sir Hemison and so looked quizzically at him for an explanation.

"Prince Amhar, I know that ye and King Arthur do not see eye-to-eye on this matter, but he is the king, and the king must be obeyed," he said simply.

"Even when the king's commands result in us fighting our own people?' Amhar challenged the Knight' premise.

"One day ye will be king and ye will know the pressures of ruling a land as large as ours, then perhaps ye will not be so quick to judge King Arthur's commands." Sir Hemison gave Mordrede and Amhar a final look and then departed.

Alone with Mordrede Amhar felt he could once again speak his mind.

"I could have perhaps not lost mine temper, then maybe Arthur could have been swayed to turn away from this disagreeable course of action." He looked to Mordrede for his response.

"Perhaps Amhar," there was a long silence and then Mordrede added, "I will seek the king's leave to join ye in the defence of Caerleon rather than fighting with farmers in Exeshulme. This brought a small laugh from the Prince.

"Mine thanks dear brother," he said. Mordred gave Amhar a slap on his shoulder and followed Sir Hemison from the room.

Chapter 19: Leaving Caerleon

The following morning Amhar and Mordrede watched from the battlements as Arthur and his Knights rode from the castle. It was difficult to pick the overall mood of the Caerleon inhabitants. Word of Amhar's opposition to the battle had spread though the populous and it appeared that he had a number of supporters in the ranks of the soldiers and all of the auxiliary staff that worked in the castle. Not that any of them would oppose the king's decision openly though. Amhar and Mordrede, for all intents and purposes, were alone in their protest to Arthur's attack upon Exeshulme.

For all of these reasons it was with jubilation that King Arthur was riding once again into battle to free the land from the Saxons. The crowd was much more subdued. It was something that Arthur noticed as he rode through the main courtyard while waving to Gwenhwyvar and looking at the faces of the stable-hands, soldiers, and other people around him. Although there was the occasional joyous wave and smile, there were far more people that seemed to Arthur to be just going through the motions. And there were others who didn't raise a hand in farewell at all. It was disconcerting.

Merlin too noticed the general absence of merriment from the people. He'd been given leave to not join them on a mission that was greatly tipped in Arthur's favour. A small village with perhaps a dozen Saxon soldiers who'd strayed into Arthur's dominion; they didn't stand a chance against Arthur's knights. Appropriately the number of foot soldiers taken on the battle was far fewer than normal. This was not so much a conflict as a surprise attack upon a small force that was not ready for it, nor would they have any chance of adequately defending themselves. This was not going to be a fight that Arthur would have to spend too many resources upon.

Merlin was with Morgan and Ivorwulf and they stood on the battlements above the main gate and watched the troupe ride out in pairs.

"What shall we do whilst the men are otherwise engaged in cleansing Arthur's outer reaches?" inquired Ivorwulf.

It seemed to be an innocent enough question, but it was tainted with a sublime mocking somehow. Both Merlin and Morgan noticed it but equally dismissed their interpretation of the question as perhaps being too sensitive about the subject to be properly objective.

"Let us practice the tapestry spying spell that ye told us of yesterday," Morgan replied, "I'd like to appear in a tapestry in Anderitum and see all that is transpiring there." Morgan looked expectantly at their guest. Merlin took up the suggestion with vigour.

"Aye, aye, by all means, let us all appear in tapestries in far flung castles and see what we can see." He was very enthusiastic about learning a new spell that he'd never before encountered.

"Perhaps we had best choose a familiar tapestry to begin with, just so ye may both practice it with ease." Ivorwulf's suggestion made sense, but it did mean that they would not be able to spy upon their Saxons to the south as Morgan originally suggested.

"What is the most recent tapestry that the women of the Castle hath completed?" asked Ivorwulf looking to Morgan for the answer.

"It was sent to Castle Mynyw, a scene of the Castle itself being constructed. Will that do for the demonstration?"

"Perfect," he said. "Let the three of us retire to thine chamber, Merlin, to begin thine instruction on this spell."

***

It was as much of a sombre ride through the South Angle held lands and toward their destination as it was a farewell from Caerleon. There was not the usual banter between the Knights. No inane chit-chat from the foot soldiers about their wives or other petty problems. Arthur would have noticed these things more than he did but he was brooding about Amhar's outburst the previous day at the Round Table. Sensing that the king needed to talk about something, Sir Galahallt rode up to be beside the monarch and made light conversation to try and bring Arthur out of his self-imposed silence.

"Noon, we're making good time, Sire. We should be near Wedmore by the end of the day at this pace." Galahallt waited for an answer of any sort from Arthur. The King looked over at his trusted Knight and realised immediately what he was trying to do. He felt gratitude for the consideration shown by his Knight and friend so didn't try to come to the point of the matter by talking about their position relative to their destination, instead he came to the point.

"Amhar vexes me Galahallt. How did he come to hath this bizarre point of view? Was it something that I did whilst rearing him? Or something that I did not do properly?" he trailed off, unsure of how to adequately put into words what he was feeling. Galahallt offered his opinion.

"Sire. Prince Amhar is his own man. He does not fight in the same style as ye; and he does not think in the same way as ye. All of the major battles to win the gains that hath been made were done when he was still an infant. He never saw the worst of the fighting, the terrible things that the Saxon, Angles and Jutes were prepared to do to maintain their stolen footholds in our country. That is why I think he holds a moderate view toward our enemies."

Arthur listed with interest to the character assessment of his son. Galahallt had a good point, as Amhar had only ever been involved in smaller battles that had in every instance gone in Arthur's favour. Arthur remembered back to the early days of the fighting, even before he'd met Gwenhwyvar. The fights were so much bloodier then, much more reliant upon brute force and random luck. With

Merlin's aide, Arthur's fighting style had become refined over the decades. He'd taken the best that the Roman's and Spartan's had written of and demonstrated throughout history and modified it to suit his men, weapons and terrain. The expedience with which Arthur now fought could be a contributing factor to his son's outlook. Amhar had never fought in a battle that was not almost assured of victory. Perhaps he was feeling sorry for the other side.

"Good advice, Sir Galahallt. Amhar needs to be taught that the enemy is as treacherous now as they were when we first began to liberate Britons from the warlords that sought to oppress them." Arthur thought through some scenarios about how he may achieve this, and thus transform Amhar's ideals to be more like his own.

"One day Amhar will be King. It is mine hope that he is King of a united Briton, beneath his rule alone. Our land for our people Galahallt,' what more could I ask for as ruler?" even though rhetorical, Galahallt could not help but answer the question.

"Nothing more, Sire."

Arthur smiled at the enthusiasm and dedication of his Knight.

"It is good that we can make these small gains then within mine own borders. We must out-wait this ridiculous alliance between the warlords. Then when they're again at each other's throats, we can begin the process of excising them from Briton once and for all." Arthur was suddenly feeling much better about everything. He was sure that he could bring Amhar around to his point of view eventually. He was sure that he was doing the right thing for the given circumstances that he found himself in at present. And he was sure that one day he'd be able to fulfil his dream and hand over the Monarchy to his son, one land, one King, one people. "Let us quicken our pace Galahallt. I see no reason to delay these matters." The king's brightened demeanour was immediately noticeable. Galahallt was pleased that he was able to offer the assistance that he had.

"Aye, Sire!" he responded, and signalled that the men should up the ante with their horses cantor. The foot soldiers dutifully began to march faster in step to the more alert speed.

Chapter 20: Exelhulme

It was not until noon of the following day that the township of Exelhulme came into view. It was a fair-sized settlement built where the Rivers Ex and Barle converged. It had some substantial buildings made of the local stone, but was for the most part the typical thatched roof, timber straw and lime wash walled huts and buildings that were so common throughout the country. Emboldened by this newfound sense of purpose, Arthur eschewed the usual gathering of his men beforehand for a final briefing. They knew exactly what they had to do. Identify any Saxons in the village and challenge them to battle. Not wanting to seem like this was an absolute massacre and Arthur at the last minute decided to leave the foot soldiers out of the fighting. They instead were deployed to encircle the settlement and ensure that none of their targets escaped. Further to this; Arthur's instructions to his knights were that all of the identified Saxons were to be challenged to battle one-to-one. It seemed fairer that way.

The commotion that Arthur and his Knights made when they appeared was exactly as they would have expected. People were glad to see the King and his Knights, however the ones that they'd come to deal with were less so and they stood out from the crowd. Some of the men scrambled inside their huts or other establishments. Others were so arrogant about their origins that they actually wore clothing with various Saxon standards embroidered into them. Arthur directed the Knights from horseback as he pointed out the obvious dissenters in the township.

"Sir Galahallt," he said, pointing to one of the men wearing Saxon standards.

"Sir Alynore, Sir Pellus, Sir Dagonet, Sir Guaen, Sir Garethe," he said, and pointed to the target that each of the Knights was to pursue and engage. Realising what was happening, the crowd was quick to join in with their king's wishes. Some of the townsfolk then began to assist in the identification of the Saxon settlers. The scene was acted out over and over again, but the one that Arthur noticed happened closest to him. A man was dragged out of his home and toward the king's horse by some of the townsfolk.

"What are ye doing? I hath lived beside ye in peace all of these months, why betray me to thine bloodthirsty king?" the Saxon was clearly disturbed about the two-faced attitude of this adopted neighbour. Arthur interrupted any further objections from the man.

"Thou art a Saxon and ye are unwelcome in mine land. Did ye think that ye could live beneath mine rule and still serve thine Saxon warlord?" he did not wait for the man to answer.

"Sir Kay," he said, directing his Knight to dismount and engage the man in combat. Sir Kay dutifully dismounted and drew his sword as he approached the man. The townsfolk that had betrayed him left the man to the advancing Knight. Somebody actually threw the beleaguered man a sword it landed at his feet. Looking frantically around him for any sign of support the hapless man realised that he had no choice but to fight for his life.

"And if I win King Arthur; what then?" the man's question and his arrogance annoyed Arthur who did not bother responding. Instead he signalled Sir Kay to begin the battle. The man swooped down and lifted the sword in his grasp. He handled it with familiarity. Arthur noticed this as did the well-trained eye of Sir Kay. This was not going to be a simple matter of dispatching an armed man. Clearly the Saxon was a fighter. So much the better, thought Arthur, his death would mean one less Saxon warrior to contend with.

There were battles of a similar nature happening around them, but this was the one that attracted the biggest crowd. Former neighbours rallied around to see the errant Saxon fight for his life. It began with lightning speed. The Saxon appeared to be examining his sword as any soldier would prior to battle. But it was a ruse, he tried to catch Sir Kay off guard with his pretend inspection, instead he lunged with amazing speed and put his full weight toward lunging directly at the Knight's throat. Only Sir Kay's brilliant reflexes saved him from a mortal wound. He twisted sideways without a moment to spare. The force by which the Saxon had hurled the lunge meant that he was now caught off-balance. His sword had not stuck his opponents' throat so he fell forward.

Sir Kay flicked up his sword as it passed him and barely caught the handle with his blade as he did so. Fortunately the Saxon's fingers were gripping the sword low on the handle and he was spared any damage to his fingers. The clash of metal upon leather-wrapped metal brought a loud approving roar from the crowd. The Saxon had but a precious second to recover his balance, which he did. The force of the blow to his sword by the Knight may have brought the sword out of his hand, but such was the determination of the Saxon he retained it, holding it tightly. The reverberation of the clash made its way through the man's wrist and forearm right down to his elbow. Under other circumstances it would have been agony, but he did not allow himself to dwell upon it at all, for to do so would surely distract him too much under the circumstances.

Sir Kay was the next to try a single lethal swipe with his sword, but it was met mid-flight by an equally forceful parry by the man. The noise of the swords brought another cheer from the onlookers. Sir Kay deliberately took a step backwards, his first thought being to feign uncertainty to his opponent, yet designed to give him the necessary distance to pull off a signature manoeuvre from the clever Knight. He swung both arms in a circle for balance, something that was always confusing in the heat of battle when it happened. The idea was to make the opponent look at both hands as if to see which still had the sword. But in reality it was to give him leverage to swing the sword high in an arch and bring it down with all of the force that he could muster.

The Saxon was not taken in by the flamboyant move. He'd already adjusted his stance to absorb the blow not only in his sword, but by allowing his elbow to bend just enough prior to his knees taking the rest of the force. He squatted down beneath Kay's sword but held it from doing any damage to his body. Then the Saxon pushed upwards with all of the strength that his legs could find and used the force to push Sir Kay backwards.

The Knight was taken aback with the brute force of the defensive parry and how it was turned around to throw him off his foothold. The two fighters began to circle each other. Sir Kay was swapping his sword between each hand in the hope of intimidating his skilful opponent. However the Saxon was having none of it and mimicked Sir Kay by doing the same thing.

The tension in the air was rising as clearly Sir Kay and the Saxon were evenly matched. Arthur looked down from his vantage point upon horseback and thought a terrible thought: what if Sir Kay lost the battle? There were deadly screams from beyond the current fracas that occupied Arthur. He chanced a look over in the direction of them to see what was happening. Sir Alynore had dispatched his target as had Sir Pellus. Arthur looked back quickly to the potentially disastrous situation unfolding before him.

Neither of the fighters was willing to make the next move. It was a torturous waiting game. They continued to circle each other looking for a weakness or something that could be exploited. The crowd began to get restless. There were jeers from the townsfolk to 'get on with it.'

Then it happened. Sir Kay saw the attention of the man waver for just a second. His eyes left Sir Kay and he looked at something over to the Knight's left, just the opportunity that the Knight was waiting for. With yet another of his decorative but ultimately deadly sword twirls, Sir Kay charged whilst carving a figure eight in the air in front of him. The number was traced twice as he approached his target, and while the Saxon readied himself for yet another perfect parry, he was ultimately deceived.

During the last part of the arc, Sir Kay suddenly changed the direction of the swing and brought it backwards upon itself before lunging forward and thrusting the sword from waist-height and into the chest of the Saxon. They both let out screams as the blade speared the ribcage of the man. Taking the advantage, Sir Kay repositioned himself and gave his sword a second almighty push, causing it to erupt from the spine of the hapless man. It took quite a pull to retrieve his sword from the man. Sir Kay did so and stepped back to watch his opponent fall to the ground, lifeless.

The crowd shouted with delight at the spectacle that had amused and terrified them and Sir Kay raised his sword in salute to King Arthur and shouted as he did so

"For a Briton without invaders!" he cried. The Knights that were not otherwise engaged in battle echoed his sentiment, and there followed a loud roar of applause and shouting from the gathered townsfolk.

Sir Kay looked to Arthur for his approval and Arthur gave Sir Kay a nod to signify that he was pleased with the Knights work. It was then that Sir Kay looked around to see if he could see what had distracted the Saxon. Amongst the jubilant faces was that of a young boy, perhaps ten years of age. He was looking down at the fallen man with a horrified expression upon his face and when the Knight approached the boy he noticed a woman was holding him by the shoulders.

"Has the boy not seen death before?" he inquired. The woman shot the Knight a look of malice, which gave the Knight a thought.

"Is this his son?" he asked the woman. She gave him another look of pure hatred and vigorously shook her head, but managed to speak through clenched teeth.

"No, Sir Knight, for if it was, ye would surely want to kill the son of a Saxon," she looked around at her neighbours and other townsfolk. There was a moment where some of the people looked at the woman and then at Sir Kay. A few of them seemed to be about to say something but then looked as though they'd thought the better of it.

"What is it?" he asked of a few of them. They began to look sheepish and non-verbally declined to answer. Sir Kay had guessed that his was most probably indeed the dead Saxon's progeny, but the townsfolk seemed reticent to implicate the boy or the woman.

"And thee woman, where are ye from?" he asked. She looked him straight in his eyes and answered.

"Born and bred right here in Exelhulme, Sir Knight. Any of mine neighbours will attest to that." She looked accusingly at some of the closest ones; who hurried to confirm her status as a native Briton. Not entirely satisfied that he'd reached the bottom of the matter, Sir Kay had no other choice but to let it go. Even if his guess was correct and this was the son of the Saxon living in Exelhulme, he'd now made a widow. The boy if he was found to be a Saxon would be cast out of the village by Arthur's order and would have had to find his way to the nearest Saxon village and hope that somebody would take him in. It seemed pointless to the Knight to insist upon uncovering some minor deception in this instance. The crowd had begun to thin out. Arthur's words cut through Sir Kay's thoughts.

"Take these Saxon swine across the river and dump their bodies near the closest Saxon village. Let them go back to where they came from."

The double meaning of Arthur's words was clear only to the Knights. The villagers would certainly have thought that Arthur meant that the Saxons should not have left their village across the river Exe and settled in Exelhulme. But in fact Arthur was sending a message that all of the Saxons should leave the country completely and return to where they were from.

"We stay here tonight and return to Caerleon tomorrow," shouted Arthur.

Chapter 21: Stoking the Fire

It was like returning from any battle and this time the foot soldiers were more their grumbling selves upon the return journey. The Knights were engaged in banter about this and that and even Arthur was in a good mood. His success at Exelhulme and his new-found plan to re-educate Amhar occupied his thinking and brought him hope that the boy could be redeemed. When Arthur thought of his own childhood, he could almost remember nothing else except Merlin telling him how he would be King one day and that he'd had to unite the land and drive out the invaders. It was all that mattered.

When Caerleon came into view he began to plan exactly how he was going to achieve all of this for Amhar. In his haste he actually managed to leave the poor foot soldiers behind in Caerleon Village whilst he rode his horse up the hill toward his home faster than they were able to keep up with. The Knights dutifully followed somewhat amused that they were running the foot-soldiers ragged. Arthur was the first through the gates and he could hear Amhar calling to the castle that the king had returned.

A stable hand rushed forward to take charge of Arthur's mount. He was almost to the main door of the castle by the time Gwenhwyvar appeared. She had assumed that it would take the usual amount of time from when the King's return was announced by the watchtower for him to arrive, but to her surprise he was here already. She looked at the Knights still coming through the gates and smiled at her husband, amused.

"Anxious to see me, dear husband?" she gently jibed him.

"Aye, mine dear and our son. I hath had a change of heart and believe that I know how to better serve him as a father." The unexpected news from Arthur delighted Gwenhwyvar.

"That is wonderful Arthur. How do ye..." asked the Queen, wanting more information about this new parenting revelation that

Arthur alluded to. But he silenced her with a kiss upon her lips. Gwenhwyvar appreciated the pleasant surprise. When they separated he said.

"I shall speak with Amhar in mine study, see that he is notified." He asked and then bowing to take his leave, he hurried past her and made his way inside. Gwenhwyvar was amazed at his unusual behaviour but was not in a position to question him further. So she motioned for a nearby servant who dutifully approached and bowed.

"Hath Prince Amhar join the king in his study immediately," she beckoned. The servant bowed his understanding of the order and hurried away to do as he was bid.

***

Arthur was pacing with excitement and anticipation. He was eager to get things sorted out with Amhar. The knock at the door came as a welcome sound.

"Enter," said Arthur with enthusiasm. Amhar entered the room, closing the door behind him and looked expectantly at his father.

"Amhar, when Merlin was raising me, he told me over and over again that I'd be king one day and that I would have to unite the land and drive out all of the foreigners that have seized a foothold in our country."

Arthur looked at Amhar for a reaction. Amhar nodded. He had heard his father speak of his childhood with Merlin many times.

"Come in, come in," said Arthur, "do not just stand at the door, sit down," He motioned to a stool nearby to him. Amhar did so and Arthur sat on the stool nearest to the Prince.

"What I'm trying to say is that there was never any other thought that entered my mind." Arthur was attempting to portray why he held the point of view that he did, but Amhar completely misinterpreted his father's words and thought that it was a prelude to Arthur admitting that there was more than ridding the country of the invaders occupying his every waking thought. Seizing upon the false premise, Amhar jumped into the conversation.

"Aye, Father, ye are true in thine words. There is always more than one way to look at a situation," said Amhar, with clear happiness written all over his face. Now it was Arthur's turn to misinterpret the meaning of the words spoken.

"Aye, Amhar, that is exactly what I am saying, and I want so much for thee to look at what I'm doing with a different set of eyes. Do not think of the Jutes and Angles and Saxons as worthy of thine pity, simply because they fall beneath our swords." Arthur stopped, the expression upon Amhar's face had changed dramatically.

"But Father, are ye not trying to tell me that ye reconsidered thine attack on Exeshulme and did not evict the Saxon men?" he looked a little forlorn. Arthur was dismayed.

"Of course I killed the Saxon men in the township; one-to-one battle with swords; Saxon against Knight. They all fell where they fought and we are well rid of them." Arthur had barely finished when Amhar flew into a rage jumping up from his stool, his face red with anger.

"What of their families?! What of their sons?!" screamed Amhar at the King. Arthur too jumped up from his stool to stand face to face with his temperamental son.

"We found none, but mark mine words Amhar; Saxon sons grow up to be Saxon warriors loyal to their Saxon warlords; had any been identified they would have been driven from mine township back to their masters across the River Exe!" the resolve in Arthur's voice left no room for doubting his intentions. Amhar was both confounded and disgusted with his father's actions and did not try to hide his feelings on the matter.

"Why not just run their wives through with a sword to prevent them from ever bearing Saxon children!" he screamed at his father. Even as the words left his mouth, Amhar realised that he'd gone too far. To accuse his father of being a slayer of women was unconscionable. Silence filled the room. Amhar's eyes dropped as he realised what he'd just said but his pride prevented him from apologising immediately.

"Leaving ye behind was a mistake Amhar. Ye will accompany me to mine next target, the village of Camlann, and together we will drive out the Saxon settlers," he said with raised hands to cut-off any objections that Amhar may have before pointing his finger right between the Prince's eyes.

"Thine King hath spoken," he said with an icy tone. Without a further word, Arthur pointed to the door leaving Amhar in no doubt that the audience was at an end and he should leave. He hesitated for a moment as he tried to find words to apologise to his father, but none came. He was too flustered. He could feel his temperature rising and the loss of his ability to think clearly. He bowed stiffly and hurried from the room, slamming the door behind him.

Chapter 22: The Approach of Lughansadh

Merlin listened patiently to Arthur, watching him pace up and down his study whilst he relayed the most recent exchange with Prince Amhar. It took some time for the king to calm down long enough for Merlin to get a word in at all.

"Arthur, I understand that ye and Amhar do not view things in the same manner; but surely he'll do as he hath been commanded by his king. Is that not a sign that beneath his unusual ideas he still respects what ye do and what ye stand for?"

Arthur stopped pacing and looked directly at Merlin. He took only a moment to think about what he'd said. But he waved it away. It did nothing to placate him in the circumstances.

"Who knows what Amhar thinks, Merlin, who knows?" he raised both hands to the air as if asking the gods above him. "I shall bring forward mine plans for the cleansing of Camlann, and we shall leave tomorrow," he said, and then corrected himself, determined to bring forward his timetable to attack the township in his realm. "No, the men need more rest after the recent journey home, and Camlann is further from Caerleon than Exeshulme...we shall leave the day after tomorrow."

Only the level-headed Merlin could talk any sense into Arthur when he was in a mood like this.

"Arthur, Caerleon village is already beginning to fill with people readying for the festival of Lughansadh. It is only five days before the festivities begin. And ye will be expected to be here for them."

Merlin gave Arthur a look of minor admonishment for forgetting such an important part of the *old-ways* calendar, and the news brought Arthur right back to the present. He was no longer mentally preparing to leave and do battle with the Saxons settled in

Camlann, he realized. The festival would go for at least five days, so it would be ten days at minimum before he could even *think* of leaving Caerleon for Camlann. Factoring in the three day journey time if they had foot-soldiers with them, then his plans began to seem quite a distance in the future.

"Wise and sage advice as ever, old friend" he complimented Merlin, bringing a hand down upon his shoulder.

"There's more to being King than just fighting, Arthur. Wait until after the festivities and then make a decision about when to ride to Camlann."

Merlin's words gladdened Arthur. His dearest friend had confirmed in inference that the attack on Camlann should proceed, but it was only a matter of deciding exactly when to do it.

***

Amhar was pacing up and down in his chamber in a scene that mirrored the one that had just been acted out in the king's study. But this time it was Mordrede sitting and watching Amhar pacing up and down delivering a tirade about how small minded and unyielding the king was.

"I cannot believe that we think *so* differently, Mordrede. Arthur cannot see that what he is doing is wrong. Why? Is he bewitched with an evil force that drives him to do these perplexing things?" it was a silly question of course. Should Arthur be under any kind of magical influence, both Merlin and Morgan would be able to recognise and circumvent it. Mordrede knew that; Amhar was just exasperated with his father's belligerent attitude toward the Saxons and the others.

"How did the conversation end? Did ye plead for the security of Camlann?" Mordrede's innocent question only served to once again highlight the manner in which Amhar had insulted Arthur. This was a part of the exchange that Amhar had thus far left out of the retelling of the account. Mordrede realised from the lack of reply that he had somehow hit upon a nerve.

"King Arthur intends to go forward with the attack on Camlann," said Amhar leaving out any reference to his insult. This time it was Mordrede's turn to become exasperated with the situation. He stood up and clenched his fists.

"Why? It does not make any sense to attack our own people!"

"That did not stop him from *removing* the Saxon men from Exeshulme. Reason hath left him Mordrede. We must take matters into our own hands."

The sudden turn of conversation took Mordrede by surprise.

"What do ye mean...how?' he asked, confounded by the suggestion.

"We shall ride to Camlann and form a party of resistance to stand against Arthur when he arrives with the Knights. He will surely not attack a defensive force led by his own son." Amhar was only formulating the treasonous plan as he spoke the words. He'd not given any thought to the consequences of such a manoeuvre, nor exactly how to enable it. Mordrede should have been absolutely horrified at the very thought of opposing the king. But instead he stood frozen thinking about how such a resistance may be the shock that Arthur needed to make him see reason.

"It will stop the king from any further attacks within the realm," said Mordrede, thinking aloud.

"Aye, exactly, then he may stop and consider what we hath been telling him all along, that there's no need to battle these people. They're already one with us, they live by tilling the same land as we do, raising families as we do, drinking laughing and trying to build a better life for themselves. What harm is there in that?" The Prince was preaching to the converted. Mordrede saw the sense in everything that Amhar was saying and hastened to agree with his half-brother.

"Surely if we stand together, his son the rightful heir to the throne and his illegitimate son, will see that we're right and he should simply stop and accept the people around as his rightful neighbours. The alliance between the warlords will dissipate, forgotten in a new realisation of friendship and living together in peace."

The idealistic vision of Mordrede painted a picture of serene happiness for all Britons no matter where they were born, living as one side-by-side, prospering together. It swept them up and clouded their common sense.

"I will seek the approval of mine mother," said Mordrede as an afterthought, perhaps born of an inkling that what they proposed sedition. Regardless of how they wrapped it in idealism, it was none the less, subversion of the king's power.

"Do ye think that she will support us? I do not want Morgan to try and talk us out of our plan. It needs to be done to assure that Arthur sees reason," Amhar said worriedly. Mordrede was certain that his mother would see their point of view.

"I will not tell her immediately, but find out her feelings upon the subject. If I think that she's kindred with our thoughts, then I'll seek her aid in helping us bring our plan to fruition."

Satisfied that Mordrede was not going to brashly tell his mother their entire plan, without first satisfying himself that she was on their side, Amhar gave Mordrede his seal of approval.

"Go then, see if ye can tear Morgan away from Ivorwulf and Merlin, the three of them hath been inseparable since he came to Caerleon." Mordrede knew that what Amhar said was true. It had not gone unnoticed by just about everyone that the three magicians were enraptured with each other's company. Mordrede grabbed hold of both of Amhar's shoulders and gave one more affirmation before leaving his chambers.

"We are right Amhar, Arthur will see it too." He smiled, making it seem more like a fact that would soon see the light of day, rather than a vain hope.

Chapter 23: Untenable Choice

Morgan and Merlin were predictably found with Ivorwulf in Merlin's chamber. The knock on the door was an unwelcome intrusion to a spirited debate about the usefulness of their newfound ability to spy upon anyone who had woven images upon their walls. The magical technique had been successfully taught by Ivorwulf to Merlin and Morgan and they'd practiced it by looking at the castle caretaker in Mynyw Castle going about his duties up-keeping the Castle in Arthur's absence. Not once did the caretaker suspect that he was being watched from afar by three magicians.

When Mordrede knocked on the door the three of them were in a happy but spirited debate about the distance by which the technique could be used. Ivorwulf had said that he had only ever used it to spy upon Caerleon from Londinium, which was a fair distance, and even then only because he had previously had visions of Caerleon during his sleep. The tapestries had become known to him through those visions, therefore he was able to view the going's-on in Caerleon through them; because they were familiar. He opposed Merlin's viewpoint that any tapestry in any castle could be used without previous knowledge of it. Ivorwulf was asking for a demonstration of this in the absence of finding an accord discussing it.

"Pick a castle in Gaul that ye hath never before travelled to, one that we all at least know of and project thine eyes to the tapestries in the grandest of the rooms!" said Ivorwulf challenging Merlin to put his magic where his mouth was.

They all turned to look at who had knocked so loudly upon the door and had the cheekiness to enter without being told that it was permissible to do so.

"Mordrede, mine dear, what is it?" asked Morgan when she saw her son standing in the doorway.

"Mother, may I extract ye from the hours upon hours that ye hath spent here and impose upon ye to spend some small portion of thine time with me this glorious day?" It was an innocent enough request. The two of them had always been close. Morgan felt like she was being ever so lovingly admonished for being so focussed upon all things magical instead of motherly.

"Of course Mordrede, I hath been spending too much time indulging mine love of the magical arts and hath neglected ye. Mine apologies; let us take a walk through the Queen's herb garden and enjoy the afternoon." Morgan hastily offered a morsel of her time in exchange for forgiveness about her unintentional neglect. His smile lit up the room, at least Morgan thought that it did.

"Excellent!" he said, turning to Merlin and Ivorwulf. "I see that the knights are about to do their inspection of the grain stores to the far north of the Caerleon fields. Perhaps our Kentish guest would like to see them? They may be of interest" Mordrede cleverly offered Ivorwulf and Merlin a chore that would take them away from Caerleon so that he could have his mother's full attention. That way he would be sure that she was not pining for further contact and exchange with the Sorcerers.

Ivorwulf jumped at the chance to see the stores.

"Aye that *would* be of interest, good Knight. I would like to see if ye employ any differences in the building of thine stores than we do. Another opportunity for an exchange of ideas?" he asked rhetorically.

"Aye aye, a good idea indeed Mordrede, we shall join the Knights. Who is making the inspection?" asked the old man.

"Sirs Kay and Alynore," he answered, "they'll be getting ready now in the stables so ye hath best hurry if ye want to catch them." The urgency that Mordrede introduced to the idea brought it to the exact conclusion that he'd engineered.

"Then let us depart immediately," said Merlin waving a hurrying hand at Ivorwulf to accompany him quickly to the stables. When the two Sorcerers had departed Mordrede offered his arm to this mother. She took it gladly.

***

Mordrede had been very clever at hiding the fact that he wanted to tell is mother something very secret. For all of her motherly instincts and magical abilities, Mordrede was still able to conceal the true nature of the discussion that he wanted to have with her. So when he brought up the subject about potentially opposing King Arthur's next planned battle, she was suitably shocked.

It came in stark contrast to the quiet surroundings of the Queen's herb garden. There was nobody attending to it at present so they were alone in the walled area. Safe from prying eyes and ears, Mordrede had simply changed the subject from the forthcoming festival of Lughansadh to Camlann without taking a breath.

"Amhar feels that he should oppose Arthur's next campaign in Camlann, and I feel the same way."

Mordrede stopped walking as he finished, and so did Morgan. She was perplexed. Looking straight into his green eyes, she sought the heart of the matter immediately.

"Oppose, Mordrede? How?"

"By riding to Camlann and garnering support to stand against Arthur when he arrives." Mordrede needed to now speak quickly so that the entire idea was laid before his mother so that she could judge it in its entirety instead of having a knee-jerk reaction to the surprising news.

"Before ye judge too quickly, please Mother, hear the entire plan." He looked at her waiting for a reaction. She could be seen to visibly take in a deep breath before answering in a calm and measured voice.

"Continue."

"If we can build up a force of Britons ready to stand with their new neighbours, the ones that hath come across the river and settled there, and with Amhar and myself at their head, Arthur will surely realise how passionately we feel about what he is doing, and seeing that the people of Camlann would be ready to stand up to their king for what they believe is right; it must surely show even Arthur that his way is wrong. We hope to appeal to his better nature and show him that we are already one people. He does not need to keep fighting the way that he does. Please mother, help us to open King Arthur's eyes to the reality of what is around him.

For too long he hath sought unity without realising that it would come in time, all he had to do was wait for long enough for the people to integrate with us. With every passing year we become more and more, one people. With every marriage of Saxon or Angle or Jute to Briton we bring them into our fold. Fighting will only make enemies of these people. Show them love, compassion and respect, but above all show them acceptance and they will end up becoming just as much of a Briton as any that were born here."

Mordrede's passionate plea touched Morgan's heart.

"Ye really believe what ye are saying," she said more than asked. He nodded his affirmation. Morgan looked up at the sky. She considered her response.

"Arthur is set in his ways. He truly believes that what he is doing is right. I hath never questioned his beliefs nor his vision for our country. And what ye are suggesting is treason, Mordrede." She looked at him making certain that he understood what she was saying.

"But I know that it is not just the plight of the people in Camlann that ye are thinking of. Ye are afraid that the King will make an error and both Amhar and ye seek to prevent that from happening; an error that would see the number of Arthur's enemies increase." Morgan pondered further the vision that Mordrede had painted for her. A show of solidarity from Arthur's two sons would surely sway the monarch. They both clearly felt strongly enough that what they proposed was right, to stand against their father.

"This is no small Matter Mordrede. I know that thine heart is good, and I know that Amhar would never knowingly hurt his father." Mordrede wanted to test the resilience of the two young men.

"What if I do not offer ye mine support? What if I asked ye both to reconsider thine actions? What would ye do?" she put the question to her son and waited in anticipation of the reply. Mordrede thought about it for only a moment.

"I would ask ye to not stand in our way, but we would ride to Camlann nevertheless." It was exactly the answer she had hoped for.

"No matter what I say, ye will try and protect the people of Camlann from King Arthur?' she sought confirmation of their resolve.

"Aye," he said

"Then it would appear that the decision is made Mordrede." Mordrede looked quizzically at his mother. What was she saying? Was that an offer of support or not? He indicated that he did not understand the ramifications of her viewpoint with a shake of his head. She obliged with clarification.

"I am Arthur's half-sister and Sorceress at his command. I will always support anything that is in the best interests of his monarch and his will. And in this instance, if thine hearts are true, and it is indeed going to assure that the number of Arthur's enemies does not grow, then I will support ye with my compliancy." Mordrede let out a small laugh. He understood exactly what his mother was saying.

"Ye will not stand in our way; but Mother will ye support us?"

"By not opposing ye, I am supporting ye Mordrede, believe me." Mordrede saw the sense in what his mother was telling him. If the

Caerleon Sorceress had really wanted to stop Amhar and he from taking this action, then there would be little that either of them could do to stand against her. It was less than he had hoped for, but somehow he felt like she was giving him more than he should have the right to expect.

Mordrede embraced his mother.

"Mine thanks, dear Mother," he said.

"When will ye leave?" she asked.

"Tomorrow, under the guise of preparations for Lughansadh," he'd already planned their exit from Caerleon carefully to coincide with the usual comings and goings prior to the festival days themselves.

"If Arthur asks me thine whereabouts, I will not lie to him Mordrede," warned Morgan. He understood.

"Aye, let us hope that he does not directly ask ye; at least until we are ready to face him with our united kinfolk."

As he said the words, for just a moment, Morgan considered the horrible alternative; what if Arthur chose to attack; brushing aside Mordrede and Amhar in order to slay the Saxons in Camlann. But she pushed the thought out of her head. It was ridiculous of course. Arthur would not attack his two sons. He would see that they wanted desperately for him to change his mind, and this was their way of expressing it to him.

"Good fortune, mine brave son," bade Morgan and kissed Mordrede on his cheek.

"Now let us enjoy the evening together. Sit with me tonight at the meal."

"I should not wish to make Sir Hemison jealous," said Mordrede, gently teasing his mother about her not-so-secret lover. She laughed at his sassiness. But the very mention of Sir Hemison gave Morgan a thought. She would feel so much better if he would accompany them to Camlann. Without telling Mordrede she was already working on a way to convince Sir Hemison to do just that. She knew that he would be in her chamber after the evening meal tonight. Then she would make her wishes known to him and ask for his assistance.

Chapter 24: The Next Morning

Amhar and Mordrede were awake before sunrise and were in the stables readying their horses when Sir Hemison appeared. They tried not to react to his presence and went about preparing their horses as if there was nothing unusual happening. But each of them was very aware that one of their fellow Knights was there with them, and they watched him without looking like they were watching him. Sir Hemison too began to prepare his horse and the two brothers leant in closer to converse without being overheard.

"Maybe he hath a chore to complete somewhere?" suggested Mordrede.

"But what?" responded Amhar. "We would hath heard about it before now surely."

They continued with their preparations. Sir Hemison seemed to be more adept at getting his mount ready, or maybe because he did it with more speed than the other two because the three of them ended up exiting the stables together. Sir Hemison bade the Prince and his fellow Knight good morning. They replied in kind. And the three of them continued to walk their horses into the main courtyard before mounting them.

Curiosity finally got the better of Amhar and he ventured to ask Sir Hemison where he was journeying to this day?

"I ride with two head-strong Knights of the Round Table to ensure that they get the chance to enable their outlandish plan to protest the King's forthcoming assault upon Camlann." He replied, looking at both of them in turn and waiting for a reaction. Clearly Morgan had enlisted his help to oversee the younger Knights in their quest to bring Arthur to his senses. It was also very clear that he was not entirely convinced of the integrity of their plan, but was willing to accompany them nevertheless.

The two brothers looked at each other unsure what to say. Realising this Sir Hemison relieved them of the burden to say anything at all.

"Shall we stand here looking at each other and wondering why I allowed Lady Morgan to talk me into this fool-hearty scheme, or shall we begin our journey to Camlann?"

"It is a long journey, the sooner we begin, the better" Amhar said, looking rather sheepish, They all mounted their horses and trotted out of the main gates of Caerleon Castle.

****

Arthur had made enquiries about the whereabouts of his son and so far hadn't been able to ascertain anything. He was a little perplexed and exasperated that none of the Knights that he had asked so far knew anything.

Gwenhwyvar too had become involved in the hunt for information as to where he was. The news had begun to spread through the castle by the time Morgan heard it from the staff. She was just entering the queen's antechamber to help finish off a tapestry that had been neglected for some time. She dreaded the uncertainty that surrounded her presence with the other ladies of the court and of course queen Gwenhwyvar. Surely the queen would ask her if she knew anything, and she had already promised herself that she would not lie in order to conceal his actions.

"Ah Morgan," said Gwenhwyvar, greeting her as she walked in, "Extracted thine-self from our Kentish visitor?" it was a small jibe at her absence from the usual female courtly gatherings since Ivorwulf had arrived in Caerleon.

"Aye, this tapestry hath waited long enough to be finished." Her reply was what was expected. All of the usual ladies of the court were present. Almost immediately talk turned to Prince Amhar. Lady Florie inquired from the queen.

"Hath there been any word yet about Prince Amhar, Gwenhwyvar?"

"None, I..." The Queen's words were interrupted by the appearance of a servant at the door. All eyes turned to the woman who stood waiting for permission to enter.

"Come in," said Gwenhwyvar, giving the woman leave to enter the room.

"Mine Queen, word from the morning watch, Prince Amhar was seen leaving this morning at first-light with Sir Mordrede and Sir Hemison. It is said that they are riding to North Rheged to celebrate Lughansadh with Queen Ganieda." With her news finished the servant bowed hoping to be allowed to leave. The Queen waved at her that it was alright to do so.

Morgan was astounded, how did these rumours start? It was typical of the scuttlebutt that went around the Castle. It would start with one person saying something to another and on and on until the original message is convoluted beyond belief.

"Strange that Amhar did not say anything to me about celebrating Lughansadh in North Rheged with Ganieda. Did Mordrede tell ye about this Morgan?" all eyes were now upon her. Morgan looked puzzled and shook her head.

"I hath not heard that Mordrede or the others were to celebrate the festival up north," she said, telling the truth even though she was omitting that she knew for a fact that it was a false rumour. The fact that Sir Hemison was with them now worked in favour of the false information that had been presented by the servant. Gwenhwyvar pondered it briefly before speaking further.

"It must be so, perhaps they had promised Ganieda whilst they were in residence there earlier; and of course Sir Hemison is from North Rheged; it would make sense that he would wish to celebrate it with his family."

"That must be it!" affirmed Lady Elamite who was in turn supported by Lady Lyonors.

"Indeed, it is the only explanation that makes any sense. Ye should not worry about it anymore Gwenhwyvar. Send word to the King that we hath solved the latest little mystery in Caerleon."

"I shall tell him in person," said Gwenhwyvar rising from her chair. Morgan silently breathed a sigh of relief. This was the first time that she'd ever found the castle rumour mill to work to her advantage. Now she was in no need to explain Mordrede's or Sir Hemison's absence along with Amhar's. They'd have the valuable time that they needed to gather their civilian force to protest Arthur's forthcoming attack upon Camlann. Morgan wished as hard as she could that the plan would succeed that that Arthur would listen to his two sons. She consoled herself that if it were anybody else, then Arthur would surely not listen. But because it was Amhar and Mordrede that were taking this action; his own flesh and blood, they would get through to the stubborn king.

Morgan took her place and tried to concentrate on the now-banal chore of finishing off a tapestry. She looked at the scene that it depicted. It was a battle scene, portraying Arthur's reclamation from the Saxons of the lands from Hengest Dun through to the River Exe. And suddenly all of the consolation that she could bring to bear on herself was not enough. A feeling of dread enveloped her and she felt cold. Something about this whole situation was wrong but she did not know exactly what. Morgan looked out of the window and hoped that she was just being a worrisome mother and not predicting the future.

Chapter 25: The Three Faeries

Sir Hemison had turned out to be quite a good travelling companion. He'd made it known to Amhar and Mordrede that he did not entirely believe in what they were doing, but had contented himself that his objections were known and did not continually bring it up. This helped Amhar and Mordrede immensely. If they had a dissenting voice to gnaw away at them throughout their journey, it would have made the journey difficult and shaken their belief in what they were doing.

Instead the day had past quite pleasantly. They'd enjoyed each other's company and the time seemed to slip by with increasing speed. Before they knew it dusk was upon them.

"How much longer should we travel before we make camp for the night?" asked Sir Hemison, leaving the decision to either Mordrede or Amhar.

"There's a small forest about half an hour's ride from here that we can take shelter within. We are in Saxon controlled lands, so it would be wise." Amhar's words were welcome. The journey across the river Severn and through Deorham and past Wedmore on the way to the River Exe and then into Arthur's south western lands was always fraught with danger because of the Saxon lands that needed to be traversed. The idea of concealing themselves in a forest away from prying Saxon eyes was a good one.

"Then let us make good time," prompted Sir Hemison, jostling his horse into a faster trot. The other two similarly prodded their mounts to keep up.

***

It was almost dark by the time the three men penetrated the forest. They looked about them for a suitable clearing and found one, it was quite narrow but very long. It offered a multitude of ways to escape should it be necessary. But more importantly, it would shelter a small fire when it was lit, hiding it's light from travelling and alerting anyone nearby to their presence.

Amhar was tending to the horses whilst Mordrede and Hemison worked on the starting the fire with some flint and tried leaves and twigs.

"Hath thine mother not taught thee to start a fire from nothing?" asked Sir Hemison.

"Mine mother hath imparted to me only those skills that are necessary to protect me from the dangers of the magical beings that dwell in the forests," replied Mordrede. He was cheekily teasing Sir Hemison, painting a picture that they had entered the domain of magical beings. Sir Hemison was not going to be so easily fooled by the boyish prank.

'Uhhh Haaa," he said, exaggerating his tone of disbelief in what had just been said. Prince Amhar joined them.

"No fire yet?" he said looking to each of them wondering what was taking so long. Then without warning the fire suddenly burst into being. The three men jumped back startled at the crackling fire.

"Did ye do that?" demanded Amhar of Mordrede.

"No," he said clearly as surprised as the other two by the sudden happening.

"Do not be afraid," a woman's voice came from behind them. The three men spun around. Standing there completely naked were three of the most beautiful women any of them had ever seen. The sight of their perfect bodies in the flickering firelight was arousing. The men were amazed and had no idea how to react to such a bizarre situation. Mordrede was the only one that had the presence of mind to say anything.

"Where did ye come from?" he said looking around for horses that may have carried the women. There were none to be seen.

"It does not matter," said one

"We are here now," said another

"Do you not find us attractive?" asked the third.

The women each began to stroke their long flowing hair, seductively. The sight of their milky-white hands running through dark hair and then over their amble breasts had an immediate effect upon the three men. Forgotten were any questions about where the women originated and how they had approached the knights in complete stealth. Instead the men's body temperatures began to rise. Morgan and Amhar began to get erections. Sir Hemison, a more world-weary man, was the only one that tried to fight his urges and make some sense of the situation that they now found themselves in. He shook his head to try and clear it. It was as though a mist had fallen around him and it was clouding his ability to think clearly.

"There is nobody in the forest but us," said the first stepping towards Amhar as she spoke. She reached up and caressed his hair.

"Make love to us," said the second, enveloping Mordrede with her arms and legs.

"Our kisses are sweeter than honey, our arms warmer than the sun," said the third. Sire Hemison could feel himself falling. It felt good. All he had to do was let it happen and he would turn his body over to her and make rambunctious love to the woman. It was what she wanted. Any thoughts of his loyalty to Morgan were pushed aside in a sudden flood of animal passion.

None of the men could remember removing their clothes, but if they had cared to look, they would have seen them strewn about, hastily torn away from their bodies. Every second that they were not having sex was torturous. Sir Hemison had his prize on her hands and knees. He was pounding his way into her from behind and enjoying every thrust more immensely than he could have imagined. Mordrede was lying flat on his back whilst his beauty straddled him. She moaned with ecstasy upon moving herself in time with his rhythm. Amhar was lying on top of his woman in the most traditional of love-making positions. He could not tell how long he had been with his newfound lover, but he was completely enraptured.

The three men continued to make rampant love to their respective women. Mordrede was the first to reach climax as he did so, surrendering his seed into the woman there was a brief moment of clarity. It took every bit of his strength to try and hold on to that occurrence. He knew that if he did not he may not have it again. He fought the urge to continue with the monumental orgasm; the distraction giving him enough resolve to think in an instant of time. These women were faeries surely? They had appeared as if from nowhere and beguiled the men into having sex with them. There was something that his mother had taught him. Some words to say whenever he felt that a faerie was near.

He remembered being frightened as a child. He would sneak past the chamber maid that was sleeping instead of watching over him, and run to his mother's room. She would never be angry to see him, or have him wake her in the middle of the night with his childish fears. The servants had told him of faeries and he was afraid that they may be in his room. He remembered how kindly his mother believed him instead of dismissing his foolishness. She had told him that there were words to say if he ever thought that there was a faerie nearby. Once spoken, no faerie could stand to be close and would flee with all of the haste they could. The words taught to him by his mother would always protect him, and he was not afraid anymore.

Mordrede pictured his mother teaching him those words when he was very young. He was eager to learn them so that he could use them every night in his room and not be afraid of the faeries anymore. Like a distant horseman riding closer and closer, the memory of the words returned to him. The faerie had repositioned herself and was biting his nipples gently and then firmly. It was arousing. Mordrede panicked he could see no end to the woman's need for intimacy. She would surely be the death of him if he did not save himself now. He looked around. Amhar and Hemison were covered in perspiration. They could barely hold their eyes open. They were tiring. How many times had the women had their way with the men? Perhaps it was more than once, maybe they had been making love for a large part of the night. Mordrede could not tell which way was up anymore. Was he standing or lying down.

In a flash of inspiration the words of the faerie expulsion spell came flooding back to him. He called out the first few words of the spell. It was the old Galatian tongue. The effect was immediate. The three women stopped their violent love-making and turned to him, each of them hissing like a cornered and frightened cat.

Mordrede drew in a breath before reciting the second sentence to the spell. The faerie that was on top of him jumped up and backed away, growling like and animal. There was only one sentence left to recite. Mordrede summoned all of his strength, propped himself up on one elbow to try and face the three of them. He shouted the final part of the spell. The faeries all screamed in agony.

Hemison and Amhar were jolted by the inhuman sound. It brought them back to the present. In rapid succession each of the faeries transformed into a black crow and angrily flapped their wings and snapped their beaks loudly before flying directly upwards and into the pitch black of the night sky.

Amhar, Hemison and Mordrede scrambled to their feet. The beating of the crows wings were still to be heard disappearing into the distance. It was an eerie sound, unnerving. Soon they were standing in the dim light offered by a clear sky and the very little light that was left from the fire that had been started, who knows how long ago?

"What happened? What were they?" said Sir Hemison loudly but with a quiver in his voice.

"Faeries," replied Mordrede.

"From where, what did they want with us?" asked Amhar not thinking before he spoke. It dawned upon the three men exactly what the faerie women wanted.

"They got what they were after Amhar. They wanted us. Had I not had the presence of mind to speak the spell of faerie expulsion I hate to think how we may have ended up." Mordrede's explanation did nothing to alleviate the growing shame that was now growing within the three men. They were all still breathing hard. They were tired, almost exhausted to the point of collapse.

Sir Hemison, like Amhar and even Mordrede to a lesser extent, was still trying to make sense of what had happened.

"If they just wanted sex, are there not male faeries? Would that not hath suited their purpose better?" he looked at his companions still grappling with the reality of the surreal situation they had endured. At this time it also began to dawn upon the men that they were all standing near a smouldering fire, in a forest completely naked.

"Let us stoke the fire and dress," said Mordrede. The routineness of the two tasks put before them somehow seemed comforting. Amhar reacted first and bent down to grab a small handful of dried leaves and twigs and he tossed them upon the fire. There were enough of the embers left to ignite the new fuel and it began to crackle to life once more. Although this time it was without the assistance of faerie magic.

The light that the small fire offered helped the three men find and identify their various items of clothing. Bit by bit they managed to recover tunics and boots and undergarments until they were once more clothed. It was good, the shock of what had happened had pushed any awareness of the weather out of their minds. Given the time of year, it was a rather cold night. The men's clothing offered respite from the cold night air. They gathered around the fire for warmth, each of them trembling.

"Lady Morgan," said Sir Hemison. Then looking at his companions he realised that he had said aloud what he thought that he was only thinking. Amhar and Mordrede guessed that he had accidentally let them in upon his thoughts.

"We were seduced by otherworldly beings, Hemison. My mother would not hold such a thing against ye," said Mordrede hopefully being of some comfort to his fellow knight. Amhar was the next to put into words the direction of his thoughts.

"Is it a bad omen? Should we take it as a sign that our mission is..."

"No, Amhar. Faeries are not an omen of anything except their selfish lives. What we are doing is for the betterment of all of the people of Briton. The real people of Briton, not those...things."

Mordrede's response was uncharacteristically vehement. Perhaps because of that, it snapped the attentions of Hemison and Amhar back to the task that still lay before them. It was easier now to talk of the reason for their journey than to continue to converse about magical creatures that had seduced the unwitting men.

"I shall make it a priority to succeed in our quest in order to win back mine own honour, and hold true the promise that I made to the Lady Morgan, to see that ye both come to no harm." Sir Hemison spoke his resolve with such confidence that it inspired Amhar and Mordrede to follow his lead. The Prince spoke next.

"Mine friends, now more than ever we must reapply ourselves to our commission; we are Knights of the Round Table and sworn to uphold justice in our land. We are meant to be incorruptible; yet this hath reminded us that there are other forces in our land that hath no regard for the good deeds of men. If we...*when* we succeed in turning mine father's opinion around and showing him that we are all one people, maybe then we will hath more of a chance to stand together against these faeries."

It was a heat warming speech. Although it did not take into account the fact that in the past the residents of Caerleon and the faeries had acted in unison to fight a common enemy. Now it was more convenient to see the faeries as the only real enemy.

Without realising that they had now each succumbed to the same wilful blindness that they hoped to cure King Arthur of, they rallied around the Prince's new mandate. Mordrede supported the new direction and ultimate goal of their undertaking.

"Well spoken Amhar; we shall ride tomorrow with all haste to Camlann and begin to recruit men to aide us in our chore. The sooner Arthur realises who our real enemies are in the land the sooner will be able to defend ourselves against them."

Perhaps it was the embarrassment of being seduced so easily by the faeries, but the three were now bonded by the experience and each in their own way now desperate to exonerate themselves from any further shame. This charge offered them a course of action to follow in order to achieve the redemption that they now each sought.

"Then we shall each swear it upon our own blood," said Amhar, looking from one to the other with all seriousness. "We shall swear to succeed in our quest, for King, Country and the people of Briton."

Mordrede and Hemison took up the mantle and the three of them grasped each other's wrist forming a triangle of bonded hands. Together at some unspoken sign to begin they all spoke together, swearing their new vow.

"For King, Country and the people of Briton"

Chapter 26: Camlann

The township of Camlann was really quite pretty. Like most of the townships along the river, it'd grown up without any adequate planning, but somehow all of the various elements that make up a well-established agrarian and artisan town had come together serendipitously. There was a central area from which the various artisan cheese makers and other food producers could barter and bargain together with the townsfolk. It was always a hive of activity from sunrise to just before the morning meal. Then the populous would disappear into their homes, or eat at one of the established inns before beginning their various days work, in the fields, in the iron mongers, in the pig-farms or a plethora of other minor industries that came together to keep the township well-fed and prosperous. The population had reached a point where it was possible to see people and not know who they were, at least for a time. Camlann had a good reputation in the area for its foods and wares and it attracted a good number of transient visitors.

Sir Hemison may have been able to go almost unnoticed in the township, except for his Knightly robes. Sir Mordrede, however, being an illegitimate son of the king would not go so easily unnoticed. But when the handsome Prince Amhar rode into town with him it caused quite a scene.

News about the arrival of the Prince and the two Knights spread quickly and soon there was a crowd gathering around them following them into the centre of the township. People were generally cheering and waving in delight at the royal visitor. Amhar looked around him at the smiling faces. He was sure that he could appeal to their better nature at the same time as invoking their loyalty to the king. He shouted from his horse.

"Follow me to the centre of town, there is something that I must say!" although it was only a prelude to a speech, it nevertheless garnered a cheer of support. People could be seen running to get to the centre of town to be there waiting for the Prince when he arrived. Others hurried away probably to fetch members of their households that had not seen the party enter the town.

Mordrede guessed what was happening and signalled for Amhar to saunter with a little less speed toward their destination. That would give the villagers more time to gather loved ones and then Amhar could address the largest possible gathering, in such short notice. Word of mouth would ensure that whatever he said would travel to the far corners of Camlann soon enough though. For the time-being the three men were content to bask in the glow of such a warm welcome from the townsfolk. They began to reach down and clasp hands randomly with the crowd. This too unintentionally solicited a cheer from the grateful crowd.

The swelling crowd and the insistence by the three men to greet as many as possible made progress to the centre of town slow. But eventually they reached their destination. Amhar looked around to Mordrede and Hemison for moral support. They both nodded in affirmation that he should begin.

"People of Camlann in the Kingdom of Arthur Pendragon, mine father and our great ruler..." the beginning of Amhar's speech reaped yet another cheer from the people much louder and longer this time. The three men, still on horseback looking over the sea of joyous faces could not help but smile at the reaction.

"We hath come here to seek support for the solidarity of all of the people living here in Camlann today." Amhar's second sentence was nothing short of vexing, but it had the same effect as the first and the people cheered loudly. He waited for the noise to subside before continuing.

"Which of ye would not stand beside thine neighbour to help them in a time of need? The people of Camlann are known as good people throughout the Kingdom." The obvious compliment to the townsfolk from the prince only served to make them cheer all the more loudly and for much longer this time.

"I need ye to show King Arthur that ye are people worthy of that reputation. Will ye do this for me?" He had become quite passionate with his speaking now and used his arms and clenched fists to signify his need for them to do this thing for him.

"Aye!" shouted the crowd as one.

"At the conclusion of the festival of Lughansadh King Arthur and the Knights of the Round Table will ride here to Camlann, will ye stand with me to prove thine loyalty to the King by showing solidarity with one another?"

"Aye," responded the crowd, louder than before and with more fervour. Even though it'd become clear by the expressions upon some of the faces that they were unsure exactly what the prince meant. A voice shouted from the crowd asking for clarification.

"What is it we should do Prince Amhar?" it was impossible to see who had asked the question, but it did gather a number of supporters from the crowd. It was followed with various repeats of the question from others here and there. The people wanted more details from Amhar. Amhar knew that he had to frame the next part of his plan carefully so that what he was asking the people to do, would not seem like insurrection.

"King Arthur needs to know that ye will fight for thine neighbour, even if that man or that woman is not from Camlann. They may hath come to thine township from across the river Exe. But what does it matter!? Will ye not stand beside one another and show the king that ye are one people united and living here together in harmony?" Unfortunately Amhar's explanation did nothing to clarify the situation at all, but it did sound like a good idea, so predictably some people began to shout support for it already. Sensing that he'd not yet won over the people entirely, Amhar tried to explain his plan a little more simply.

"When the king rides into Camlann, I want him to see all of the men standing together as one, ready to raise a scythe, an iron or anything else that could be used as a weapon, to prove to the king that ye are one people in his kingdom. Will ye show the king thine loyalty? Will ye show the king thine unity!?" the questions had no other answer as far as the crowd were concerned. They shouted over and over, caught up in the moment.

"Aye!" "Aye!" Aye!"

Support for Amhar's plan was unanimous. The townsfolk were prepared to show their loyalty to the king by standing beside all of their neighbours in a symbol of solidarity. It was what Prince Amhar wanted. It was what King Arthur wanted. They were only too willing to do whatever it took to show the king that they were loyal subjects worthy of the praise that was bestowed upon them by their peers. The people of Camlann were indeed good people, one and all, whether born in Camlann or now living there. The feeling of joy was palpable. The crowd so jubilant that they actually managed to grapple the Prince from his mount and toss him with elation into the air.

Thinking that it would be better for him to let it happen than to try and stop it, Amhar relented and allowed himself to be man-handled by the exuberant crowd.

Unnoticed in the general melee of delight, one of the men was slowly edging his way out of the crowd. He had heard what Prince Amhar had said and seen the effect that it had had upon the townsfolk. He needed to report these things to his master. Smiling and thumping peoples backs so as not to arouse suspicion that he was extracting himself from the celebrations, he gradually made his way toward his horse that was tethered near the main inn.

With any luck he would reach the stronghold of Cymen by the end of tomorrow. That would be more than enough time to report upon events in Camlann before the onset and then end of the festival of Lughansadh.

Chapter 27: Cymen, Son of Aelle

Cymen listened to the report from his spy planted in Camlann with great interest. The story that he was telling was almost too good to be true. He waited for the man to stop speaking, contemplated for a moment and then said;

"Prince Amhar and Sir Mordrede wish to unite all of the people of Camlann in a show of solidarity to King Arthur shortly after the Celtic festival of Lughansadh?"

It was a rhetorical question; a summation of the news that the man had brought to Cymen. He continued.

"Then the good Prince and Knight should get exactly what they have requested. Send thine message to mine brothers, they will be most interested. Then tell them to join me here in mine castle along with their most skilled warriors. He started to pace up and down his throne room whilst he mulled over the ramifications of the news. Then he said to nobody in particular.

"The population of Camlann is about to become bolstered with trained Saxon warriors...Arthur, Amhar and Mordrede won't suspect a thing!" Cymen ran through the scenario in his mind; the strategy couldn't possibly fail. The malevolence of the plan filled him with satisfaction. He could not stop himself from verbalising one more time.

"We will rid ourselves of Arthur, his two sons and the Knights of the Round Table in one felled swoop! All of his lands will become ours, the folly of a united Briton standing against Saxons will come to an abrupt end shortly after their pathetic celebration marking the beginning of the harvest. Except it is we that shall harvest...all that we hath ever desired."

Cymen almost bent over with the ecstasy that was flooding through his body. He will soon rule over an empire greater than is father King Aelle had ever dreamt of. Indeed all of Aelle's sons will rule more land than any other Saxon Lord in the history of their people. Cymen, together with his brothers Wlencing and Cissa would become the new Kings of Briton.

Chapter 28: Lughansadh

Caerleon was absolutely alive. The festival had begun in earnest and everywhere people were celebrating and dancing. Music filled the main courtyard of the castle. King Arthur and Gwenhwyvar watched from their thrones, which had been moved to a vantage-point in the grounds from which they could see everything, and more importantly everybody could see them. Their faces were pictures of delight. This was without doubt the largest festival of Lughansadh that they had ever been a part of. The number of people filling the grounds was far in excess of any previous year. Arthur made the observation to Gwenhwyvar and she agreed.

"The land is bountiful, Arthur, people are having larger families and now we are seeing the fruits of thine years of monarchy," she said needing to raise her voice so that he could hear her, even though they were sitting close to each other. Arthur nodded, he agreed with his wife's summation of the increase of attendance. There certainly were a large number of children running around and playing in the crowd.

Arthur was enjoying himself immensely, but he did regret that Amhar and Mordrede were not with them to share the experience. The errant thought must have shown briefly in Arthur's expression because Gwenhwyvar over to him and took his hand. He looked over to her

"What is it, Arthur? Everyone is having such a wonderful time; how can you look so distant?"

He was apologetic in his response. "I beg thine forgiveness Gwenhwyvar; I was just thinking how nice it would hath been to have Amhar and Mordrede with us on this joyous day. However I am sure that the festival is equally as engaging in North Rheged with Queen Ganieda." He looked at the Queen hoping that his explanation had sated her. It had. However as happenstance would have it, Morgan and Ivorwulf were passing them. Gwenhwyvar hoping to set Arthur's mind at rest called out to the Sorceress.

"Lady Morgan, please reassure thine brother that Amhar and Mordrede are ensconced in a wonderful festival in North Rheged. Try to see a vision of them for us!" Gwenhwyvar looked expectantly at Morgan for an appropriate response. It was Ivorwulf that responded though, perplexed.

"What do ye mean, they're not in North Rheged?" he enquired of Morgan. For her part Morgan looked shocked.

"I said naught!" she cried out looking at Ivorwulf and then almost guiltily at the King and Queen. Neither of them had seen Morgan verbally respond, so they were equally perplexed by the outburst from Ivorwulf. He sought to justify himself to the three vexed faces.

"I heard ye Morgan, as plain as anything...Mordred and Amhar are not in North Rheged." He sounded very assured of what he was saying. "They were thine exact words."

Morgan realised that Ivorwulf had somehow overheard her thoughts, and had mistaken it for her speaking. This was a terrible situation. She was now in a position where she'd have to lie directly to the king, her brother, and the queen, her sister-in-law, about the location of Mordrede, Amhar and of course Sir Hemison. The Royals could see the worried look on her face and immediately suspected that all was not well. Arthur even stood up to take a step closer to Morgan.

"Aye Morgan, we didn't see ye speak these words. Surely Ivorwulf is mistaken. Seek to hath a vision of Mordrede, Amhar and Sir Hemison, together with Ganieda celebrating as we do, the festival of Lughansadh."

In spite of all of the merriment around them, there seemed to be silence. Morgan looked from one to the other of the small party surrounding her. The fact that she did not answer immediately only served to raise the suspicions of the queen. Now Gwenhwyvar stood up and took a step toward Morgan.

"Morgan do as the king hath bid." It did not sound like a threat, but rather like a piece of good advice. "Put Arthur's mind to rest," she further bade of the Sorceress. Morgan would have to choose her next words very carefully if she was to continue the premise that the three were in North Rheged. However, for a second time, Ivorwulf managed to read her mind, as if it was a leaking bladder of wine.

"Camlann?" he said, looking at her as if she had said the name herself. Upon hearing this Arthur felt a sudden rush of blood through his head, he could feel his pupils expand and then narrow. As Morgan seemed unwilling or unable to answer, he turned to the Kentish Sorcerer for an explanation.

"What say ye, Ivorwulf, are ye seeing a vision of mine son in Camlann? Is that where he is now?"

This time it was Ivorwulf's turn to be flummoxed.

"I beg the king's pardon. Twice I thought that I heard the Lady Morgan speak, answering thine questions, but clearly I was mistaken."

Ivorwulf's feeble attempt to cover the fact that he had somehow read Morgan's mind did not sit well with Arthur, who was quite accustomed to witnessing such feats of magical prowess. Clearly Arthur had summed up the situation in his own mind and was now hell-bent upon validating his suspicions. He turned to Morgan and said forcefully.

"Tell me, Morgan. Is Amhar in the village of Camlann!" He was very angry and made absolutely no attempt to hide it. Morgan could see the resolve in Arthur's eyes and she knew that she had no way of hiding the truth from him. Her eyes fell and she nodded her confession.

Gwenhwyvar, Morgan and Ivorwulf could physically feel the rage in Arthur well up like a swollen river. Gwenhwyvar acted quickly and grabbed his hand. He looked angrily at his wife. She indicated the multitude of people around them celebrating loudly.

It was extremely difficult for Arthur, but he took the non-verbal message that Gwenhwyvar had sent him. 'Be calm before thine subjects'. He swallowed. His throat felt like a knotted rope. Breathing deeply three or four times he managed to suppress his anger at Amhar's insolence and did his best to put on a smile as if he was still enjoying the happenings around him.

The trio that knew exactly what was happening, watched the king intently. Arthur turned to view the jesters that were performing gymnastic feats just over from their thrones, and managed a smile and even some applause before shouting.

"Again!" as he instructed the lithe performers to once more do their somersaults. Disaster was averted. The king once more looked to be enjoying the festival happening all around him. Gwenhwyvar and Morgan visibly breathed a sigh of relief. Arthur took his place again on his throne, Gwenhwyvar followed his lead. Ivorwulf looked to Morgan for guidance in the awkward situation. She indicated that he should follow her. They both bowed courteously to the king and queen who acknowledged their salutation.

As they continued their previously interrupted journey through the frenetic crowd, Ivorwulf took the opportunity to apologise to Morgan.

"Please, Lady Morgan, I beg thine forgiveness, I did not mean to hear thine thoughts, but they were so clear; more so than any other's thoughts that I hath over my life occasionally intercepted." He tried to justify his improper eavesdropping. The damage however was done, the truth of the whereabouts of Morgan, Amhar and Hemison was now known to the king. There was no way to undo what had just transpired. Morgan was sanguine and strangely relieved now that the truth was known. She did not like hiding it from Arthur, it did not feel right.

"The fault was mine, Ivorwulf. Had I not hidden the truth from mine brother, then I would not hath felt so guilty about it and may hath had more control of mine stray thoughts. Think nothing more of it." Although a gracious response, it seemed to do little to assuage Ivorwulf's feeling of embarrassment. He tried to alter the subject to discover the outcome of what had just transpired.

"What will the king do?' he asked. Morgan replied as best as she could guess.

"Arthur will confront Amhar in Camlann at his earliest opportunity."

"But the festival will run for two more days at least," responded the Kentish Sorcerer.

"And then he must prepare and then travel to Camlann. Surely there is time enough for the king's emotions to subside and to approach Prince Amhar with a different outlook." Ivorwulf's musings were somehow very comforting to Morgan.

"I hope that ye are right, Ivorwulf, I really do," said Morgan. They continued through the crowd without any further conversation. Both were clearly contemplating the possible outcomes from the destined meeting between father and son.

Chapter 29: Cymen, Wlencing & Cissa

The three sons of Aelle were together once more. They'd ruled their various lands given to them by their father with little contact over the years. But circumstances had brought them together. They were in the main hall of Cymen's castle. It was the geographically closest to Camlann. It was Cymen that was addressing his brothers.

"The opportunity is before us. We insert our closest men into the village of Camlann pretending to be refugees from mine lands and looking to be brothers with the villagers. When in time Prince Amhar offers the united front of the Camlann villagers to King Arthur we strike, for he will not be expecting it. We dispose of Arthur, his son and the Knights of the Round Table in one decisive move." Cymen finished outlining the plan and embellished it by clenching his fist symbolising the crushing of their enemies.

There were no words of rebuke, or concern or even the thought that they may fail. Nothing but guttural moans of support came from Wlencing and Cissa and their closest advisers. Emboldened by the lack of critique Cymen pressed his advantage.

"The combined force of our strongest and most skilled men will be able to accomplish in one day what all of the other warlords hath failed to do in these past thirty years; conquer the country completely." Again the men nodded and grunted with pleasure at the very thought of Arthur's demise and gaining all of the land that they could ever possibly want.

"Bit by bit the men will leave here and trickle into the village. Some will say that they are from Arthur's other lands and have come to resettle in Camlann. Others will say that they are just passing through, returning home after the Celtic festival. And still others will claim to have been persecuted in mine land because of suspected Briton blood in their veins; now they seek a life beneath the benevolent King Arthur. The villagers of Camlann will hath no reason to suspect anything except what they are told by the men." Feeling perhaps that Cymen had been speaking too much his brother Wlencing took up the diatribe.

"Prince Amhar will be glad to see the numbers of Camlann villagers that will stand beside him when his father comes to purify his territory. Naively he will be an innocent lamb lead to the slaughter when the fighting erupts. A gold coin for the man that kills the prince and ensures there will never be another successor to a throne that we will overthrow." This garnered a loud acclaim from the gathered men all cheering at the thought of being rewarded so handsomely for doing the deed.

Not wanting to be left out of the proceedings, Cissa upped the ante.

"Two gold coins for the man that kills King Arthur." This too caused an outcry of approval from the men. The three brothers were now standing side by side and looked with satisfaction at the uproar that they had caused. They looked at each other and through the din of the chest beating and boasting that one or the other soldier would be the 'first' to kill the Prince or the King; they managed to speak to each other. Wlencing said to his brothers.

"And then we shall proclaim ourselves the new rulers of Briton." He smiled with smug satisfaction. Cymen responded.

"Long live us, the kings of Briton." He almost laughed aloud at the very sound of calling himself king. Wanting it to become reality as quickly as possible Wlencing prodded the other two into action.

"Enough talking, dispatch the first twenty men immediately; then the remainder in small batches over the coming days. We want our full contingent to be in place when Arthur arrives."

Chapter 30: The End of Lughansadh

The remainder of the festival was excruciating for Gwenhwyvar, Morgan and Merlin. They knew that Arthur was seething with anger at Amhar's insolence but that he was not showing it to anyone. As far as the Knights were concerned the king was enjoying the proceedings around him. The servants too did not suspect that anything was wrong. The Queen had been particularly careful to keep an open ear for any scuttlebutt from the gossip-mill that was the Castle fraternity, which may even hint that all was not well. Thankfully there was nothing.

Merlin new better than to approach the king when he was in a mood like this; he did his part to uphold the appearance that all was well, as did Morgan and the queen. Instead of trying to reason with Arthur, Merlin used his time to work out a way to try and diffuse what was going to be a volatile situation when father and son came face to face once more. He was going to need all of his wiles if he was to be in any way effective.

It was after the closing ceremony at dusk for the festivities that Merlin decided to make his move. The king had given a speech to the gathered people thanking them for their participation and telling them that it was the best festival of Lughansadh that he had ever been a part of. He had certainly won the favour of his subjects, not that he needed to, but they were even more proud to live beneath his rule than ever before. The general feeling of good will that emanated from the king and queen's subjects did its part to quell Arthur's anger.

Arthur had just bade farewell to everyone and retreated inside the walls of the castle and made his way to his library to be alone. Merlin made it look like he was only passing by just as the king entered the library. He nodded and said.

"A fine speech Arthur, ye make me look forward to next year's festival already." Merlin made as if to walk away but the king stopped him.

"Join me in mine library old friend," he said. Merlin smiled and dutifully did so. Arthur closed the door sealing out the hustle and bustle of the servants clearing away the decorations other remnants of the festival. Rather than approach the subject that he so desperately wanted to talk to Arthur about, Merlin spoke of anything but, in the hopes that Arthur would lead the conversation in the direction that Merlin wanted.

"The first harvest was bountiful Arthur, a sure sign of even better harvests ahead." It was not quite a question but it nevertheless provoked a response from the king.

"We hath been fortunate, our farmers are hard workers, truly dedicated to their calling. As much as our honouring of the old ways, they are responsible for our years of plenty." Arthur's response was much like Merlin's comment, somewhat open-ended. He pretended to think about what he had heard for a moment and then built upon the conversation.

"The ways of our forefathers hath put us in good stead to wrest the hearts and minds of the people from the tyranny of our occupation by Rome, and focus their attention on the betterment of our way of life," said Merlin.

"Aye," responded Arthur, "the..." and he trailed-off as if lost in thought. Merlin allowed the King this lapse in their exchange. Arthur turned away from Merlin and walked to the window and looked down at the scene below. He did not take in anything that he saw. Instead he said just one word.

"Why?" then followed silence. Merlin knew exactly to what the king referred. But he did not have an answer so he did not offer any response. Confused by the lack of reply Arthur turned to face his sage. The look upon Arthur's face said everything that Merlin already knew. Arthur was in agony; his son's blatant defying of his plan to cleanse Camlann of its Saxon blood, vexed him ineffably.

Merlin breathed a large sigh and moved to sit upon one of the stools closest to Arthur in the hope that it would somehow encourage the King to do likewise. When he had settled himself he looked up at Arthur, still standing at the window.

"He is an idealist, Arthur, just as ye. He seeks the purity of absolute truth in the life he sees around him."

"But he does not see that my truth is the ideal that he should strive for?" countered Arthur, the injury in his voice apparent. Merlin's eyes dropped.

"We all seek our own ideals, Arthur. Yours were an extension of mine. I imparted them as I raised ye. Amhar is a product of a different age. Not the violent age in which ye drew Excalibur from the stone and became king. By the time Amhar came of age, thine lands were vast, more than any before ye. And even as a Knight in thine service, Amhar hath only had to fight occasionally to win more concessions. Most of thine victories hath been won by negotiation over these last ten years. This is what Amhar sees as effective, and perhaps why he is so averse to resorting to fighting in order to achieve our ultimate goal." Merlin could have gone on for much longer and in more detail about why he thought Amhar had taken such an opposing view to theirs, but he did not. Merlin already felt that he was moralising to Arthur, and he did not want the king to feel that he was being lectured.

The summations of what Merlin though were Amhar's reasons for his actions were perhaps just enough to help Arthur try and see his son's side of the story. Arthur slowly made his way to the stool opposite Merlin and took a seat.

"If I ride to Camlann and fight, I risk causing a rift in mine own house. How can I raise Excalibur against mine son and rightful heir to the throne? What would Gwenhwyvar think of her husband at war with his son? How many of mine loyal Knights could I rightfully ask to stand at mine side in such a conflict?" the barrage of difficult questions hit Merlin with a force. None of them had an easy answer.

Amhar had placed his father into an untenable position. Merlin began to ponder upon the nature of the situation which faced Arthur. He was busy trying to fathom more reasons for Amhar's apparent complete disregard for his father's wishes, but also how to overcome the youngster's show of defiance without seriously injuring the pride of both parties. None of Merlin's collected history of life's experience or his learned scholastic achievement could provide him with a solution to this puzzle.

"'Tis a Gordian knot," said Merlin after quite some time, "a puzzle without a solution." But even as he said the words he was reminded of Morgan's encounter in the Labyrinth with the Minotaur who similarly offered her a rope with a Gordian knot tied into it. Believing that she would be unable to undo it, he hoped to get out of a bargain that would have freed her and Gwenhwyvar if they passed various tests.

"Magic is the solution Arthur." Merlin's face was beginning to light up as if dawn was spreading across his old features. Magic helped Morgan overcome her impossible task. This situation was no different. Magic could solve this problem too.

"How?" queried the king uncertain of the simplistic nature of the offered solution. Merlin's mind was racing ahead through all of the plausibility's and possible outcomes of the given scenarios that he was running in his mind. Arthur could see the furious pace that the wizard's thoughts were turning, it gave him hope.

"Ye cannot back down now, it would appear weak, but ye cannot attack for fear of hurting thine sons. What if Morgan and I were there to ensure that not a hair upon their heads would come to harm, by casting a spell to slow them down and ensnare them as if in a spider's web, cocooned away from the tirade of battle?" The offer was too good to refuse. Arthur demanded detail.

"Tell me exactly what ye hath planned!" he said excitedly. "Leave nothing out" he followed. Merlin leant closer to Arthur.

"There could not be many Saxons that ye need to strip away from Camlann. Morgan and I shall ride with ye and fold a spell around Mordrede and Amhar that will make their reactions slow. It will be as if they are walking through waist-deep mud. The Saxon refugees can be picked off by thine Knights. Do not involve thine person in the battle at all. But instead give the order for the ethnic cleansing just as ye did in Exelhulme. Thine orders will be carried out. Excalibur will never hath even been drawn from its holder. Father will not hath raised his sword to his sons. They will be incapacitated." Merlin finished the briefing with a flourish of his arms.

"Why hath ye not used this spell before in any of our battles Merlin? It could hath been very useful in many that I can recollect." Merlin lifted his finger to the side of his nose.

"That is because I hath not invented it yet. But with Ivorwulf's help, Morgan and I will create this very spell and cast it for the first time when we reach Camlann." The enthusiasm in his voice and the exultation upon his face made it difficult to bring any criticism into the conversation. Arthur wanted to be absolutely certain. He was going to ask for a demonstration of this new-found power prior to facing Amhar and Mordrede in battle and hoping that it would save them from harm. But the king stumbled with almost embarrassment at seeing how completely convinced the Sorcerer was that he and his fellow magicians could carry off this plan.

"But...what if....how..." Arthur started various sentences of objection but the contagious enthusiasm from Merlin silenced them all before they were given a voice. If Arthur's experience of a lifetime with Merlin had taught him nothing, it was to rely upon the old man when he was absolutely certain of something. Arthur saw no reason in this instance to do otherwise. He capitulated with a sigh and a laugh of relief that the situation would be able to progress. He felt relieved.

"Aye Merlin; cast thine spell and spare mine sons from harm. The ethnic cleansing of Camlann shall go ahead as I hath ordered. I shall give the orders to prepare for our departure." Arthur stood up. Merlin almost jumped up from his stool.

"I shall consult with Morgan and Ivorwulf immediately. We hath magical work to do Arthur." With that he bustled out of the room in a most excited manner.

Chapter 31: The Council of Magicians

Merlin was alive with energy. Ivorwulf and Morgan could see it as he approached them. They could feel it too. He had found the couple in the kitchen they appeared to be mixing various dried herbs and spices together.

"Good, good, ye are mixing a brew for a magical purpose; what is it?" he asked as he approached them, wide-eyed and excited. The response was something of a let-down. Ivorwulf replied.

"A spiced porridge for the morning, Merlin; nothing beyond that" He was almost apologetic in his tone. Realising his mistake Merlin looked as if he was attempting to brush it away with a flurry of his hands.

"No matter, no matter, we hath work to do. To mine chambers immediately. We are to conjure a spell that hath not yet been written." The offer was too intriguing to refuse, and certainly more interesting than a spiced porridge dish. Merlin almost herded them away from the kitchen table.

"Hurry, hurry, there is no time to waste." He said bustling the two of them before him. Mordrede attempted to turn around to query Merlin on this new spell of which he spoke, but Merlin would not have the progress to his chambers impeded with frivolous questions.

"More details when we are behind mine closed door" he said. "Until then let us hasten our pace" he said. The infectious nature of his excitement helped expedite their travel up the great staircase and through the passageways to Merlin's chamber. When they were finally safely sealed inside he turned to them and said

"Arthur will go forward with his attack upon Camlann to rid them of any Saxon interlopers." This news shocked both Ivorwulf and Morgan. They were about to object with any number of reasons as to why such a thing should not happen but Merlin interrupted them.

"Our job is to find a way to shelter Amhar and Mordrede from themselves. To make their actions sluggish and unwieldy; in essence to allow the king's Knights free reign to execute Arthur's orders, whilst they battle with the coordination of a toddler just learning to walk. They will be spared becoming involved in the heat of the fighting and not a sword shall be raised against them in anger" He smiled at the proposal put before them. It all seemed perfectly reasonable the way that Merlin put it. But the actuality of how it would be done, hung in the air like a standard flapping upon a pole.

"That is the task mine friends. Together as a council of magicians we will see that it is done." Mordrede looked from Merlin to Ivorwulf who returned her look and then looked to Merlin. There was a moments silence and then both of them began to talk.

"I recall something similar that may form a part..."

"There is a spell that could help in a small way..."

"Excellent, excellent!" shouted Merlin, clapping his hands together. "Tell me everything that ye both think will make up a part of this spell, and I shall tell ye mine thoughts. We shall bring together all of our combined skills and knowledge. Surely there is nothing that we cannot achieve? By the end of this night, we must have come up with a spell that will make it happen." Merlin reconsidered his final sentence of his inspirational speech.

"By the end of this night, we *will* hath a spell that *shall* work!" He was delighted with his revised words of encouragement. At that moment it felt, to the three of them, that it was a certainty; and all they had to do was go through the motions to achieve their goal. They gathered their thoughts and all began to speak at once.

Chapter 32: The Infiltrators

Mordrede and Amhar looked around them. The villagers had gathered together to practice exactly how they would stand together and show their solidarity to King Arthur when he arrived. The men were a little slow at taking direction. Amhar wanted them to look like a band of united farmers rather than a Roman legion ready to attack. Instead they seemed determined to mimic the precision lines of the Knights of the Round Table or that of the Saxon armies. The two Knights were beginning despair.

"No mine friends," shouted Amhar to the crowd, "not like a battalion ready for battle. Gather in groups standing shoulder to shoulder." The less than specific direction from the Prince failed to resolve the situation. He looked at Mordrede for inspiration on how to overcome the misunderstanding. Mordrede also felt that the men seemed more like an attack force than a show of support for each other. But instead of trying to overcome the crowd's determination to form a line he worked with the problem rather than against it.

"Stand in line behind one another. Form more than one line." The crowd did their best to follow the order. The result thankfully looked more like farmers heading out to their fields than anything else. Surprised at his own success, Mordrede smiled to Amhar.

"That looks less intimidating surely." He said seeking affirmation from Amhar. The prince nodded.

"Perfect Mordrede; now they look like simple villagers trying to show their resolve rather than..." he trailed off and changed his direction of conversation.

"Mordrede, do ye remember when I first won the support of the villagers?"

"Aye."

"How many villagers do ye think were present at the time?"

"Around one hundred, men, women and children," he said.

"That was my recollection as well. Look at the crowd now. How many men do ye think are there?"

Mordrede looked and noticed for the first time that the numbers seemed to have swelled considerably. There were definitely many more villagers, especially men than he would have thought were native to Camlann. He offered a theory.

"Perhaps word hath spread, and the villagers from the fringes of the town hath come in to join?" But even as he offered his proposed explanation it did not seem to be able to account for the sudden increase in the numbers. Amhar looked at Mordrede with an expression that showed that he did not think much of the Knight's hypothesis.

Amhar signalled to one of the nearest men to come over and talk with him. The man at first looked a little intimidated, but managed to overcome his shyness and dutifully hurried forward to meet with the prince.

"Aye Prince Amhar?" he said as he approached.

"How long hath ye lived in Camlann?" asked Amhar.

"Mine entire life, Sir Knight," the man responded.

"Are all of these men villagers of Camlann?" Amhar further inquired. The man suddenly looked like he knew that he was not in trouble for anything but was just being used as a source of information. He visibly relaxed.

"Sir Amhar, some of these men were passing through Camlann at the end of the festival, on their way back to their homes and they heard of our gathering and hath decided to support ye. Others hath come from nearby villages so as to do the same thing. We hath been speaking to the newcomers and they all seem to hath either stumbled across our gathering by happenstance, or deliberately journeyed here to be with us and support it," he said with a clear glint of pride in his eyes.

Amhar and Mordrede were astounded.

"That is wonderful news!" said Mordrede.

"Aye good news indeed; mine thanks for bringing it to light," said Amhar. The man pleased that he had been the bearer of good news, left to re-join the practice with a spring in his step.

Amhar and Mordrede felt flushed with success. Amhar put into words what they were both thinking.

"Mordrede, do ye know what this means? We hath more support than even we previously thought, or could hath hoped for. Arthur is sure to relent when he sees the brotherhood of these villagers all standing together in peace together side by side. We hath won our victory even before the King arrives." Amhar's optimistic view of the situation should have twitched a vein of caution in Mordrede. But perhaps he too was so keen to succeed with this plan that he was partially blinded to logic and reason.

"Aye Amhar. It is a relief knowing that our defiance of the king will all be for a good cause and that even he will see that we are right in this matter." Just as he finished talking Sir Hemison joined them.

"I am pleased with the new lines that ye hath organised, Sir Knights. They look less like a threat and more like a protest. Just as ye hath envisioned." Then he added "There are so many more villagers than I would hath thought. Some say that there are men that hath defected from living in Saxon lands and come here to find a new way of life. I'm not sure how many men that constitutes though."

Amhar responded.

"We hath heard this too Sir Hemison. Our message of liberty for all hath touched the hearts of many more than we had dared to hope. It is a good sign."

"Camlann stands to benefit from such an influx of farmers and artisans. It could easily become the Anderitum of this part of the land." The thought of Camlann growing under the new regime of freedom from persecution appealed to Amhar. The seed that he was sowing today could reap a crop of culture, trade and prosperity for the entire region. If only his father could see what was being accomplished by *not* fighting and persecuting the Britons that he would brand as Saxon.

"It is a good thought Mordrede. One that I hope comes to pass." The three men looked at the crowd of men before them and to differing degrees of measure, all felt hope that they were doing the right thing.

Chapter 33: A New Spell

The three magicians of Caerleon, which is what they'd become known as in the castle, were on the battlements above the main gate. The fact that Ivorwulf was technically a prisoner seemed to have been forgotten. He clearly enjoyed the company of Merlin and Mordrede and was accepted as the unofficial third Sorcerer in the castle. Ivorwulf was showing no signs that he wanted to return to Kent and the employ of his former master. So his unofficial and unspoken recruitment into the fold was taken for granted. The three wizards looked at the scene below them.

Four Knights were on horseback in the main courtyard. At a prearranged signal from Merlin they were to ride as fast as they could from their starting point, through the gate and out the other side, where they would then finish their race to nowhere.

As usual the word that something magical was about to happen had got around and a crowd had gathered. Arthur was at the main doors along with Gwenhwyvar. They watched from their vantage point.

Merlin turned to his two compatriots.

"Ready?' he asked. Both indicated in the affirmative. He then raised his arm and shouted at the top of his lungs "Ride!" With that command the four Knights jostled their mounts into action. All eyes had turned to the horses and the ensuing race to get through the gate first. People who obviously had their favourites to win the competition began to shout support for their chosen Knights.

Unnoticed by the crowd, the three sorcerers had joined hands and were concentrating furiously. Had anyone seen the looks on their faces they would have surely been worried. Such was the frowning of concentration that each of them looked to be in excruciating pain.

Words were being mumbled beneath their breath. Whatever language it was, they were all speaking in unison. At some point in their rhetoric they all opened their eyes and raised their hands pointing to the horses. Nothing could be felt, there was no sound nor flash of light, but the effect was astounding.

The horses and their riders all slowed down. It was like they were suddenly wading through a raging river. The steps of the horses became laboured and slow. The men riding the horses could see and feel the sudden lack of progress. They too seemed to react too slowly to the situation. They dug their heels into the flanks of their horses to cajole them into faster motion. But even that motion was slow and ineffective. They could not put any force into their actions. Something was pushing against them. It was like the strongest of winds, and yet the air was still. The overcast day did not threaten any wind. But it felt like they were battling their way through a storm.

Arthur and Gwenhwyvar looked at each other in amazement.

"Merlin hath delivered exactly what he said that he would. How could I hath ever doubted him?" Gwenhwyvar could not think of an appropriate answer so she contented herself with clasping his hand instead.

The Wizards were too observing the effect of their newly created spell with a great feeling of achievement. It was more than exciting to work together to cast a spell that had never before been done. But the feeling of satisfaction eclipsed anything that any of them had felt before.

"Exactly the effect that we were hoping for," said Ivorwulf.

"We can now stop Mordrede and Amhar and Hemison from riding forward in the attack. They will be safe," said Morgan with relief.

"Excellent work mine friends, this is perfect, just perfect!" said Merlin gleefully. They watched as the race in slow-motion proceeded through the gate. There was a clear winner although only by the length of a horse's neck. But nobody noticed such was the awe that people felt from witnessing the three magicians perform this feat of enchantment.

The race continued in excruciatingly stretched-out time through the gate and outside of castle. People had left their positions in the audience and had ventured forward to inspect the spectacle of the Knights on their horses.

"Watch!" pointed Merlin to the brave servants and other aides that walked up to the Knights.

"See, see! They are completely unaffected by the spell. It remains around only those upon which it was cast." The proof that they needed was there before them. The spell was a resounding success. They had everything that they needed to continue the ethnic cleansing of Camlann and ensure that Hemison, Amhar and Mordrede did not come to any harm in the looming battle.

Chapter 34: The Following Day

Arthur was ecstatic. After the display of prowess by Merlin, Morgan and Ivorwulf he felt that there was nothing that he could not achieve. He'd ordered the preparations for the journey to Camlann and they had proceeded with a frenetic pace. It was only Gwenhwyvar that had talked Arthur into waiting for the following day to depart, otherwise he would have left as soon as everything was ready.

As it was, the day of departure was sunny and clear. The ladies of the court dutifully watched along with their children as their fathers rode past them and waved goodbye. Merlin, Morgan and Ivorwulf rode behind the king, followed by a large compliment of his Knights. Only Sir Percival was left behind, in charge of Caerleon's security in the king's absence.

Arthur waved to the crowd and twisting around on his mount managed a final wave to the queen. Gwenhwyvar laughed. All this time and he still seemed like the young king that she had met. Full of life and vigour and determined to unite the country. This, in her mind, was just another step in the journey that would bring Arthur his final victory.

Ladies, Lyonors, Florie and Elamite were standing the closest to Gwenhwyvar. Florie spoke putting into words what each of them was feeling.

"Another battle; another sure victory for Arthur." Florie's words were greeted with favour by the others who all said 'Aye' or 'Surely' or other words of affirmation.

Arthur's latest battle, if it could be called that, was a pre-determined victory. It was more of a slaughter of unwanted Saxons infesting Camlann. It was not as if they would be able to put up a fight of any kind. Arthur would return, his lands secure and his authority confirmed.

***

Arthur was in good cheer. He talked to Morgan, Merlin and Ivorwulf about various things for the entire morning of the slow cantor toward their destination. In turn, the three brother Knights also had their turn chatting with the king. All was well and was evident in his manner. This minor mission would be no trouble to any of them at all. And the plan to ensure the safety of the three wayward Caerleon Knights was well understood by all.

Unnoticed by any of them, a terror was descending from the sky above. Four black shapes of indeterminate form or substance were hurtling toward them in absolute silence. It was shortly after noon when the lead horses, sensing something even before any of the Magicians did, reared up almost throwing the Knights and king.

"Easy!" called Arthur to his mount. This was echoed by the other Knights also trying to calm their suddenly unnerved horses. And then the four black shapes fell to the ground ahead of the troupe causing the horses to once more rear up in in fright. It was difficult but the horses were brought under control. Everyone was astounded they looked at the four masses of...whatever they were. Some looked up to see where they'd come from, but the clear sky gave no clue.

"What are they, Merlin?" shouted one of the Knights to the old sorcerer.

"I do not know!" replied Merlin. He looked to his two companions for their assessment of the shapeless masses of dark lying on the ground before them. They were similarly vexed. Just as they gathered up enough bravery or curiosity to venture a little forward for a closer inspection the four shapes suddenly shot up from the ground and took human form.

There was a haggard old woman that looked as if she'd been in a fight in a tavern. She was bruised and bloodied. She was old, but fearsome looking. Her straggled hair and crocked features were a fright to behold. Behind her three men all with straggly dark hair looks equally as scary. There was an unmistakable look of malevolence in all of their eyes. The woman spoke, addressing the crowd.

"Which of ye is King Arthur of Briton?" her tone was icy cold. Arthur didn't need to identify himself, all eyes automatically looked toward him. He was still trying to calm his agitated horse as he looked at the woman who addressed him.

"I am King Arthur, who are you?" he said with equal loudness.

"Good," said the old woman, her face twisting into a smile that sent shivers up the spines of the Caerleon men.

"I am Queen Carmun of Hibernia. These are mine sons, Dub, Dothur and Daun." As she spoke their names each stepped arrogantly forward and glared at Arthur.

"What do ye want here in mine land?" demanded Arthur, looking from one to the other.

"Ye are mistaken, Arthur, this is now mine land. Ye shall worship me as thine ruler and mine sons will be made regents to govern the far corners of this land in mine name." Her tone left in no doubt that she was absolutely serious.

With no other reply in his head Arthur nevertheless questioned the seriousness of the claim.

"Your land? You, the ruler of Briton? With what army do ye propose to take this land from me Carmun? These three boys?" he motioned with his hand at her sons. Merlin interjected.

"Arthur, they are nothing more than troublesome faeries of some description." He then turned to address Carmun.

"Stand aside wretched thing or feel the weight of mine wrath." He said it quite casually for he was certain that a simple faerie expulsion spell would rid them of this nuisance. Carmun did not respond, but she stood her ground resolutely. This annoyed Merlin. He signalled to the other two magicians.

"Together - the spell of expulsion," he directed them. They followed his lead and the three of them began to chant in the old Galatian tongue the spell that would make faeries feel very uncomfortable indeed. But it had absolutely no effect upon the four menacing creatures. They were well into the spell when each of them realised that it was not working. Merlin was the first to break from the chant.

"What treachery is this faerie!?" he said accusingly at Carmun. But she turned her evil smile toward the old man and said.

"I am not a simple faerie, Merlin, sorcerer of Caerleon. I will not be so easily disposed of." With that she raised her hand and a bolt of lightning flashed from her hand and struck Merlin from his horse. The other horses all jostled again frightened of this new occurrence. The situation was becoming unmanageable. All watched with horror as Merlin fell to the ground. Morgan and Ivorwulf dismounted immediately to go to his aide.

Arthur was thinking of the practical nature of the situation that had thrust itself upon them all. The horses were being spooked by everything that these magical beings did.

"Dismount!" he shouted "Draw thine swords!" her further commanded. This was an order that the Knights were accustomed to following. They did so automatically. As each of them found their way to the ground they gave their horses a small slap to drive them away a short distance, taking them out of the immediate battle area.

The Knights, following their years of training and experience, formed a line in front of Arthur. The king was being threatened and he would be defended to the last man.

Morgan and Ivorwulf had in the meantime reached Merlin and were helping him to his feet. They had already examined him with their eyes that could see through flesh to ensure that there were no bones broken. He had been lucky and landed on a bush that had for the most part broken his fall. They helped him to his feet. His ears were ringing. It was as if he had been hit by a full sack of grain. But there were no other ill effects. Nothing was scorched, not his skin or his clothing. His vision was unimpaired. The other two could sense all of these things about Merlin so there was no need to discuss his condition. Instead they turned their attention to the problem at hand.

"What kind of being is this, Merlin?" asked Morgan.

Merlin shook his head, both to clear it and signal that he had no idea what they were facing. Ivorwulf spoke before either Merlin or Morgan had the chance to turn the question upon him.

"I hath never before seen such power from a...woman." He paused as if he had said something that invoked a thought. It had. He gathered his thoughts and spoke.

"Merlin, Morgan, stretch out with thine feelings. What say ye about this woman?" he asked. They dutifully leered at the old hag and realised exactly what Ivorwulf was intimating. First Merlin spoke and then Morgan as if one had started the sentence and the other finished it.

"This does not feel like a magical being at all"

"She seems like a simple woman."

The realisation that they were fighting with a being that could not easily be identified as magical made each of them shiver.

"What else could she be then?" asked Morgan of the two, not really expecting an answer.

Meanwhile, Arthur was regarding his newly proclaimed enemy from behind his men. The hag had not used her lightning again to strike any of them down. That was interesting. Maybe, just as when Merlin did something utterly fantastic, there was a period of recovery needed. Arthur decided at that instant to test his theory.

"Two Knights, each to the three boys; two more to the old woman!" his orders were clear. The Knights somehow worked out by their approximate distance to their intended targets which would attack the three youths and which would attack the old woman. The Knights moved forward fearlessly.

The woman raised her hand again menacingly causing Sirs Lyonell and Dagonet to pause briefly. But the King's orders were given and they would not show fear in the face of an enemy, no matter how intimidating. Sure enough Carmun shot out two more bolts of lightning from her hand one for each of the Knights. They were knocked off their feet, their heads ringing with the force. But they were able to gather themselves up faster than Merlin was able to do so.

Arthur watched this with intense interest. Making allowances for the difference of age between his Knights and the old Sorcerer, he was sure that the Knights were not as affected by Carmun's power as Merlin had been. Surely she was weakening.

The six other Knights had reached their targets swords at the ready to deal a decisive blow, but out of nowhere the young men suddenly had swords in both hands. The sudden appearance of the weapons shocked the Knights. Where did they come from? They'd not been drawn from anywhere except from the air itself. How was this possible? All of these questions were still going through their minds when the sword play began. It pushed aside all ponderings as it became immediately apparent that the youths were excellent at wielding both swords simultaneously. They were easily able to match the skills of the Knights attacking them.

More than that, whenever a Knight tried to circle around to split the focus of the enemy, he was able to continue fighting both at the same time by turning sideways and taking on both attackers. The boys didn't seem to need to see where the Knights were standing to be able to easily parry away any blows that the Knights tried to inflict upon them. It rapidly became obvious that two Knights per youth would not be enough to deliver the easy victory that Arthur wanted.

"Sir Garethe and Maris; slice off the head of that hag!" shouted Arthur. It was a calculated risk. He knew that Carmun would defend herself again, but then he intended to continue to attack her until she was unable to defend herself with her magical hands. At least that was the plan that he had formulated in his head. Arthur turned to see how the six Knights were faring with their battles.

Summing up the situation he further ordered three more Knights to join in the attack on the boys. At that moment Carmun again used her magic to knock down Garethe and Sir Ectorde Maris. But they did not fall completely to the ground.

"Lyonell, Dagonet; she is weakening. Attack again if ye are able" This was all of the encouragement that the Knights needed. They rallied and charged toward the old woman. Once more she shot her lightning at them, but this time it was significantly weaker. It stopped the two Knights in their tracks, but did not knock them over.

"Garethe; Maris!" Arthur's instruction was clear. They were to take over the attack once more. They did so and when Carmun shot her magical lightning at them both. It felt like a force but not one that would completely stop them in their tracks. They continued their attack reaching their intended kill and both raising their swords. Carmun ran toward them both and using both of her hands punched the two Knights in their chests before they had a chance to swing their swords. Her speed for such and old woman was astounding. But her strength was unbelievable. Both Knights went flying with an "ooooffff!" as the air was knocked out of their lungs.

"Second Knights!" shouted the king indicating that Sir Lyonell and Sir Dagonet should now attack the hag.

Chapter 35: An Underestimated Enemy

Dutifully, even if somewhat cautiously, the Knights Charged and met with a similar fate. Both of them knocked more than a body-length away by the strength of the old woman.

The three Knights engaging their enemies were not having any success either. The most hideous thing happened when the numbers ganged-up on the boys. They seemed to duplicate their torsos. With a disgusting sound of flesh and bone growing at an unimaginable rate, they each sprouted an extra torso. Each torso was complete unto itself, with head, neck and arms, holding swords of their own. Only from the waist down was there normalcy to be seen. One waist and one set of legs. It really was one of the most disgusting things that any of the Knights had seen in many years.

Armed with two heads and four arms, each brandishing swords, the boys were more than a match for the three Knights that were attacking each of them. Arthur could see that absolutely no progress was being made on any front. He looked over to Merlin. Even from the distance Merlin could see the apprehension in Arthur's eyes. Merlin for his part was beginning to panic but he didn't want it to show.

"Levitate them as high as we can and then let them drop!" he ordered his fellow sorcerers. They all turned and concentrated on the old woman first. It should have had an immediate effect with the three of them using their powers, but there was nothing. Realising that something was wrong. Merlin turned their attentions to Dub, Dothur and Daun.

"The three boys instead," he shouted. They concentrated and tried their best to lift the boys from the ground. Nothing happened. The boys were still fighting with amazing precision and dexterity. The Knight could not seem to even land a single blow.

"The new spell" ordered Merlin. It was his hope that as it was their newest spell that it would be more front in each of their minds. Clasping hands and then concentrating to their fullest potential they began to form the spell that would slow down the three boys. Or should they now be counted as six? Not a thought that was necessary or welcome under the circumstances.

The Caerleon magicians formed their new spell, the one that they were so proud of. Then releasing it at Dub, Dothur and Daun they waited the microsecond that it should have taken to cripple their strength and speed. Again there was absolutely no effect.

Merlin and Morgan had felt this feeling before; when they were at the mercy of Hellekin and the Minotaur on Skellig Mhor. What hope was there to fight magic beings if their own magic was ineffective?

Carmun for her part had now disabled four of Arthur's Knights and was turning her attention to him. Seeing the look on her face, the remaining Knights gathered around Arthur, swords again raised. Without orders, Sir Pellus charged forward in the hope of surprising the old woman. He failed. Again she used her superior strength and speed to punch him out of her way. He let out a yelp of pain as her fists both impacted him and he flew through the air and crumpled to the ground.

Arthur could think of only one thing. Stall for time.

"What drove ye from Hibernia Carmun? Why come to this land to rule?" The ruse worked. This line of questioning seemed to provoke the old woman.

"It is enough for ye to know that now I shall rule Briton instead of Hibernia," she hissed.

"So ye were exiled from Hibernia? No longer a queen then, surely?" he said. This too elicited a growl of disapproval from Carmun.

"Kneel before me, Arthur; pledge the allegiance of thine men to mine sword!"

With her screeched words, suddenly Carmun was holding a sword. Arthur chanced a look to his three magicians. They looked to be in the midst of working magic and yet he could see no results from their efforts. He thought to continue upon his line of questioning in the hope that it turned up something that any of them could use against her. But what? How could he stretch out this situation for long enough to gain the upper hand, or to at least expose a weakness in her?

"What did the Hibernian people do to vanquish ye, *Queen* Carmun?" Arthur put an emphasis on the title in order to mock her. This infuriated the old woman. Raising her sword like a seasoned professional warrior, she spat her retort at Arthur.

"Stop cowering behind thine men, *King* Arthur, face me in battle, prove thy strength!" She too used the royal title as a way to mock.

"Enough!" shouted Arthur. Everyone stopped and looked at him, such was the force of his words and the resolve in his tone. Even the three magicians that were unsuccessfully trying to launch fireballs at Carmun and the boys ceased their efforts. There was an uneasy lull in the battle. Then with equal force of tone and volume Arthur took up the challenge.

"So be it, Carmun. Sword to sword; ruler to ruler. We shall battle for the future of Briton. He motioned for the Knights around him to part. They did so. He stepped forward brazenly ready to fight Carmun.

She looked pleased in her own malevolent way.

"Good. Two would-be rulers of this land. One fair sword battle to determine who shall rule Briton. Agreed?" she screeched.

"Agreed!" Arthur shouted back at her.

There was a collective gasp from everyone around. What was Arthur doing? How could he win a sword fight with a magical creature that could not be stopped by three sorcerers and multiple Knights? Had Arthur completely lost his mind? All of these thoughts were going through the Knights and magicians' heads. Unknown to them all, the exact thoughts were also racing through Arthur's head. He had effectively gambled the throne of Briton upon a single sword battle against a foe that would almost certainly win.

Chapter 36: The Sword Fight

The crowd gathered in a large circle around the two soon-to-be fighters. The sense of anticipation for what was to come was almost unbearable. Carmun's sons had returned to a recognisable human form. It was a great relief to the Knights that had been in battle with the misshapen things. They no longer had to stomach the grotesque forms that they were previously engaged with. This distraction, no matter how hopeless it seemed, was still welcome and preferential to battling the three creatures.

Arthur and Carmun regarded each other from a few arm-lengths apart. They began to circle each other, first in one direction and then in the opposite. Both had their swords in their hands, partially raised as pointing to the other. Carmun's eyes began to narrow. Arthur recognised this immediately as a prelude to a charge. He was correct.

With a shrill screech she suddenly clasped her sword with both hands and charged at Arthur pointing her blade directly at his head. Arthur, instead of the usual manoeuvre that he would adopt to deflect such an attack, similarly charged at Carmun. When they were in range of each other Carmun made a mighty push with her sword as if to pierce Arthur's forehead. Arthur swung his sword around in a short circle and parried it away. They continued on their chosen trajectories and as they passed each other, Carmun shoulder-charging Arthur, taking him by surprise and almost knocking him off balance.

The crowd audibly gasped at the sight of King Arthur almost losing his balance. He recovered and swung around in preparation to fend off any immediate follow-up blows from Carmun. There were none. She had run a few steps to almost the boundary set by the onlookers and then turned to once more face Arthur from afar.

Arthur knew three things about Carmun now. She was definitely weakening since her last show of amazing strength. The sword that she carried seemed to be similarly made of a metal somewhat akin to Excalibur for it had not shattered when he thrust away her blow. And more importantly she seemed unwilling to engage him in a blow after blow battle, perhaps because of his first observation, that she was weakening. Perhaps it was not a battle technique that she was comfortable with. Whatever the reason, he would find a way to use it against her.

Carmun had gathered herself and with a similar narrowing of her eyes began another charge but this time displaying a very ornate way of swinging her sword around and around her head in a manner that was probably meant to conceal from which direction her actual blow would come. Arthur again did not use his typical defence for such an attack. Instead he mimicked her and with a similar charge and twirling of swords he too shouted aloud as they came together once more.

Both swords managed to find each other somewhere around face-height and again Carmun successfully deflected, retreated almost immediately. Arthur did not take an opportunity to prolong the exchange. He was still assessing her. This second blow told Arthur more about his enemy. He was now surer than ever that a sustained attack was going to figure at some point in his strategy, he just had to pick the correct moment. Furthermore, although weakening, Carmun was swinging her sword with the same ease that Arthur could move Excalibur. This fortified his belief that her sword was too magical. It would be light in the hands of its intended user. For the first time ever, Arthur had to think in the heat of battle about how to effectively combat a magical sword similar to his own.

Both of the warriors were so immersed in their situation they did not notice what was going on around them. The three magicians were all horrified at the proceedings, Merlin most of all and it showed in every feature on his face. Everything that he'd worked for throughout his entire life had been wagered on this one fight. He and his fellow sorcerers were powerless to use their magic against this evil thing, whatever she was. Merlin could hardly believe that this was happening. He was so panicked at the proceedings that he almost did not notice the expression on one of Carmun's sons.

He'd blindly looked around the crowd, but not really taken in what he'd seen. It must have been on his second pass that it dawned upon him. Daun, or was it Dub or Dothur, he couldn't tell them apart, was worried. He looked form one of the boys to the next. It was there; they were clearly concerned about their mother. But why? What did they know about Carmun that would make them so bothered in her current situation? Knowledge is power and Merlin knew if he could find out, then that knowledge could be used to help Arthur.

The two had once more come to blows, or rather a single almighty blow. Carmun failing for the third time to actually land an injury upon Arthur screamed in frustration. She again retreated to a safe distance to ensure that the fighting did not progress beyond a single action.

Merlin, unnoticed by anyone backed away from his viewpoint and circled around behind everybody and surreptitiously took up a position beside the son that he'd seen with the worried look. He spoke softly to him.

"Thine mother fights well; but Arthur is better, he shall win eventually."

The boy shot a look of hatred at Merlin, his only reply to the comment. Carmun began her circling of Arthur once more. Arthur guessed that it was because she needed time either to come up with another strategy to fight him, or more than likely because she was exhausting herself with her single mighty blows that were not finding their mark.

Not wanting to give Carmun time enough to gather any more strength, he began to mock her.

"I should hath expected that a Hibernian woman would fight poorly," he said. Carmun hissed at him and charged again, a repeat of her first movement. Arthur more easily blocked her thrust and this time instead of allowing her to retreat to a safe distance he spun around and followed her taking a swipe at her back and cutting a gash in her shoulder blade. She screamed with pain and shock.

"Ma!" shouted the boy beside Merlin in distress. At that moment Merlin knew exactly what Arthur had already surmised. Carmun was weakening. Somehow she must have used up all of her available strength in the fight with the Knights. Merlin shouted at Arthur.

"She is weakening Arthur, finish her off!"

Dothur screamed his protest at the summation of his mother and brutally bashed Merlin in the face with the back of his clenched fist. Merlin crumbled beneath the onslaught. Momentarily distracted by the exchange all eyes turned to see what was going on between Dothur and Merlin, Morgan and Ivorwulf ran over to the old man's assistance.

Arthur made the most of the perfectly timed distraction to remove the dagger from the handle of Excalibur. He secreted it in his hand so that it could not be seen, turning the short blade around so that it was hidden by his hand and wrist.

Carmun only had her eyes off Arthur for a moment. She turned her malevolent gaze upon her quarry once more. He could see the hatred on her face. She was breathing hard. Arthur did not charge. Instead he strode purposefully toward her, effectively taking the fight to her this time. She seemed unprepared for the advance and quickly readjusted her sword to her other hand to more effectively battle him from this direction.

Another piece of information was gleaned. She was ambidextrous with her sword play. She could fight with both hands, as any good swordsman could. But which was her preferred hand? Most surely it was the other one, the one that she had used up to now. As Arthur approached he did exactly what Carmun had done and seemed to throw his sword over to his other hand, but instead of actually throwing it to his other hand, he only feigned the movement. This effectively put Carmun off her guard as she tried to adjust her stance and sword fighting hand before he was within striking distance but it was too late. She had to fend off his attack with her pose upset by the turn of events.

She slashed at Arthur with a grunt and muffled cry. He belted the sword downward and almost succeeded in knocking it out of her hand. But she rallied and skilfully ducked down to instead of countering the force of Arthur's blow she worked with it so as to ensure that she did not lose grip of her sword. Her instinctive reaction saved her from a humiliating turn of events against her. She twisted around on her heals and jumped up in the air whilst swinging her sword downwards. The force of her downward travel in collusion with the force of her swing took Arthur by surprise.

He barely managed to fend off her sudden attack. Jumping backwards so as to get out of her immediate range, Arthur had to quickly reconsider some of the observations that he'd made about his enemy. Clearly even in a weakened state, she was capable of summoning up strength that could easily overpower him. He had to wonder, was it a one-off occurrence or could she do it whenever she absolutely needed to. He could not waste time thinking about it. Better to put the question to the test.

Arthur took only a moment to gather himself and again with a shout he attacked. Charging at her as if he was jousting with the sword, Carmun was ready for it, but at the very last moment Arthur pushed forward his leading leg to slide along the dirt and duck down whilst simultaneously swinging up to strike her sword out of his way and then jab Carmun in her thigh.

She bellowed in pain and in a massive swing to push Excalibur out of her flesh she managed to dislodge Arthur's sword from his hand. The sword flipped over and landed in the ground blade first. It was tantalisingly close but it may as well have been five paces away. Arthur was on his knees at the mercy of Carmun. She realised her advantage and wished to exploit it as quickly as possible. Her scream was unbelievable. It was a mixture of victory, malice and pain. She swung her sword up and over her head ready to split Arthur in two with its force. Arthur flicked Excalibur's dagger from his hand toward her and it flew through the air lodging itself in her stomach.

She gagged in pain, unable to complete her deathblow. Arthur regained his footing and reached down pulling Excalibur from the ground. He raced the one step that he was away from Carmun and pushed his sword through her chest. Both of her arms flew backwards in agony and she dropped her sword. There were cries of victory and dismay from the crowd. Carmun's sons all bellowed as if they were the ones that had been struck.

Pressing his advantage, Arthur reached down and pulled the dagger from Carmun's stomach. Putting it up to her throat he cut her from left to right. Blood spurted out, covering his hand. Pulling back Excalibur, he watched as the hag fell to the ground. In a display that none of them were expecting, Arthur again jabbed Carmun's prone body with Excalibur, this time piercing her head just above the bridge of the nose.

Chapter 37: A Ripe Plumb

The look of abject horror on the three boys was apparent to all. Arthur looked over at them and then pulled his sword from their mother's face. He wore an expression of contempt while walking over to them slowly.

"What manner of creatures are ye, and what is the real reason that ye came to Briton?" he asked as he stopped in front of them, his tone leaving no doubt that he was in no mood for evasion or trite replies. The Knights were fearful of Arthur's life. What was to stop these boys from dishonouring the verbal treaty that Arthur had made with their mother, and continue their inhuman fighting? Arthur seemed to have not thought of such a possibility or if he had considered it, he did not care. He faced-down each of the boys, demanding they answer his questions. Dothur began the reply.

"Our mother was a witch, she was feared by all who knew of her existence in our homeland," Dub said, taking up the explanation first.

"She was paid tribute for many years from the farmers in Hibernia, far and wide; for fear that she would ruin their crops if they did not," Daun said, completing the summation of the answer to King Arthur.

"The Christians incited revolution amongst the farmers, and together they rose up against her. Our magic did not work upon them and after the ensuing battle, we were banished from Hibernia. Our mother said that we should wrest control of Briton from ye. After a lifetime of uniting the factions of Briton, thine Kingdom was a ripe plumb for the taking. It should hath been and easy battle. After all we had no fear of thine magicians and as ye hath seen, we are more than a match for thine Knights."

Arthur was satisfied with the account. It did nothing to assuage his bad mood though. He'd been intercepted by a witch, whatever that was, though he was sure Merlin would explain it to him later.

And his mission to further cleanse his borders of invaders had almost come asunder because of more invaders, this time from Hibernia. In fact, his entire life's work had almost been ruined because of this Hibernian trespasser and her misbegotten spawn had so completely coveted Briton.

If Arthur was in a dark mood at the conclusion of the battle, it was darkening by the moment. He chose his words deliberately; his tone menacing.

"Leave these shores for evermore and never return or meet the same fate as thine mother!" he practically spat the words with venom at the three boys. He turned rather dramatically and marched back to the body of Carmun where he leant down and pulled out his dagger from her prone body.

"Merlin are thine powers restored!?" he shouted impatiently. Merlin snapped his fingers causing a spark to fly from them.

"Aye," he confirmed.

"Then burn this thing NOW!" he commanded. Morgan, Ivorwulf and Merlin sprang into action and summoned the fire spell, each unleashing a fireball directly at the body of Carmun. Arthur stepped back just in time before it exploded with a fire so intense that it shocked all of the onlookers.

"Garethe, Alynore; find the horses, retrieve them!" he further commanded. More than just the singled-out Knights hurried to fulfil his wish.

"We continue to Camlann, let nothing more stop us!"

As he finished his proclamation he turned and glared at Dub, Dothur and Daun. They jumped into the air and transformed into the shapeless black forms that they'd arrived in. Some of the Knights watched as the trio of flying things spiralled upwards and then took the direction of the coast. Perhaps they were going to Magna Frisia, perhaps Gaul. It did not matter, providing they never again set foot in Briton.

With a firm resolution to continue the mission that they had set out to accomplish, the party recovered their mounts and gathered themselves together to continue their journey,

Chapter 38: The King Approaches

The three Knights had been running another practice drill of how the now-small army of men would be positioned to greet King Arthur when he arrived. All had gone very well this time and practice it seemed, was all that they needed to perfect their brotherly stance. They managed to look both resolute and non-threatening at the same time, exactly what Mordrede and Amhar had hoped for. Hemison too was very impressed at how well the large crowd took direction. If he did not know better, he could have almost sworn that they were already a trained army that had somehow found their way to Camlann and this historic moment in time.

"All is in readiness," reported Arthur to Amhar and Mordrede. "The only missing part of this puzzle is King Arthur. If he left Caerleon directly after the festival then he should be here already." It was something of a puzzle.

"Perhaps his heart is not in this senseless killing?" offered Mordrede. It was a tempting thought, and showed that Arthur had realised his mistake and was now taking a more moderate view.

"I can only hope so," responded Amhar.

While they were still speaking there seemed to be a small kerfuffle in the crowd. Somebody was running through the men and heading directly toward them. He was shouting something. Having gained the attention of the three Knights they all looked up curious to see what message this man was bringing them. As he got closer it was easier to make out the words that he was shouting repeatedly as he approached.

"King Arthur approaches. He is only half a day's ride away!" The man repeated the news a few more times as he closed the distance between them.

"Where is he?" demanded Amhar.

"Further around the bend of the River, and settled in for the day at the edge of the forest."

It was approaching sunset now. Arthur was sure to not try and cover the distance on this day. Amhar did a quick calculation in his head. He knew the area that the man was referring to and wanted to confirm that it was truly half a day's ride from the Camlann.

"So King Arthur will arrive before noon tomorrow; he will start early and approach from the north. The point where we meet him should be there," said Amhar, confirming his best guess for how events would unfold tomorrow late in the morning. He was also pointing to a position along the river bank where there was a natural clearing. It would be the designated point where Arthur would more than likely reach the outskirts of the settlement. The two other Knights agreed with Amhar's summation of how and when Arthur would approach Camlann.

"We shall call the assembly for one hour before noon. It would be best for the men to not be standing idle for too long before we make our demonstration to the King." Mordrede offered his idea of a timeframe that they should work within. Both Hemison and Amhar agreed with him. Hemison completed the exchange.

"Then it is settled. We meet at the river bank, further along, exactly one hour before noon. I shall tell the men and have them pass the news along." He moved off to begin spreading the word about tomorrow.

Mordrede and Amhar could hardly believe it. Their moment had come; the point in time where they would change the way that Arthur looked upon people within his realm.

"When Arthur sees our display of solidarity, his heart will reach out and embrace all men and women living within his borders," said Amhar.

"There will be no more talk of Saxons invaders within our midst. It will just be the people of Briton living together as one," said Mordrede.

Both Knights firmly believed that that is exactly what would happen. Neither of them would sleep very much this night, they were so full of expectation. By noon tomorrow a new unity would embrace all of the peoples within Arthur's monarchy. Word would spread far and wide. There may not ever be a reason to come to blows with the Angles, Jutes or Saxons again. If they did not feel threatened, then what possible reason could there be to come into conflict with the King?

They had both sown the seeds for a new era in the land of Briton. All they had to do now was hold their nerve and make the King see their point of view. It was exhilarating and frightening at the same time. The sun would rise tomorrow over a land filled with doubt and mistrust of perceived foreigners. And it would set upon a unified land. Amhar felt that he was bringing to fruition everything that his father had worked for his entire life. But he would do it without raising a sword against his fellow man. It was all so perfect it brought tears to his eyes.

Chapter 39: Insurrection

The following day Hemison, Amhar and Mordrede were busying themselves with the final preparations. The villagers tried to go about their normal pre-dawn duties and then their morning meals. But the sense of anticipation in the air to see King Arthur and show him what a unified and loyal people they all were, prevented much from being done that would have normally been done. The crowd gathering for the general assembly at the pre-arranged position along the river bank did so long before they needed to be there. This pleased the three Knights and helped lower their nervousness somewhat. At least they did not have to worry about gathering the villagers together. But from this point they had longer to wait for the King to appear. Time it seemed began to move slowly.

The day was sunny. It was not overly hot, nor was it cold. The weather had given them the kind of perfect day that they felt should have been bestowed upon this momentous occasion.

Everything was going to plan, even if it was somewhat earlier than scheduled. The men were all in their lines facing the direction that Arthur was expected to emerge from the trees. Hemison, Amhar and Mordrede were to their left on a small hill. Their vantage point made it easy to see everything around them. More importantly, Arthur would be able to see them, and hear then if they shouted loudly enough.

Amhar was practicing what he was going to say. He was testing his speech on his fellow Knights.

"King Arthur, father. See how these men that ye would call Saxon hath integrated completely with the community of Camlann. These accepting villagers are prepared to stand together in a show of solidarity and not see that there are Saxons or Angles or Jutes in their midst. They only see other members of thine village. A village of loyal citizens willing to prove their loyalty to ye by standing together as one. Will ye not see then what thine people see? Britons all around us! Nothing else! Join us, father. Rule as the benevolent king that ye are over a land of Britons and lay down the malice for those that do not deserve it. What say ye, Arthur, king of Briton?"

Amhar finished his speech and looked for a reaction from his compatriots. Both were clearly moved by his words. It was obvious from their pause before offering their critique. Hemison began.

"Amhar, that was a fine speech indeed. If King Arthur's heart does not melt at hearing those words then I do not know what else could."

"Stirring Amhar; Arthur will see the light of a new day and a new way to be ruler of our land," prompted Mordrede.

"The king!" shouted a voice from the crowd.

Everyone turned to look at who had shouted. A man in the first line of the assembly was pointing at the tree-line. Sure enough King Arthur emerged from the trees on horseback closely followed by Knights immediately recognisable to Amhar, Mordrede and Hemison. The three brother Knights were flanking the King, and bit by bit appeared almost all of the full contingent of Knights from Caerleon. It seemed that only Sir Pellus and Sir Dynadane were not in attendance. Pellus, they guessed must have been left in charge of security at Caerleon. Dynadane was acting as regent at Stamfyd. There were no Knights currently in residence at North Rheged, Pen Rhionydd, Mynyw, Cellewig, or Humbor. So with the two exceptions, Arthur had brought all of his available Knights with him to Camlann. It was an unexpected show of strength from the king.

Arthur had stopped to regard the sight before him; his Knights taking up their positions to his right and left. Mordrede could make out the figure of his mother.

"Mother is with them, and Merlin too," he said, pointing to where he could make them out. There was a third figure on horseback that they did not immediately recognise, but did not give much thought to at that point. The sight of Arthur's force was formidable.

The assembled crowd began to cheer. The noise was incredible. The shouting and the distance both conspired to rob Amhar of his speech at this point in time. He would both have to wait for the men to settle down and for the king to approach closer before he could deliver his explanatory message about what the king was now facing.

***

King Arthur was in a dark mood. He could see Amhar, Mordrede and Hemison set apart from the crown of gathered people before him. They were mostly made of men, formed in lines that mimicked the lines of the old Roman battalions when they went into battle. He could not tell if the shouting was rejoicing or mocking and at that moment he did not care either. Littered amongst the crowd were obvious Saxon infiltrators. They may as well have worn the standards of their overlords so much did they stand out from the rest. And their numbers were greater than those that he had to extinguish from Exelhulme. This was not going to be an easy task to excise the invaders from the villagers of Camlann. It was lucky that he had decided to bring most of his Knights with him.

"What is he doing?" asked the king of his Knights. Garethe and Galahallt were the closest to Arthur, having taken up positions directly to his left and right. Neither of them were able to offer any insights. To both it looked like Amhar, Mordrede and Hemison were observing a crowd of Britons and Saxons.

"Maybe Prince Amhar hath brought the villagers out to watch as ye execute the infiltrators," but even as Sir Garethe gave his proposed explanation it fell short of illuminating the situation.

"Why not then just bring us the Saxons?" asked Galahallt. Poking a hole in his brothers take on the event that was unfolding before them.

"There are so many," observed the king. "It is a good thing that we are skilled fighters and that I brought most of the Knights of the Round Table. Otherwise how would we have dealt with this situation?" he was irritated at not knowing exactly what was happening. Were his three errant Knights somehow prisoners? What was the meaning of this assembly? Arthur struggled to find any other explanation other than the obvious one. The one that he had at the forefront of his mind when the left Caerleon.

"Amhar intends to defy me and fight us rather than allowing me to remove the invaders from Camlann. It is exactly as I had feared. Is there no end to his impertinence? To his...his...stupidity! Why does he do this? Does he want to wrest the crown from mine head and make himself ruler of all!"

Most of the Knights surrounding the king did not bother offering alternative views that may have vindicated the Prince. From where they all were, it looked exactly as Arthur had feared. Prince Amhar, Sir Mordrede and Sir Hemison were openly defying the king and were prepared to fight to show their resolve.

Sir Galahallt offered a small ray of hope that all was not as bleak as it seemed.

"But Sire. The villagers cheer for ye..." he did not get the chance to finish his sentence.

"They jeer at me, Galahallt!" Arthur was in no mood to entertain such a thought. He shouted over his shoulder.

"Sorcerers, to me!" He commanded his three magicians to come forward and they dutifully motivated their mounts to join Arthur. Ivorwulf was the first to speak when he approached the king.

"King Arthur, I recognise the way that these Saxons are dressed. They're in the service of Cissa, Cymen and Wlencing; Aelle's sons"

"Are ye certain Ivorwulf?" demanded Arthur.

"Aye, Sire. I hath travelled far and wide to help implement our treaty. I recognise this kind of attire. They are most certainly from Aelle's sons' forts and castles."

The very mention of King Aelle inflamed Arthur's temper. As far as he was concerned, the decision was made; he would attack.

"Position thine-selves to cast the spell, when ye hath done so we will attack." He dismissed the wizards with a wave of his hand. Arthur turned to his men.

"The Saxons are easily spotted amongst this crowd. We will attack and pick them off, line by line. Shout to the other villagers to stand clear as ye approach thine targets. I do not want any of our own people to be hurt. Above all, show no mercy to the foreigners. Strike then down with impunity, do ye understand!?" he was angry bordering upon being absolutely livid.

The orders were perfectly clear. None of the Knights wanted to oppose Arthur whilst he was in such a mood. It was bad enough that three of their number were in opposition to them instead of faithfully carrying out the orders of their King.

"Ready. On my command!" ordered Arthur. He looked over to the three magicians. They were in conference slightly away from the line of Knights on horseback. Once they'd disabled Amhar, Mordrede and Hemison, the slaughter could begin.

Chapter 40: The Plan

The three Sorcerers were preparing themselves to cast the spell of sluggish motion. They'd all agreed to use the fullest of their abilities to project the spell the distance between them and the three Knights and Merlin was concentrating, building up the energy within himself. So was Morgan and if they'd only looked at Ivorwulf, they would have seen that he was facing away from them and even away from their target. He was mouthing some words in the direction of King Arthur and his surrounding force.

Morgan was concentrating so fully what when Ivorwulf spoke to her she almost jumped out of her skin.

"I do not like the chances of our success Morgan. Look at the blood lust within King Arthur's eyes. He will charge with his Knights, causing a fracas that may end up with Prince Amhar, or Sirs Mordrede and Hemison being injured. Perhaps all three." Ivorwulf looked genuinely concerned. And at that moment, Morgan became alarmed. He was right of course, the spell may not be enough to ensure that her son and her lover were not harmed, nor her nephew, the Prince.

"Perhaps we should simply levitate them out of harm's way?" suggested Morgan trying to think of an alternative.

"We discussed this at length Lady Morgan. The sight of three flying Knights will cause panic with these simple village folk. Who knows what the outcome would be for them? Perhaps a panic that would cost more lives that Arthur intends to butcher today?"

Everything that Ivorwulf said made perfect sense to Morgan's panicked mind. She looked over at Merlin. He was positively glowing with the force of magic that he was about to output. She could see it as a silver shadow projecting out from his form. Ivorwulf leant in to speak further with Morgan.

"See, Merlin is just about ready to cast the spell. He will effectively trap the three Knights where they stand. Think of what harm they'll come to if they're unable to properly defend themselves when all around them are unhindered, as they'll soon be?" Morgan turned to him.

"But what can be done?"

"We must not join Merlin in this endeavour, together we must find a better way!"

Ivorwulf's sudden shouting scared Morgan. In a split second she reacted as a mother would defending her child, and as a wife would defending her husband. She leapt forward and pulled the spell from Merlin's body and just as quickly flung it around him so that he became trapped in the very magic that he had hoped to project.

It was all over so fast Morgan barely had time to think. But in the immediate aftermath she looked in horror at her handiwork. Merlin was immobilised. He was motionless, like a statue. She could not see him breathing but she knew that he was still alive. There was no expression upon his face. His eyes were open in the moment that he felt his magic being separated from his body. He did not even have time to alter his expression to one of either surprise, or wonderment as he felt his magic taken from him.

"What hath I done!" screamed Morgan. She felt a wave of alarm spread through her entire body like no other fear that she had before encountered. She turned her head to look in desperation at Ivorwulf. He had reached forward as if he were trying to grab hold of her clothes, but his hands fell short. Ivorwulf have taken hold of Morgan's magical abilities. Just as she had done with Merlin, Ivorwulf did to her. He dragged her magical abilities from her body. Morgan felt the depletion of her other-worldly abilities. It was like someone had cut a hole into a bladder of wine and the contents poured out emptying the vessel and leaving a thin remnant.

Morgan could feel her magic being used against her. She saw the Kentish Sorcerer rip it from her being and fling it around her body as she had done to Merlin. It was like nothing else she had experienced. Her mind was alert but her body slowed down. She felt like she was immersed completely in thick mud and could hardly move. Even her breathing slowed to be imperceptible. And just as quickly as Merlin had become immobilised she too was motionless.

This was exactly what Merlin had gone through. Morgan's mind was alert, it was completely unaffected by the spell of sluggish motion. Ivorwulf had put them out of action. She had allowed herself to be scared by his words and he had used her fear to remove Merlin from the forthcoming battle. Now she too had paid the price for her trust of this stranger from Kent. She was frozen and unable to help. But surely Arthur would see what had taken place and send the Knights to their aide?

***

Arthur was impatiently waiting for his three Sorcerers to effectively put Hemison, Mordrede and Amhar out of action. He looked over to them to see their progress. They seemed to be chanting away together and pointing their hands, just as he had seen them do at their demonstration in Caerleon. But it was taking too long. Perhaps he was just on edge he thought.

"What is taking the wizards so long?" he said to nobody in particular. Sir Guaen watched the magical trio and then looked over to the Knights that would soon be on the receiving end of a magical spell.

"Perhaps the distance requires more...magic?" he answered, hoping that what he said made at least some sense.

"Aye, perhaps," said Arthur ,not in the least satisfied with the lack of progress that he was observing.

Chapter 41: Spells Within Spells

Ivorwulf was safe behind his spell of beguilement. To Arthur and his Knights, he and Morgan and Merlin looked like they were busy casting the spell of sluggish motion.

"Fool," he said, sneering at the king. He began to chant a second spell of beguilement. But this time it would be a different vision that he needed to project. The most elaborate beguilement spell that he'd ever before cast. He glanced at the recently imprisoned Morgan and Merlin. They were motionless and unable to cause him any harm. That was good, for he needed to concentrate with all of his might to pull off his next two feats of deception. It would be a deception on a scale that no magician to his knowledge had ever before achieved. But he would accomplish it; he knew so.

Turning to Sir Hemison, Sir Mordrede and Prince Amhar, he concentrated and pushed the spell of beguilement upon them. Then stealing himself he brought every bit of magical energy that he had to bare and did the same toward King Arthur and his Knights of the Round Table. It exhausted him. He'd never before felt so drained. But if everything went according to his devious plan, then he would not need to perform any magic from this point on. Now all he had to do was wait.

***

Sir Hemison was the first to see that something was terribly wrong.

"The men are restless, some are jeering the king rather than cheering for him?" he said to his compatriots; indicating toward the assembled villagers. But neither Amhar nor Mordrede were listening to him. Instead they were staring in horror at the men that they'd somehow mistaken for King Arthur and his Knights.

"Aelle's sons!" said Amhar.

"Aye, that is them for certain," replied Mordrede. Hemison looked at them both and then over to where the King was; or rather where he had mistakenly thought that he had seen the King. Instead he saw Wlencing, Cissa and Cymen, King Aelle of Sussex's three sons, now warlords in their own rights. They were flanked by the most fearsome set of warriors that any of them had seen.

"They look to attack!" said Hemison. It was easier to think about the looming battle with these terrible foes rather than wonder about how they had ever mistaken these men for the king and their fellow Knights. The one or two times that he tried to think about how he could have made such a mistake, a fog came down making it hard for him to concentrate properly.

Amhar and Mordrede were experiencing the feeling too. Thoughts of the king were pushed aside because they resulted in a feeling of malaise affecting their ability to think clearly. But it was easy to fall back upon their training. These three well-known Saxon warlords were ruthless and known by the men. This was an attack of some sort, an unprovoked attack within King Arthur's monarchy. They must have hoped to annex Camlann. There was no other reason for them to be there. But as luck would have it. They were faced by the assembly of men that were gathered to greet the king. If only King Arthur would arrive now, he could help the three of them in their sudden dire situation.

"See how they hesitate. They think that we hath assembled a defence force to protect Camlann from them. We're greater in number, we should take the advantage and attack them before they attack us!" Mordrede's words made perfect sense to Amhar and Hemison.

Prince Amhar had been thinking along similar lines even as Mordrede spoke. He did not know why Aelle's sons had suddenly decided to attack King Arthur's realm, but he did know that they had a larger fighting force. Even if it was made up of farmers and artisans; they could be lead in a battle to defend their township from this insurgence surely.

"No more time to think. We attack. Give the word!" Amhar shouted to Hemison.

***

The Camlann villagers were confused. They'd thought that King Arthur had arrived and they were ready to give him the greatest welcome that he had ever had from any settlement within his borders, but instead there was a band of Saxon raiders opposite them. What were they to do? People asked one another about how this could have happened? But nobody had any answers. Did this Saxon war party plan to invade Camlann? The situation that they suddenly found themselves in was frightening. Where was King Arthur? When would he arrive? They needed him now more than ever. He and the Knights of the Round Table would save them from this menace.

Everywhere the Camlann villagers were looking for guidance from the Prince and the two Knights of Caerleon.

Only some of the newly arrived men did not seem to be particularly bothered with the peculiar turn of events. They stood their ground and were producing weapons from within their robes. It was lucky that these men had defied the previous orders to not bring weapons to greet the king. For if they had not where would they all be now? Small conversations were exchanged to confirm the lucky happenstance.

"It is good that ye brought a weapon with ye stranger," said one Camlann villager to a couple of the more recent arrivals.

"Aye we will need to defend ourselves from these Saxons, surely," said another

"Then let us await the word from Prince Amhar and we shall do just that, attack these marauding invaders" said one of the men in reply.

***

King Arthur's eyes were wide with fear. The men that he had thought were his two sons and Knight, were in fact the three sons of King Aelle.

"How could we hath mistaken these vile Saxons for our own!?" he Arthur at the Knights around him, but they had no answer. There was no explanation that made any sense. Some of his Knights were pointing at the assembled crowd. Arthur managed to tear his attention away from the objects of his horror for just a moment. He looked at the villagers. There were Saxons everywhere. How could he have mistaken these people for his subjects at all?

"What treachery is this?!" he screamed at his men.

"Saxons; everywhere!" shouted back one of the Knights.

"It is a trap!" screamed another.

"What are we to do Arthur, there are so many!" bellowed Sir Galahallt at him. Arthur did not have time to ponder how he had come into this bizarre situation. All that mattered was that he was facing the three sons of his bitter enemy and a plethora of Saxon foot soldiers.

"We hath the advantage," shouted King Arthur to his men hoping to offer some words of comfort before the battle. "They hath only three on horseback, and we are Knights, better trained and more experienced than any of them. WE ATTACK!" it was perhaps the shortest motivational speech that he had ever given before any battle. But it had the same effect as if it had been a well-rehearsed tome designed to get the best from his men.

As one they cheered in acceptance of his revelation. They would fight to the bitter end and drive these trespassing Saxons from the village of Camlann; or die trying. Arthur drew Excalibur. The distinctive noise that it made leaving its sheath was all that the men needed to mark the moment before the cry to charge.

"Forward!" shouted Arthur, and as one the line of Knights prodded their horses into a violent charge toward the line of the enemy.

Chapter 42: The Truth in Intentions

Approximately six months earlier, Ivorwulf and Karal were in the Castle of Cymen. The lord of the domain was sitting in a chair that was meant to mimic the throne of King Arthur of Briton. A fabrication not lost on either Karal or Ivorwulf. Clearly Cymen saw himself as a king rather than a Saxon warlord. Cymen's two brothers were flanking him and all three were regarding the Jute-Kentish visitors with some distain and much suspicion.

Wlencing summarised the reason that they had agreed to meet with Karal.

"So Karal of Kent. Ye hath a plan to topple the mighty King Arthur of Briton and lay open his lands to conquest? Please regale us with this magnificent plan, that will succeed where all else hath failed!" His goading was meant to be insulting.

Ignoring the mocking tone of Wlencing, Karal indicated to his wizard.

"I hath in mine employ a sorcerer mightier than Merlin of Caerleon. Together we conceived an intricate scheme to relieve Arthur of his crown and ensure that we can all expand our borders as far as we wish. More importantly with the end of Arthur's reign there will be no more bolstering of his Knights of the Round Table. It will be the end of any that threaten any one of us. Because whilst there is one of us threatened by invasion from Arthur, we are all at risk."

Karal wanted to restate that they all held their landholdings only by the grace of Arthur's current force size, which was still not yet large enough to threaten them all. But eventually it would be, and they all knew it.

"With each passing year, more and more Britons side with Arthur. He increases his force and influence over the land. Soon he will to our borders in Kent and claim them as his own. Perhaps he will first try to take back Anderidae, which he feels was cheated from him all of those years ago." Karal pointed at the three boys, hoping that he could make more urgent his tone by insinuating that one of them may be the next to fall to King Arthur and his men.

Cissa was annoyed at the delay. He was keen to hear this supposedly brilliant plan to help them all rather than postulate upon the expansionist plans of King Arthur.

"Enough of thine talk of dread Karal. What is this plan that will save us all from the menace of Arthur?' Cissa gave Karal a look as if to emphasise that he should get on with the explanation. Karal nodded obediently.

"Firstly we push Arthur into a position where he is afraid to attack any of us," he said, just about reaching his stride when he was rudely interrupted by Cissa once more.

"How?" he shouted.

"We form a pretend alliance between all of the warlords that share borders with Arthur and then let him know the substance of this false alliance. Each shall come to the others aide should Arthur choose to attack him." Karal was once more interrupted, this time by Cymen.

"Ye will never get all of the warlords that border Arthur to agree to such nonsense!" he said dismissively.

"They will not need to agree to it, only pretend to agree to it, that will hath exactly the same effect that we need it to have, as if it were a truly organised and ratified alliance between us all." He waited for another interruption but when none came, he continued.

"Arthur will feel trapped within his own extensive lands. What will he do? He dare not attack any of us for fear of a massive retaliation that he may not survive. What would ye do in such a situation, if ye were King Arthur?" he handed the question to the three brothers and awaited an answer.

Cymen was a little flummoxed, how indeed would he react if he were in that situation?

"I would take the time necessary to train more of mine subjects into a greater fighting force. So that in time, I would hath the numbers to fend off any retaliation from the allied forces." He presented his answer as a flaw in the proposed plan that Karal was delivering. But instead of rising to the challenge of fending off the criticism, Karal looked to Wlencing for his answer. Realising that each of them had to reply before Karal was to continue Wlencing dutifully thought about what he would do. He thought that his brother's solution was a good one, but wanted to prove that he was more thoughtful. His solution would need to be cleverer.

"I would concede a good deal of land to one of the bordering warlords and make the others jealous and damage the treaty between all. With the treaty in ruins, the lands could be recaptured and each of the neighbours picked off one by one." Wlencing was proud of his ultimate solution even though it intimidated that the proposed allies were in reality petty and jealous.

Karal nodded in agreement that Wlencing's plan was a good one. He looked to Cissa the most vocal critic during these proceedings so far. Cissa was backed into a corner. Both of his brothers' schemes were excellent and he now felt the pressure to come up with something equally as innovative to get himself out of the simulated situation. His eyes could be seen darting from side to side and around the room as he looked for inspiration to trump his siblings.

"I would secretly let Arthur know of the deception in return for exemption from attack on his word as King."

Cissa had sold-out his brothers in the unusual scenario but instead of being horrified at his insolence, they were instead very impressed at his conniving. They both looked at him and nodded in favour of his proposed solution.

Karal and Ivorwulf exchanged a look. They were not oblivious to the selfish machinations on display. Regardless of the outcomes that each had proposed, it did not affect the next point of the plan that Karal intended to make.

"With the help of mine sorcerer, we will ensure that the course of action that Arthur takes is to rid his monarchy of any Angles, Jutes or Saxons that are now living within his borders."

The outcome was not what any of the brothers were expecting. They could be seen grappling with the idea and exactly how it would somehow in the long-run benefit them. Wlencing was the first to verbalise his frustration with his inability to see the bigger-picture.

"What good would that do us, Karal? If Arthur embarks on an ethnic-cleansing programme, how does that play into thine hands!?" he was clearly annoyed at the nuances of the plan being presented to them.

"Because we can implant men into one of his proposed battles, men that would on the surface seem to be happy to live beneath Arthur`s rule, but in truth, they would be mine men, and your men Cissa, and your men Wlencing and your men Cymen. All ready to fight Arthur in his own territories when he is not expecting such a well-organised and heavily armed and skilled battle. He will be taken completely by surprise. What King would expect a simple ethnic-cleansing exercise to result in a battle that will topple him from the throne and wrest control of all of his lands from his dead hands?"

The melodramatic outcome of the plan was now laid bare before them all by Karal and then there was silence. The very thought of being able to surreptitiously attack Arthur when he least expected a massive attack was very tempting indeed. All that they needed now was the detail of the plan. How could this miracle be accomplished?

"Very well, Karal, ye hath our attention," Cissa said. "What could ye do to make this situation come to pass?"

Chapter 43: Protection from the Spell of Beguilement

Karal and Ivorwulf knew that they had the brothers exactly where they wanted them. They'd offered a plan whereby they would deliver King Arthur to one kind of battle when in fact he would be faced with a completely different kind; a devastating attack within his own realm that he would never see coming. The outcome was a foregone conclusion, even for the great King Arthur. It was the most tempting thought that had entered the brother's minds in many a year.

"Speak, Karal" said Wlencing impatiently. "How can this be done?" Karal paused dramatically and looked at the ceiling. Then he returned his gaze to the men and continued to outline the intricate scheme to overthrow King Arthur.

"This is where mine brilliant sorcerer comes into the plan," said Karal, indicating Ivorwulf.

"Ivorwulf will ally himself to the two famed Sorcerers of Caerleon, Merlin and Morgan as a kindred spirit," he said indicating them all in the room. "A fellow other-worldly practiser of the magical arts. He will be present at one of the battles that King Arthur chooses to rid himself of *our* kind"

"Using his magic, he will ensure that Arthur and his men cannot tell his own subjects from the ones that we'll secret amongst them. The battle will be Arthur against his own subjects. And the beauty of this plan, the one thing that makes it the most devious of all plans that hath ever been devised against Arthur...any of the men that we plant in the battle will be completely immune to the magical spell that Ivorwulf will cast. With that he took hold of bad that Ivorwulf was holding and threw the contents across the floor scattering them before the three Saxon brothers.

Small white stones all around the same size sprinkled the flagstone floor of the room. The brothers looked at them. Wlencing and Cissa actually bent down to recover one each for a closer inspection. They gazed at the unremarkable stones with blank expressions, failing to see how these things figured in the plan. Each of them looked to Karal for an explanation and he did not disappoint.

"These are magical stones that will protect our men from the spell that befuddles Arthur and his men. So, only our men in the crowd will be able to see who is friend and who is foe. The battle will be a slaughter as King Arthur and his Knights struggle to see the truth before them, whilst our men will be able to see with absolute clarity." Karal waited for the reality of what he was proposing to sink-in with his audience.

Each of the men was in their own dream-world imagining exactly what such a battle would be like. King Arthur and his famed Knights of the Round Table unable to tell enemy from king's subject when they and their force would be able to see everything un-obfuscated. It was almost too good to be true. Karal had presented the most tempting offer that any of them had heard in their lives.

Each of the men was looking to the other for a hint of what they thought of the plan. But there was no hiding in their expressions exactly what each of them thought. Without any verbal consultation they all turned to face Karal and Ivorwulf. Cymen spoke on behalf of them all.

"How many men from each of us would ye like and when can this plan be put into action?"

Chapter 44: Attack

King Arthur charged forward on his mount shouting at the top of his voice.

"Victory for mine subjects; death to the Saxon invaders," his words emboldening his Knights, causing them to surge forward with him. The ground between the two forces was covered in hardly any time at all. He did not even remember slashing his sword downwards and slicing off the head of a Saxon that was curiously unarmed. Next he set his sights upon two more of them that for an instant he thought were both holding swords, but just as suddenly he perceived that they were not. No matter, he thought, two more dead Saxons was a good thing. All that he cared about was killing the invaders and protecting the villagers of Camlann.

Sir Galahallt too was busy maiming and killing the invaders at a pace that even he was surprised at. He glanced over to see his brothers Guaen and Garethe similarly engaged in beheading and slicing off the limbs of the Saxons that were all around them. It was difficult, but it almost seemed like they were calling out to King Arthur in mercy and horror, but that of course could not be the case. He put such a silly thought to the back of his mind.

"Flank them both left and right!" screamed Arthur to his Knights. They dutifully obeyed. His men began to heard the crowd as if they were sheep. This battle seemed to be as if they were doing just that, it was so easy to kill these Saxons. There were the obvious ones that were backing away but that did not matter at this early stage of the battle. Soon enough, they too would be at the end of a sword from one of the Knights.

***

The Camlann villagers were terrified. Somehow this Saxon warlord was massacring them. The direction from the Caerleon Knights to fight was resulting in nothing. They were farmers and artisans not soldiers. How could they possibly defend themselves from this mad-man?

Sir Hemison was trying to direct the men to form around just one of the attacking horsemen. If they could just take-down one of the riders then they'd be motivated to do so again and again. Just one attacker at a time was all that they needed to concentrate upon but they simply could not be corralled to do even that.

Sir Mordrede was equally having absolutely no luck in directing any of the men to fight in a coordinated way. He was getting frustrated shouting directions at them.

"Concentrate on that one on the brown horse. If ye can topple him then the rest can be done just as easily!" he shouted. It was useless. The Camlann villagers were not engaging with the Saxon invaders they were doing their best to escape from them.

Prince Amhar was similarly observing the rout that was going on around him.

"Do not run villagers. We need to defend thine land and thine Village until King Arthur arrives. He will be here and help us. Of this I am certain!" his words of encouragement were lost on the crowd.

They were only seeking to get out of the situation that had been thrust upon them as quickly as they could. Deep in his heart he did not blame them, but they were all that he had to fight with until his father arrived to help them. Where was he? How much longer could they hold out without his intercession? This was turning into a massacre of epic proportions.

***

Sir Alynore was just finishing off a Saxon that was screaming for mercy when a moment of clarity descended upon him. He'd just killed a villager of Camlann and had even been to Camlann many times since its liberation from the lands of the neighbouring Saxon warlord. The clothes of this man were clearly that of a Camlann artisan of some description. The Knight looked in horror at what he had done. Something was terribly wrong. He looked around him at Arthur and the Knights of the Round Table, then attacking the villagers of Camlann, whilst the Saxons amongst them were holding back. They were sacrificing the Camlann Villagers, as if to tire-out the king and his Knights before they themselves attacked. It was horrifying. He had to do something.

***

Ivorwulf felt Sir Alynore's horror at seeing the reality of the battle playing-out before him. The man must have a particularly strong will to fend-off the spell of beguilement so soon into the fighting. Either that or as was more than likely, his spell was so thinly-stretched that it was bound to break apart in places. Ivorwulf concentrated directly on Sir Alynore. He spoke the words of the spell again. He was determined that one Knight would not bring his plan asunder.

Without knowing it, Sir Alynore was clubbed into stupidity once more by Ivorwulf's magic. All around him he was surrounded with Saxons that needed to be killed. With renewed vigour he began to slice and hack away at them.

***

Arthur was both directing the Knights around him to take on various targets at the same time as fighting. He was a little perturbed at first that these Saxons seemed to be running and screaming rather than fighting. But he soon put that feeling aside and replace it with one of gratitude for his luck. He and his men were vastly outnumbered and had no hope of winning such a war if all of the

Saxons surrounding them were bloodthirsty and accomplished fighters. It was fortunate indeed that such a large number of them seemed to lack any fighting skills at all. He was slashing yet another one of them with his sword and unsatisfied that the blow was deadly enough, he returned to hack at the man's head. When the body fell to the battlefield lifeless he turned his attention to the next. Spying three of the brigands that had circled around Sir Galahallt he shouted.

"Galahallt, behind ye!" it was timely advice. Sir Galahallt had just dispatched two of the Saxons and needed a new target to concentrate upon. He dutifully twisted around on his horse to see where the King had indicated and spied the three of them. They appeared to be trying to get away from the battle by heading away from the village instead of the back toward it.

Galahallt did not give the unusual strategy any further thought, he reared his horse around and made toward the men. They were clutching each other as if in mortal fear. His sword found the back of the neck of the middle one and as he pulled it out he managed to slice it to the left cutting the ear off one of his companions. Then satisfied that he was basically immobilised with pain he motioned his horse over to the third fellow who had broken away from them and was attempting to run toward the river in the hope of safely.

Galahallt's sword found its mark and the hapless man died screaming. Now he was free to return to the second and finish him off as well. It was all almost too easy he thought to himself.

***

There were three overall men in charge of the Saxon warriors. There was one representative each from the forces of Wlencing, Cymen and Cissa. In all they numbered around thirty men. It was the maximum number of men that they thought they could safely secret amongst the villagers without raising the suspicion of anyone.

All of them were in possession of magical stones that protected them from the Spell of beguilement. From their vantage point it was easy to see the rout that was taking place. They had positioned themselves at the back of the assembly and were preventing the Camlann villagers from leaving. At the pre-arranged signal from Ivorwulf they had produced their swords that where hidden within their clothing and taken up a line that would assure that the Camlann villagers could not escape the swords of the Arthur and his men. Those that tried to escape what they saw as a Saxon invading party that had replaced Arthur and his Knights were horrified to find that Saxons had them completely surrounded.

Mayhem had erupted.

"Keep them contained!" shouted one of the leaders to the men.

"Drive them forward!" commanded another.

The battle was going exactly as they had been told by their masters it would. Arthur and his Knights were busy slaughtering the king`s subjects. Soon they would be battle-weary and then it would be the time for them to attack. A final Saxon victory over King Arthur and the Knights of the Round Table was all but assured.

Chapter 45: Frozen in Time

Merlin and Morgan were watching in horror, but were powerless to do anything *but* observe. They could hear each other's thoughts as well, and in an instant of time Morgan shared with Merlin the sudden panic that gripped her and the reason that she tore Merlin's magic from him and enveloped him within it. Then too late they both realised the treachery of Ivorwulf who had planted the seed of doubt in her mind. He, possessing the same ability as Morgan to steal magic, had used it against her and she too was imprisoned in it.

Ivorwulf was standing just ahead of them watching the unfolding of the battle with satisfaction. He turned around and walked back to them.

"See Merlin, Morgan...Arthur tires. Soon he will hath the combined elite force from Aelle's sons to deal with, and he will not be able to overcome them." He laughed maliciously at them loudly and for a long time.

"If only thine expressions could show what ye both are feeling, it would be all the more amusing."

Why?

He heard the word in his head, it was Morgan's voice but her thought that he could hear. He reached over and stroked her motionless face.

"Silly woman! Why? To be absolute Caesar of Briton, of course," he answered with a laugh.

"Soon Arthur will be dead and I'll declare mine-self ruler in his place. But do not feel too betrayed fellow magicians. Even mine former employer will feel the sting of treachery. For ye see, he thinks that this is all for the benefit of him, and the sons of Aelle. Simple-minded fools all of them." Ivorwulf swept the air dramatically with a wave of his hand.

"It was never mine intention to hand over the crown to anyone. Here see the deviousness of mine plan in thine minds." He leant forward and touched the forehead of both Morgan and Merlin. In a moment of time he recounted the meeting that he and Karal had with Wlencing, Cissa and Cymen half a year before. The plan that was laid before the men and how sorely tempted the three were by the very thought of it.

"They supplied the men that we seeded here in Camlann, shielded with stones that protect them from mine spell of beguilement, of course. They can see as clearly as we." He leant over to study the frozen face of Merlin.

"And certainly more clearly that ye old man," he said spitefully.

"But that is only the beginning of mine cunning. For ye see, another opportunity presented itself to me during mine abduction from Londinium. Remember the faeries in the cave. Did ye not think that we escaped with ease? See what really happened." Again he touched the foreheads of the imprisoned magicians. They could see through his eyes as the events unfolded in the cave that they appeared in, all after escaping from Karal's house.

Chapter 46: A Secret Bargain (The Cavern)

Ivorwulf looked at the scenes surrounding him with horror. Queen Aine was attacking Morgan; the Knights Sirs Galahallt, Guaen and Garethe were all incapacitated; Merlin was most certainly mortally wounded; and Morgan was close to death.

He turned on Nimue, who was similarly looking at the happenings around her with alarm, but she made no aggressive move toward Ivorwulf. He looked at her as if to either challenger her to begin attacking him or do otherwise. It was then that he noticed the distress upon her face. Nimue was looking at Morgan wilting beneath the onslaught of Queen Aine and moved as if to offer assistance but then thought the better of it and did not. She was conflicted, he could see that now. She wanted to assist Morgan and Merlin. She was looking from one to the other. Ivorwulf took the initiative and stepped toward her.

She looked alarmed but he held up his hands in a gesture of surrender and he offered her his hand. She looked down at it as if she were expecting a fireball to erupt from his fingers at her. But nothing happened. He offered her his hand again, more urgently this time. She instinctively reached out and took hold of it.

***

Nimue was in a place that she'd never before seen. A fog covered the ground and occasionally billowed up like a roman column and then formed a ceiling of fog above her and Ivorwulf. Then the reverse happened, the fog floating eerily above her occasionally formed a column which funnelled more fog to the ground below. There was only the two of them in this strange place, and they were no longer in the cavern.

"How did we come to be here? Where is this place?" asked Nimue of Ivorwulf. He did not answer but instead asked his own questions of her.

"Ye wish to aide Morgan and Merlin, why?" His tone left in no doubt that he wanted answers. Nimue tried to push aside her curiosity about her current predicament and concentrate upon Ivorwulf.

"I feel for them both. They hath been kind to the faerie people in Briton in the past. There is no need for them to suffer simply because we wish ye to cast a spell for us."

She looked at him resolutely. He believed her answer. He walked in a half circle around her. She turned so that she always remained facing him.

"But mine dear Nimue, I hath every intention of taking up ye most kind offer." His response shocked Nimue.

"But ye..." she began to object and show her disbelief of what she was hearing from the sorcerer, but he cut her off.

"The price that ye are to pay is too tempting to refuse. But ye hath interrupted a scheme of mine own. And I will see mine plan completed before I avail mine self of the faeries' most kind offer. Let ye mind be in no doubt whatsoever, Nimue. I will cast the spell that ye wish and in return I will take every spell that ye three faerie rulers offer me as payment. How could I possibly refuse?"

Ivorwulf was smiling broadly. He was so complicit now he hardly seemed like the same man. Again Nimue was going to object but he held up his hand.

"Mine plan does not concern the faeries of Briton, Gaul, Magna Frisia or any other nation that hath magical beings. Suffice for ye to know that Merlin and Morgan are an integral part of it and I need them to be undamaged. So then, in addition to mine payment from the faerie rulers, I need to rescue Merlin and Morgan from this situation without it looking like I hath agreed to thine terms.

They must both continue to believe that I despise faeries and all that they stand for. That is what I want Nimue. Give it to me and the continuance of thine race that ye so desperately seek shall by yours," Ivorwulf said, finishing his proposal.

Nimue did not hesitate.

"I accept thine terms, Ivorwulf. When can the spell be cast? When will thine plan be completed so that we may benefit from thine magic?" Nimue had become suddenly extremely pragmatic. It did not matter to her what Ivorwulf's plan was, only that he had agreed to theirs. This pleased Ivorwulf immensely.

"Gather thine people three moons from now at the stone circle. Hath all of the ingredients waiting for me and the spell. I shall cast it and the faeries that are present will all become fertile once more. But ye did not answer mine other demand. How do we rescue Merlin and Morgan and let thine fellow rulers know of our bargain without the Caerleon sorcerer and sorceress finding out about our arrangement? We must seem to overcome ye and triumph and then make good our escape as if we are the victorious party."

He was demanding, but Nimue did not care. She thought for a moment and said.

"Possession! A faerie spell that I shall teach ye right now. Ye will inhabit the body of another and be able to pass on to them thine vitality." Nimue waited for a reaction from Ivorwulf to her plan.

"And who shall we inhabit?" he asked. The thought of learning a new spell, especially one that he had never before heard of, *was* alluring.

"I shall inhabit the body of Morgan and magnify her powers so that she may overcome the attack from Queen Aine. Ye choose one of the Knights and invigorate him to attack. When we hath prevailed and driven away the Queen and King and their forces we shall simple step backwards out of our temporary body and be returned to our solid forms once more. Just ensure that nobody sees ye do this. I will seek out mine fellow rulers afterwards and alert them to our secret arrangement. They will be gratified indeed Ivorwulf. Mine thanks," she said, finishing off her hastily constructed strategy.

Ivorwulf was nodding in satisfaction to her plan.

"Aye Nimue, a good plan; we shall be victorious and escape and it will look as if the faeries are driven away. Then let us waste no more time. Teach me the spell of possession so that our deception may begin."

Chapter 47: Merlin's Defeat

Morgan and Merlin saw the memories that Ivorwulf had projected into their minds. Their hearts sank. They had been betrayed twice over by this evil man.

Had we not noticed ye in the tapestries on Caerleon's walls we would never hath sought ye out and brought ye to our home.

Merlin's thoughts were as clear to Ivorwulf and Morgan as if they were alone in a silent room with only each other for company. Ivorwulf clasped Merlin's chin in his hand as if Merlin was a small boy and shook his head.

"Oh Merlin, I had been observing ye for years from the tapestries throughout Caerleon. Only when I wanted the two great magicians from Arthur's court to notice me did I allow ye to see mine figure secreted amongst the weavings."

Every word that came from Ivorwulf mocked Merlin and Morgan. They'd been completely fooled by the pretence of this traitor. He was clearly only interested in his own lust for power. And there was nothing that Merlin could do about it. He would have started to cry but his eyes were as motionless as the rest of his body. Morgan felt the despair welling up within him. But beyond that there was something else as well. Her feet had no feeling, and she could tell that Merlin was experiencing the same numbness. No, different to that, not numbness, nothingness. The stray thought was picked up by Ivorwulf who had turned to see how the battle was progressing.

"Aye Merlin, thine defeat is total. The spell that Morgan ripped from ye and cast to imprison thine body was augmented by mine own. Soon the both of ye will be turned to rock. There is nothing that can stop it. Nobody to save either of ye. All that I hope is that ye both retain thine wits for long enough to see Arthur die at the tip of a Saxon sword."

He snorted and turned walking away from them for some distance so that he could gain a better vantage point to view the fighting.

***

Sir Hemison, Mordrede and Prince Amhar were doing their best to corralled the men and get them to fight the oncoming enemy. But they were not meeting with very much luck. In desperation they managed to come together in the melee so that they could confer with one another. Sir Hemison outlined the problem in a single sentence.

"If we do not make some head-way soon the men will be even more disheartened than they are now. We must claim some small victory." Both Mordrede and Amhar knew that he was correct. And then the idea seized Mordrede. With a fanatical look in his eyes he shouted at his compatriots.

"I shall battle with their leader and kill him that will help turn the tide." His solution was immediately embraced by the other two Knights. In the absence of any other ideas and under the circumstances, it sounded positively inspirational.

"We shall flank ye and ensure that ye make it to thine target Mordrede," said Amhar encouragingly.

There was nothing more to discuss. With a loud yell from each of the Knights they strapped their horses forward and directly toward the enemy leader. In the shouting and yelling as they three of them closed the distance only Amhar had the fleeting thought that this Saxon leader for which they were heading, fought in a remarkably similar style to his father. He dismissed the thought as two of the leader's horse-borne minders seeing what was happening pushed their horses forward to try and intercept the three men.

***

Sir Galahallt and Sir Garethe could see the forthcoming attack from the only three of the enemy that were on horseback. They barely had time to register what was happening before they conferred with each other in a moment of time by looking to see if the other had also seen the forthcoming danger; then they shouted and together rode out to meet the menace. There was no need for further instruction but the brothers shouted direction at each other nevertheless. Sir Galahallt was first.

"I shall take the one on the right," his brother shouted in reply.

"I shall take the one on the left. Guaen!" he screamed in the hope of attracting the attention of the youngest brother. It only seemed fair; there were three aggressors and there were three brothers to fend them off.

Alas Sir Guaen was otherwise occupied and did not hear the call from Garethe. The only other thought in the minds of Galahallt and Garethe was that one of the other Knights would see what was happening and come to help them with the rider in the centre.

They met on the battlefield and Sir Mordrede in a masterful show of horsemanship coaxed his horse to jump as soon as that moment happened. It caught Sir Garethe and Galahallt by surprise. Both had hoped to land at least one blow to the centre-rider before engaging their chosen targets. They were both robbed of that chance and swords clashed and skilled fighter engaged skilled fighter. They were evenly matched and all as determined as the others to succeed in their chosen missions. None of them managed to land a single slash or blow on the others in the immediate stages of their clash.

***

Morgan and Merlin could see the dexterity by which Mordrede handled his mount. He had avoided the brothers and was now closing on King Arthur. If he succeeded in his attack, he would murder the King of Briton. If he failed and Arthur was victorious Morgan would lose her son.

Something ignited in the very depths of Merlin. He could feel it. From the total despair that he was feeling there was a...*strength* of some kind. Perhaps it was a fight-or-flee instinctive reaction that he was previously unaware of. Unsurprisingly, he could feel the same thing happening in Morgan as well. Facing the prospect of her son dying on the battlefield at the hands of his father was more than Morgan could bear.

Chapter 48: A Final Fragment of Magic

Arthur only saw the danger when it was upon him. He was engrossed with finishing off some stragglers that were trying to avoid his sword and made short work of them. Excalibur sliced through the cowardly Saxons with ease, but suddenly there was a scream from ahead of him, he glanced up and perceived a man on horse brandishing a sword. He immediately thought that it was one of his Knights, perhaps coming to his assistance, not that he needed any for the men he was fighting were offering little to no resistance.

It was that incorrect assumption that put Arthur in mortal danger. Arthur looked around for his next target and then looked up to see which of his Knights was charging toward him. To his horror he saw that it was a complete stranger – aSaxon warrior. Arthur barely had time to raise Excalibur to fend off a mighty blow delivered by the man. The sound of sword on sword filled both their ears.

****

Mordrede tried to get in as many hacks, slices and jabs in as short a time as possible to this ugly Saxon that he was engaging. To his horror, each of them was easily fended off. The might of the defence was such that he feared that his own sword might break under the strain. What manner of Saxon was this, and from where did he get that amazing sword? Questions that mattered not in the heat of the battle; he had to find a way to deliver a death blow to this man as quickly as possible.

****

Arthur was surprised at the dexterity and speed of this Saxon warrior that had engaged him. Excalibur made it easy, however, to fend-off the skilful swordsman. Arthur decided at that moment to call upon the full power of his magical sword to finish off his attacker. He didn't have the time to fight a fight of skill or chivalry with this man; he needed to win this battle as there were plenty more to be fought this day.

***

Merlin couldn't feel his legs up to his knees, nor could Morgan. But it didn't matter to either, the creeping death that was overtaking them. All that mattered was to separate Mordrede and Arthur. They were both careful to not verbalise in their minds the thoughts that they knew each was harbouring deep in their subconscious. It was a mind-bending exercise. The familiarity with each other and the certainty that each was doing the same thing was what spurred them on. They could not think directly of what they were doing for fear that Ivorwulf would overhear them. So alone and yet together they both worked toward a single goal.

Merlin shot a loud thought to Morgan, knowing that Ivorwulf would hear.

The paralysis takes hold; I can feel it building as if it were the first spell that I taught ye.

His words masked a deeper meaning. The first spell that Merlin had taught her was to create fire from the air. Their unspoken plan must have something to do with the air. It was difficult to think only in undertones and not allow Ivorwulf to hear. No, wait, it was nothing to do with the air. Merlin had made direct reference to the very first spell that he'd taught her. He must be indicating to put into practice those very same feelings as she remembered it took all of her will to make that fireball appear and light the fire in his chambers.

That was what he wanted now; everything that she had. And at that moment she was prepared to do it. Every last piece of magic, will power, energy that made her including the very magic of life itself would need to be forfeit if they were to do anything at this desperate time.

She was prepared to drain herself of every last vestige of life if it would save Mordrede and Arthur. Merlin knew that Morgan had received his message and was preparing herself to make the ultimate sacrifice. He too was drawing upon everything that he ever was, everything that he was at that moment and everything that he ever would have been if circumstances had been different. Nothing would be held in reserve, nothing at all.

At that moment the earth surrounding them became as clear as the surface of Callyfyrth Lake. The magnificence of life was made known to them. Merlin and Morgan could see the entire plan for the land. They could see its past, prior to the occupation by Rome. They saw the people that shared a common language religion and way of life. Then through the Roman occupation they saw the strange benefits that their culture had derived from the foreign land; roads, mathematics, architecture and art. All were derived from the contact with Rome. Now they could understand what Amhar and Mordrede had been extolling. All of the people of this land were one now, there were no such things as foreigners. There was no need to battle anymore. The future was revealed. Briton would become a land of agriculture and industry; overflowing with artisans of descriptions that defied their understanding. Everything that they saw was so incredibly beautiful that it moved them to the very core of their beings.

It touched them in a way that nothing else had done so before; not even the alluring touch of magic that they shared, and how they came to harness it and use it for their own ends. The future would have no need for magic. The men and women of this land would create a new kind of magic that would build a nation the likes of which they had never imagined possible. That is why the faeries were infertile. Their time had come and gone and they were no longer a part of the greater scheme of things. That is why religion was becoming so prevalent; it would replace magic as an ethic to follow for quite some time, but not forever.

More than that they could see so far into the future that there was a time when life and death were the purview of ordinary men and women that could will things into existence without using magic, but draw upon the divinity within each of them to effect good everywhere.

They saw, men and women, animals and birds, trees and lakes all working together to create a better life, a perfect life living together in perfect harmony. At that moment, they surrendered their life forces to feed a last fragment of magic that would erupt from them and spill out on to the battlefield and beyond.

Chapter 49: Knowledge of the Truth

Arthur raised his sword and called upon the full force of Excalibur to end the battle he was fighting. He swung the sword upwards, ready for the deadly blow.

Mordrede could see the blow coming, and reacted instinctively. The way that the two horses had become entangled during the close proximity fighting he had no way of manoeuvring his horse into a defensive position. He swung his leg out of one leather and wooden stirrup and over the neck of his mount. Then bringing his foot to rest on top of his other foot, still secured in its stirrup, he looked for an instant like he was dismounting. But in fact it was to crouching down to reposition himself as he could not move his horse.

Arthur perceived that his enemy was dismounting, but it did not matter, soon Excalibur would cut through him as if he was not even there. Mordrede stooped down on his stirrup. It allowed him to drop his guard from fending off the coming blow and instead thrust his sword at the torso of his enemy.

Mordrede's sword pierced the chainmail at the point where its sleeve met with the body of the heavy garment. The tiny iron loops had become worn down with the many years of use and gave way allowing the sword to enter. The angle that Mordrede pierced Arthur's body meant that his sword cut through the body and directly beside the King's heart.

Arthur screamed with pain but did not let the injury divert his death-blow to his enemy. Excalibur impacted at Mordrede's neck and carved a perfect line downwards through his torso to his stomach before the natural arch of the blow drew the sword outwards from there.

***

Ivorwulf only became aware that something was happening behind him when it was already too late. He was so engrossed in the battle between Mordrede and Arthur that he failed to perceive the building-up of a magical force behind him. He turned, surprised by the sudden feeling that enveloped him.

Merlin and Morgan were glowing with a brilliant white light the likes of which he'd never before seen. It was so pure that it made the sunlight of the day seem dull by comparison. That was all he had time to take in before that same light shot out from their bodies and past him, spreading out over the field of battle. It had a devastating effect upon Ivorwulf's spell of beguilement.

The spell became visible for a moment and then shattered into pieces too many to count. The fragments of his carefully cast spell melted away before his eyes. He could see it, feel it; his spell was destroyed. He was furious. He began to speak the words again but even as he did so he knew that it was not working. Something was preventing him from mending his spell of beguilement. Turning around he ran back toward Morgan and Merlin determined to wring both of their necks with his bare hands. He stopped with fright in his tracks and stared at the pair of them. First at one and then at the other and then back to ensure that he was not seeing things. His first thought was that they'd cast a spell over him. He concentrated and tried to cast a spell that would protect him from what he thought was a masquerade. Opening his eyes he realised that it was true. Merlin and Morgan had turned to stone. He walked forward, reached out and touched the 'face' of Morgan. It was cold, hard granite.

Walking over to Merlin he did the same thing, just to assure himself that what he was seeing was real. They were no more. The great magicians of Caerleon were gone from this world. It took a few moments for him to gather his thoughts. They were many. How had this happened? The manoeuvre that he instigated should have paralysed them at least for the duration of the battle, but this outcome was completely unexpected. The strength of the magic that each was encased within was so powerful that it had robbed them of their human bodies, replacing them with rock. Perhaps he had in the end underestimated the power of both Merlin and Morgan?

And yet through all of his wonderings there came a sole thought that stood out above all others. He was rid of the only two other sorcerers in the land that could even hope to oppose him. This serendipitous happening had served to further his plan to become absolute Caesar of Briton. A feeling of malicious happiness began to well up within him. Looking with distain at what was once Merlin, he spoke.

"Goodbye, Merlin the magician, sorcerer of Caerleon; rest in stillness for all of eternity knowing that in the end I was the more powerful Wizard."

***

Across the battlefield, men formerly influenced by the spell shook their heads as if something had hit them but left no mark. There was the general feeling as if a weight had been lifted from them. Senses were returned to their former sharpness. Camlann villagers all looked at the dead and wounded lying around them and at the Knights of the Round Table that had caused all of this carnage.

King Arthur watched as Mordrede fell from his mount, dragging the sword that had pierced his body out and down with him. The horror of what had just happened occurred to him. He'd been bewitched into thinking that his illegitimate son was a Saxon enemy. He'd murdered one of his sons!

"Mordrede!" screamed Arthur in rage and sorrow. Arthur's anguish drowned-out the searing pain that he should have been feeling from his wound. Arthur's cry cut through the air, penetrating the ears of all the Knights.

Sirs Hemison, Galahallt, Garethe and Prince Amhar all who had been blinking at each other in disbelief, turned as one to see Mordrede lying at the feet of Arthur's horse. Even from this distance they could see the blood flowing freely from the king. All of the Knights instinctively went to the aid of their ruler, but Amhar who was more shocked than any of them, and perhaps because of the accompanying surge of adrenalin closed the distance between them before any of the others. He dismounted just in time to take in the horrific scene and was luckily in a perfect position to catch his father as the king fell from his mount.

Numbness was overtaking Arthur he looked into Amhar's eyes and loved his son now more than he ever had before.

"Father," began Amhar, his voice trembling. He was so full of emotion that he could barely speak, but he forced himself. Arthur brought up one hand to touch Amhar's mouth.

"Let me speak," said Arthur, his voice weak. By this time the other Knights had arrived and were gathered around the king in a circle. Amhar began to weep openly, trying his hardest to hold it in for fear of missing a single word spoken from his father. The King's blood began to cover the thighs of Amhar.

"Time for ye to be King now, mine son," he said. His eyes began to close, triggering a new rush of dread and sadness within the Prince. Arthur felt nearby to the ground where he was being supported by his son. His hand found the grip of Excalibur and with all of his might he lifted it to hand it to Amhar.

"Take Excalibur," he said. They were the final two words of King Arthur's life. He died his eyes still half open, unfocussed upon the sky above. Amhar had reached forward and gripped the sword just above his father's hand when he saw death descend upon the king.

"Noooooooooo!' he shouted in absolute despair. The surrounding Knights looked on helplessly. Their beloved leader was dead. Sir Mordrede, the King's illegitimate son lay dead barely one pace away.

The scene was almost too much to comprehend. The Knights starting with Sir Galahallt and following on in slow succession all knelt before their new ruler, King Amhar. He would now rule just as Arthur had done and Uther before him. The royal line was unbroken. It was a small solace amongst the tragedy before their eyes.

King Amhar wept openly and without restraint. He buried his head into his father's in a final embrace. The sorrow would have overwhelmed him as nothing else had before except someone was calling him; no, not someone, something. He could feel the might of Excalibur in his hand. It gave him strength to fend off the despair that could have so easily enveloped him. But more than that, there was a compulsive need to press the handle of the magical sword to his forehead. It was completely irresistible. He brought up the sword slowly and it touched his forehead.

***

Merlin and Morgan were standing before him and he was at the edge of a beautiful lake somewhere. It looked like it was the lake near to Cellewig castle. The sense of relief to see his mentors was incredible. He wanted to run forward and embrace the both but he could not move. He was fixed where he was. Looking down at his feet he could see neither shackles nor anything else that would hold him in place. He was perplexed. He looked up at the magicians in the hope for understanding about what was happening.

"Amhar," said Morgan. "Ye are still on the field outside of Camlann near the now deceased body of thine father."

"Everything is clear to us now Amhar, the past, the present and the future," Merlin said.

"I do not understand, Merlin...Morgan; what is happening?"

Morgan tried to explain. "We have planted this message within Excalibur for ye to see, it is a record of the events that hath lead up to this battle."

With those words, King Amhar saw the entire plan that Ivorwulf have laid out. The false treaty between all of the Jutes, Saxons and Angles; Ivorwulf's own deception of Karal his master and the plans of the sorcerer to wrest power at the defeat of the Knights of the Round Table and the death of King Arthur. He saw the secret deal with Nimue to cast the spell of fertility and bring the faerie population back from the brink of extinction. And the final piece of magic that both he and Morgan cast to break Ivorwulf's spell of beguilement.

It was difficult to take in, but he did. It was absorbed by his consciousness completely. He understood everything about how they had come to be in this situation. And yet he somehow felt that Merlin and Morgan were holding something back from him. He looked into their eyes. They were both fading away.

"Do not leave me; I need ye both now more than ever!" he said anxiously. They only smiled and became less solid and more transparent. Morgan and Merlin had one final message for the king. Merlin started the sentence and Morgan finished it.

"Ye were right about the people of this land being one..."

"...there are no foreigners in Briton, only people."

The two magicians had now completely disappeared. For a moment he was alone at Llyn Callyfyrth. He pondered on everything that he now knew.

***

King Amhar brought the sword down from his forehead. He surveyed the scene before him. The Knights were still kneeling around him in a circle. There was a look of expectation on their faces. He gently placed the head of his father on the ground and stook up facing all of them.

In the distance he could see the Saxons that had formed part of the insidious plan to lure them to this place. They were all looking at the Knights sizing them up, and preparing for their attack. Amhar knew that there was no choice but battle. They would not listen to his reasoning about all Britons being one; they were the muscle that Ivorwulf was going to use to excise the Pendragons from the country. He pointed with Excalibur at them.

"These men hath been sent here to kill all of the Knights of the Round Table and to Kill Arthur and mine own person too. They wish to end the Pendragon bloodline and vanquish the Knights of the Round Table forever. We are outnumbered almost three to one. Stand!"

The confidence and strength in his voice gave all of the Knights renewed spirit. They stood and turned to face their true enemies.

Chapter 50: The First Battle of King Amhar Pendragon

The thirty skilled fighters sent from Cissa, Wlencing and Cymen, formed in a neat line and as one beat the handles of their swords against their leather breastplate repeatedly. The sound would have terrified normal men, but the Knights and king from Caerleon were not so easily intimidated. They too formed into a single line albeit one much shorter than the line that they were facing. Both sides held expressions of determination. Neither would back-down there was too much at stake.

Amhar weighed-up the enemy. He knew that they would be the cream of the forces from the Saxon warlords. There was no need to take them on at ground level. Amhar commanded his men.

"Mount!"

Each of the Knights found their horse and dutifully climbed up into position. If this seeming-advantage made the Saxons worried, it did not show. They remained beating their chests in ominous time.

Amhar was in the centre of his Knights. They splayed out to his left and right.

"Forward!" he shouted, and jolted his horse into a level cantor toward the enemy.

It was a strategy he had seen Arthur use time and again against a force superior in numbers; ride toward them slowly to give them time to worry about what was about to happen. The Knights fell into the rhythm that the king set for them.

***

The triumvirate that were the leaders of the Saxon war-party all gave each other a signal from where they were standing. Each had taken up position in their line along with their own men. Many battle strategies had been discussed leading up to this moment that was now upon them. The pre-arranged signal was to decide which of their fighting plans they would put into place first. The decision was made and the news communicated to all of the Saxon warriors. They would be ready for the Knights and their horses.

***

Amhar and the Knights were about fifty paces away from their enemy when the king shouted

"Charge!" and all of the men spurred their mounts into flight.

They galloped toward the Saxons at great speed. The Caerleon Knights met the line and reared up their horses, which were trained to react in this way. They kicked some of the Saxons maiming some and winding others. It was a clever move to try and decrease the numbers of Saxons available to fight. But the Saxons were not concerned with losing a few men here and there, temporarily or for the rest of the battle. Swords were drawn and the Knights ignored unless they were directly threatened by a Caerleon sword. The Saxons cruelly turned their swords upon the horses and jabbed through hide and muscle; slicing legs and tendons, piercing hearts and heads necks and flanks.

The horses all died with agonising noise. Sir Brumean was unlucky to be pinned beneath his falling horse and suffered a crushed leg. He screamed in pain but tried to fend off two Saxons that had descended upon the hapless man. Although his fighting was brave and selfless, he was slain by the Saxons, a sword piercing his neck and rupturing his jugular vein. He died in a pool of his own blood on the muddy ground outside of Camlann.

Elsewhere Knights had been thrown from their horses and were scrambling to their feet. Sir Ectorde Maris witnessing in an instant what the Saxons were doing to the horses had taken the initiative and jumped from his horse. He was a brave Knight and jumped into the

Saxon line hoping to surprise them with his valour and fearlessness. It worked. The Saxon that he landed upon was knocked from his feet. Sir Ectorde Maris neatly dispatching him with a single slash from his sword to the man's throat. But the boldness of the Knight's trick was also his undoing. Now he had to fight Saxons to both his left and right. And although accomplished at such fighting he had never before had to take on two to his left and two to his right.

A Saxon warrior maimed him with a jab to his tendon and felled the Knight. One other warrior took the opportunity to jab him in the hand that held his sword. Ectorde dropped it and barely had time to look up at who'd disarmed him before a sword pierced his face in his left eye socket. His death was agonising but mercifully quick.

Sir Bors De Ganys had too jumped from his horse, although only at the very last second after he realised what had happened. He unlike his now dead compatriot had jumped backwards so that he could more adequately size-up the men that he was about to fight. He seemed to be facing only two at the current time. One that was within range must have succumbed to the kick of his horse before it had been killed. So much the better thought Bors, he charged forward with only two Saxons to occupy him.

The fighting was excellent from all three men. They were highly-charged individuals the trio. Swords clashed high and low. But none of them managed to get in any serious blows to the other. The speed at which Bors parried away the thrusts from both of his assailants was admirable. He was completely immersed in his form and function. Strike, parry, thrust, swipe; with every move he looked for an opening that he could exploit. Finally one presented itself to him. One of the Saxons must have thought that he could try something different in the close-quarters fighting and went to swing his sword in a large arc aiming for Bor's helmet. With a single deadly thrust the Knight plunged his sword into the man's chest causing him to scream loudly. His arms went limp and the body began to fall forward. Sir Bors De Ganys tried to remove his sword from the man, but the body was falling forward toward him ultimately preventing him from doing so.

The remaining Saxon that he was fighting saw what was happening and exploited the situation with deadly consequences. He raised his sword in the same manner as his now deceased friend. It gave him a huge swing of his sword up and over so that it could fall with devastating force. The man aimed for the Knights arms that were both trying unsuccessfully to pull his sword from the dispatched enemy. Both of Bor's hands were severed just below the elbow. He shrieked in agony and blood spurted from the stumps. The second last thing that the Knight saw were his hands still holding onto the grip of his sword falling to the ground with his sword still lodged into his conquest. The last thing that Sir Bors De Ganys saw was the Saxon that had severed his hands once more swinging his sword with a long deliberate and well-aimed throw. Bors head was decapitated and it rolled across the battle field.

King Amhar had made a significant error in his attack but did not know it at the time that his horse was killed. The king scrambled up from where he had been thrown by his dying horse. He could feel the strength of Excalibur running through him. He knew everything about how to handle the sword. He was no long a child being taught swordsmanship by this father. No, now he was king and he knew that right now was the time to call upon the full power of Excalibur if he hoped to win this battle. Three Saxons approached him swords forward. He slashed the away advancing blades splitting each of the swords. The bearers looked in dismay at their suddenly shortened weapons. Amhar could see the expression on their faces knowing that they were thinking *What do we do now*?

He did not give them time to contemplate their next moves. Charging forward he thrust Excalibur into the centre man who looked down at where it had entered the very centre of his chest in abject terror. Without the need to remove the sword before using it effectively again, King Amhar simply swung it left cutting through the body of the first Saxon as if it were not even there. Excalibur then severed the sword arm of the man that was standing next to him. Blood pumped out from the stump and he was, suddenly, no-longer a threat.

Repeating the move Amhar moved Excalibur to the right and had to cut through the torso of the centre Saxon once more because it had not had time to fall to the ground when he did this. The Saxon to the right tried to jump back instinctively, but he was too late. Excalibur slashed through his pectoral and blood spurted out.

Injured but not critically, this man became the focus of Amhar for the time-being. The king gave him a look of utter disdain. If looks were swords, the man would have surely died on the spot. The Saxon thrust what was left of his sword at Amhar who simply parried away shattering the stump and handle in the process. The man stood there defeated, still with a look of disbelief on his face. Amhar finished him off by beheading him. The man's rolled over the ground.

Looking up and to his left Amhar could see the Knights all involved in skirmishes of one sort or another. He acted as he thought best and ran over to aid the Knight that was nearest to him. Sir Galahallt was involved in a three way battle. The brave Knight was admirably fending off the three attackers, but was not making any headway with his attack. Amhar aimed to help Sir Galahallt even the odds. He approached alerting one of the Saxons that was beleaguering the good Knight. This made the battle a little more even as two of the Saxons continued their onslaught with Galahallt and the other turned to face the approaching King.

Amhar could see that this was a huge man. Amhar was unimpressed with his height however. It may have intimidated others, but not the feisty king. The Saxon thought to use his height, weight and long arms to attack the king before he was ready and surged forward sword raised high and plummeting downwards towards Amhar's head. Amhar simply deflected the blow with a flick of his wrist. His opponent's sword did not shatter in this instance. But the ease at which Amhar had overcome his attack put a look of concern on the Saxon man's face.

He repositioned himself and prepared for another assault. But Amhar was not waiting for it, instead he charged forward and with a guttural scream aimed his sword at the man's chest and thrust forward. The Saxon thought that he could deflect such a simply attack manoeuvre with a slice downward from his sword, aided by his mighty weight. Too late he realised he was completely wrong. Trying to deflect Excalibur was like trying to brush away log in-flight. His sword simply clattered off the advancing blade and before he knew it, his heart was shattered within his body. The Saxon man died instantly.

Turning his attention to another of the two men engaging Galahallt, Amhar shouted at the nearest to him.

"Find some sport with me Saxon, if ye dare!" the insult had the exact effect that the king had hoped for. Leaving his friend to continue the battle with the Knight one-on-one, the other Saxon warrior turned his attentions and revile against king Amhar.

"This way Knight of the Round Table; come and meet thine death!" The man indicated that Amhar should make the first move in this game of force and skill. Amhar accepted his offer and was about to attack when there came a cry of agony from Sir Galahallt. Amhar did not see what had happened but the Saxon warrior must have somehow gained the upper-hand. Amhar was dismayed. Sir Galahallt had a sword sticking through the side of his throat. The warrior withdrew his Saxon blade and blood spurted from the jugular vein. It was a mortal wound. There would be no way to mend it without the aid of Merlin or Morgan.

Sir Galahallt fell backwards writing in agony and shock on the ground. Infuriated Amhar retaliated immediately. He took the dagger from Excalibur's handle and threw it at the man that he was about to attack. It penetrated the man's cheek and he bellowed in pain. His compatriot looked up from gloating over the dying body of Sir Galahallt, just in time to see Excalibur flying through the air toward him. The magical sword speared the man in the torso and he staggered and dropped his sword.

Amhar strode up to the man with the dagger in his face. He was stumbling around in distress. Amhar put the man out of his misery by gripping the man by his shoulder with his left arm and then pulling the dagger out with his right and immediately re-inserting it into the man's heart. Death was immediate.

Then without waiting for the victim to fall he marched up to the man with Excalibur embedded within him and gripped the handle of Excalibur. This had a curious effect on the Saxon warrior who momentarily seemed to forget the searing pain that was wracking his body. Instead he looked with dread at what Amhar was going to do. Amhar slotted the dagger back into the handle of his magical sword. Then clasping the handle with both hands moved it up cutting the man's torso in half. The warrior died screaming, blood gurgling up in his throat before he ceased to be.

Again King Amhar assessed the situation to his left. Sir Guaen was in danger. Two men were attacking him and he seemed to already have been injured at some point in the fighting. His sword arm was bleeding profusely. Amhar wasted no time; with a raucous shout he charged toward Guaen's assailants. Two of them turned to face the approaching enemy. If they had hopes that they would be victorious simply because the numbers were in their favour, they were wrong. Amhar smashed down with Excalibur and chopped off both of the hands from the first man and with the return flick of his sword he sliced through the head of the second, neatly shearing it off at an angle. Half of the man's head slipped away from the rest of his body; he was dead before he even knew it.

The Saxon that had engaged Guaen was distracted enough by the goings on to allow Guaen to get in a death blow of his own. Guaen ran the man clean through with his sword. Not being a magical sword and given the amount of effort it would have taken after such a ferocious battle, it was more of an accomplishment than it seemed to anyone who had seen what happened. He pulled back freeing his sword. He did not bother to watch his victim fall to the ground rather he consulted quickly with the king. They looked up and down the line of fighting men.

"This way," indicated Guaen, pointing down toward the left of the line, the direction that Amhar had been heading in anyway. Amhar did not debate the assertion.

"Aye," he confirmed and they both charged toward the next Knight in peril. It was Sir Dagonet, but even as both approached the two men that were attacking him it was too late. They were still three of four paces away when one of the men managed to disarm the Knight. Sir Dagonet looked directly into the eyes of the man that had managed to best him on the battlefield. There was no anger, nor surprise. Instead he was defiant till the end. He gave the man as look as if to say that his death would not help the Saxons win this war, they were outmatched by the might of the Knights of the Round Table. The Saxon warrior although perplexed in the moment of registering the defiant look that the Knight was throwing at him, did not hesitate to finish his task. He speared Sir Dagonet through the throat, the sword penetrating completely and coming out the back of his neck. There was no scream of pain, there could not be. The honourable Knight died where he stood.

Amhar and Guaen simultaneously let out a cry. This alerted the Saxon to his next targets. It looked for just a moment as if he was to shout a diatribe at them but he never got out a word. Amhar was the first to reach him and parrying away the feeble attack from the man the king sliced off first one of his arms at the shoulder and then the leg on the opposing side. Both limbs fell to the ground at the same time as the warrior. Vengeance had been swiftly metered out by King Amhar.

Two more Saxons came out of the melee, and with swords flashing, began to fight with Guaen and Amhar. Guaen had taken a beating but his strength was renewed with the anger that he felt over witnessing Sir Dagonet's death before his eyes. He fought like a wild animal almost forgetting the graceful way that he had learnt over the many years in the serviced of the former king. Charging forward screaming at the top of his lungs and with arms and sword flying at incredible speed, he easily intimidated the hapless man that had thought to take him on in battle.

Amhar, as usual, did not have any doubt that he would win against the man that had chosen to engage him. Still feeling the incredible power of the sword in his hand he made short work of his assailant's sword, breaking it cleanly in half, length-ways. The precision of the cut effectively gave the Saxon warrior two sword to fight with. Although amazed at what had just happened, he adapted to the situation with frightening ease. Taking one of each half of his sword in both hands he crouched down in a threatening way. It looked for a moment as if he was going to spring toward Amhar.

The king knew that he needed to act immediately and not give the man any chance to make use of his dual weapons. He swung his sword in a fancy manner that would be more appropriate in showing-off to trainees than a move that would be useful in actual battle. Excalibur circled around in Amhar's hand two or three times, mesmerising the man. In effect keeping him off-guard by not knowing which direction the thrust was going to come from. In a flash of speed Amhar threw his still spinning sword to his other hand catching it and thrusting it forward in one easy motion. Excalibur skewered the man's face; he jumped backward in agony and writhed upon the ground bellowing in pain.

Guaen in the meantime had bested his enemy. Amhar only saw Guaen pulling his sword from the dead man's body. He did not see exactly how Guaen had managed to get the upper hand and take the decisive and winning blow.

Another death scream was heard by them both just as they re-joined each other. It was Sir Bedwere. They could see him only about five paces away. He had two swords sticking into his body at the torso and thigh. There was no telling if these were the first or second blows from the swordsmen that had victoriously beaten the Knight. As both swords were pulled out from his body there followed two spurts of blood. Sir Bedwere fell forward with a sickening thud upon the blood covered ground.

There was only Sir Alynore left down at this end of the battle line. Somehow he had managed to occupy four of the Saxons. But now that the two who had been otherwise occupied with the former Sir Bedwere were freed-up, they too could concentrate upon felling the good Knight.

Time appeared to slow down for both Amhar and Guaen. They could see the Saxon reinforcements running toward Sir Alynore. Guaen shouted something at the top of his voice in the hopes of drawing their attention but it did not work. It was almost as if they had somehow communicated without speaking and were acting like a pack of wild dogs. Amhar and Guaen ran towards Alynore knowing that they would almost certainly be too late to offer any assistance for him against six aggressors. The feeling of dread that passed through both men made their hearts feel like they were dropping into their stomachs

The crowd of Saxons surrounding Sir Alynore was so thick that neither Amhar nor Guaen saw the first blow that critically wounded the Knight. They did see the second blow though. The man that delivered it was in clear view, as his compatriots had stood back knowing that the Knight was beaten. They waited for the inevitable. Sir Alynore was lurching backwards blood streaming down the side of his face. One of his ears had been cut off, he was crying out in pain. The Saxon that ended Sir Alynore's life used both hands to cleave his sword through the Knight's ribcage. Even at the distance Amhar and Guaen were at they could hear the cracking of bones within Alynore, it made them both sick. Sir Alynore fell to the ground.

The band of Saxons that had contributed to the small victory all cheered and were in the process of slapping each other on the back when Amhar reached them. Two of them turned to face this upstart that dared interrupt their celebration. Excalibur sliced the both of them clean through. The remaining four almost dropped their swords in shock. Only at that point did they realise that they were in trouble.

Sir Guaen joined Amhar and shouted a profanity at the men, but it could not take their attention away from Amhar and his incredible feat that he had just displayed. There was an attempt by the men to regain their composure in the prelude to a combined assault. A desperate one that they hoped for an instant would save their lives. They were wrong. Amhar did not give them the chance; he raced forward and swinging Excalibur left and right, up and down in a blur of motion that Guaen had never before witnessed in all of his years fighting; suddenly the four Saxons were dead. Their victory was short-lived.

Amhar was breathing hard and was exhausted. He looked at Guaen and they both looked back up the direction that they had come. There were still Knights involved in battles that were stacked against them. Now Amhar realised what he had done wrong. If he had started at one end of the battle line he could have simply proceeded through and killed as many Saxons as he could with Excalibur, saving his men from being outnumbered. But he had not.

He was at what was the far end of the battle line and he now had to make his way back to the other end where all of the fighting was still going on.

"Guaen," he said through panting breathes. "Garethe."

Sir Guaen immediately looked around to locate his brother. Amhar must have noticed something and was trying to communicate it to him but was completely drained of energy. Sure enough Guaen's eyes came to rest upon Sir Garethe involved in a tussle with two Saxons.

"I can feel," gasped Amhar "the power of the sword...but I am only...a man." Amhar was trying to relay that the magical sword still felt to him like it could cut through anything, but he, its operator, was not so magically imbued. Fatigue was overtaking him.

Guaen did not have time to interpret what the king was trying to impart to him. He raced toward Garethe in the vain hope of being able to offer him some assistance. He cursed the Saxons that had killed their horses in the opening minutes of the fighting. He desperately wanted a horse now more than ever before. Amhar did his best to follow, but was not as quick as Guaen.

As Amhar ran toward the battling men he thought vainly of somehow removing his chainmail so as to give himself less of a burden to carry, but he realistically did not have the time. His Knights were in peril. They were outnumbered, fatigued and more vulnerable than at any time before. Amhar had to fight-off thoughts of the Knights that he had already lost. If he began to dwell upon them now he would most certainly lose the rest as well. He had to stay focussed upon the living. Amazingly, this gave him a boost.

The distance to what was the centre of the battle line seemed so much greater on the way back toward it than it did on the way down away from it. The Knight that was fighting beside Sir Garethe fell backwards onto the ground. It was Sir Kay. Amhar could see him scrambling to get to his feet. He rolled over onto his side in order to get better leverage to lift himself up. But a sword plunged through him. He cried out and was silent. Another of the Knights of the Round Table was forfeit in this conflict. Amhar could see that Guaen was close to reaching Garethe. At least there was some solace to be found in the midst of all of this carnage. Side by side the two brothers were a formidable combination.

From deep within his being he had to draw upon every reserve of energy that he could. By the time he reached Guaen and Garethe they were busy fending off blows from Saxons that had managed to surround them. Amhar thought that he had best concentrate his efforts on the remaining Knights as the two brothers would be able to hold their own. He was not averse to giving them a little help though. As he passed by the struggle Amhar lashed out with Excalibur severing the spine of one of the attacking Saxons. The odds were made a little more even with a single blow.

There was shouting from behind Amhar and in front of him. The Saxon warriors were communicating something. Maybe it was his fatigue or their thick accents or a combination of the two, but he could not make out exactly what it was that they were shouting to each other. There was no time to think about it now. Sir Lyonell was directly ahead and in danger. He was faltering against the onslaught of swords. He was facing-down two Saxon men. Amhar interceded and took out one of them with a not-so-carefully aimed swipe at the man. The result looked far more professional than the randomness of the move exhibited. The Saxon victim turned around as if he had been rudely shocked. And then half of his shoulder, still connected to his arm fell away from the rest of his body.

More shouting from the Saxons; again Amhar failed to make any sense of it. Amhar watched as Sir Lyonell gained the upper hand in the now one-on-one battle. His opponent was clearly rattled at seeing his companion so easily slain. His distraction was his downfall. Sir Lyonell saw an opportunity and stabbed the man in the throat. He died chocking on his own blood.

"Quickly Lyonell," shouted Amhar, "Sir Degore is in need of thine assistance!" Amhar indicated the beleaguered Knight a little way off. But an opportunistic Saxon saw that Sir Lyonell was paying attention to Amhar and not to his own back. This man had a bow slung around his back. He quickly took it off and produced an arrow from within his robes. By the time Amhar noticed what was happening it was already too late to shout a warning. The Saxon took aim and released the arrow. Amhar screamed out but the arrow found its mark and pierced Sir Lyonell's back. The Knight spun around in shock and pain. He located the source of the arrow that penetrated his body.

Surely enough, the same Saxon was readying another arrow. Sir Lyonell looked around for a shield that he could use to defend himself from the arrow. There was one only a few paces away. He could not believe his fortune as he ran toward the shield. He also presented a much more difficult target now that he was on the move, or so he thought. But the Saxon bowman was an excellent marksman. He released the second arrow and it flew through the air. Just as Sir Lyonell reached the shield that he could have used to protect himself the Saxon's arrow thrust its way through Sir Lyonell's eye socket and into his brain. The brave Knight died before he hit the ground.

Amhar saw the futility of Sir Lyonell's death; he could take no more and screamed at the top of his lungs.

"NO MORE!'

It was almost as if the intensity of Amhar's tone stopped the remaining battles around him. There was more shouting between the Saxons. Amhar surveyed the scene. Behind him Sir Guaen was victorious against the men that he was fighting, but he could see that

Sir Garethe was now lying on the battlefield, prone. Sir Guaen was kneeling beside the body.

At the feet of the largest group of the Saxons, Amhar could see the body of Sir Hemison. He had succumbed to the greater numbers and been killed in battle also. There was only Sir Degore left. He had backed away from the greater number of attackers. The look upon his face told Amhar that he was completely exhausted and unable to continue.

There was more shouting from the Saxons to one another, but this time Amhar understood what they were saying. They were afraid of him. His exploits with Excalibur had not gone unnoticed by the remaining warriors. It was then that he noticed it. They had begun to bunch up. Their faces betrayed their shared demeanour. Amhar counted his enemies. The warriors led here to destroy the Pendragon bloodline so that Ivorwulf could declare himself as ruler of the country. There were about eight of them left.

Amhar took the initiative. He threw Excalibur from one hand to the other catching it neatly each time. It made the Saxons nervous. He took a step toward them. They could be seen to flinch in response. He pointed the magical sword at them. The effect was immediate; some of the men actually ducked as if it were an arrow that could strike them down from afar. At that moment Amhar knew what to do.

"Leave this place in peace or die in battle against mine crown and mine sword!"

Amhar's words seemed to echo even in the open ground. The Saxons could be seen looking at one another as if to find someone to make the decision for them. Amhar guessed that the senior men must have already fallen in battle. The remainder were without leadership.

All it took was for one of the remaining Saxons to make a decision and then the rest followed. One man actually ran away from

Amar, even though he too would have been exhausted. The others followed in rapid succession. The battle was over. King Amhar was victorious. An empty victory for a battle he did not want to fight; a war that had cost him the majority of the Knights of the Round Table.

Chapter 51: Stone Pillars

King Amhar looked at the utter devastation surrounding him. He felt an unbelievably heavy sense of loss. His friends, some of which he had grown-up in front of, and fellow Knights were all but dead. Victory against the evilness of Ivorwulf had come at a high price. The very thought of Ivorwulf triggered a warning in Amhar's thoughts. The Kentish Sorcerer that would-be Caesar of Briton was still a danger. His army-for-hire were gone, but he remained alive and dangerous.

Amhar did not have to search for long to find the object of his concern. Ivorwulf was where he had been for the entire time, in the area away from the main battle, a perfect vantage point from which to view everything that had happened. Even from this distance Amhar could see that Ivorwulf was seething with rage. His plans to extinguish the Pendragon bloodline from Briton had not yet been finished.

Amhar now faced the thought of battling with a powerful Sorcerer in order to claim his victory and ensure Ivorwulf's plans came asunder.

"Amhar," the voice was familiar. It sounded as if it was right beside him.

"Merlin?" Amhar looked around for the old Sorcerer, which he knew was dead. There was nobody there.

Again Merlin called his name. Amhar looked down and at Excalibur. There was something there. He lifted the sword; it was still immaculately clean in spite of the killing that it had performed that day. Reflected in the sword was Merlin, standing right beside him. Amar looked again to his right. Merlin was not there. He was only in the reflection of Excalibur's blade.

"Merlin, how can I..." said Amhar in distress, but Merlin held up his hand to quell Amhar's question.

"One final show of magic before it passes from this land and into the realm of memory and myth," said Merlin.

"What is it?" asked Amhar.

"Do not fear Ivorwulf's powers. Do what must be done!" Merlin disappeared from the reflection in Excalibur.

Amhar did not stop to ponder Merlin's instructions. He marched toward Ivorwulf. As they came closer together Amhar could see the naked hatred on the Sorcerers face. He spoke; practically spitting the venomous words at Amhar.

"I shall see the Pendragon blood-line gone from this land, mine land. Die!"

Chapter 52: A New Future for Briton

Ivorwulf raised his hands levitating Amhar high into the air. Ivorwulf smiled as Amhar let out a cowardly scream. Then bringing his arms down suddenly the wicked man forced Amhar to the ground crashing his body into the rocky ground beneath him. Amhar let out the sound of an *oomph* as his lungs were deprived of all that was in them.

The Sorcerer laughed loudly at the agony that he had caused. He could not resist gloating.

"King of Briton no-more, Amar! Kneel before Caesar Ivorwulf thine Emperor."

The manic wizard again levitated Amhar high into the air but this time instead of hurling him to the ground he flung him toward a large boulder near the bend in the river. Amhar flew through the air and impacted against the side of the rock. There was another sickening thud. Amhar slid to the ground as was motionless for a while. Even from the distance though, Ivorwulf spied that there was still life left in the battered man.

Again, he levitated Amhar into the air. This time he brought him down softly about ten paces before him. Amhar would not have had the strength now to stand on his own two feet so Ivorwulf assisted him.

"Now in the final moments of thine life Amhar pay homage to the almighty Ivorwulf." The evil magician forced Amhar's body to bow down before him. Satisfied that he had had enough fun torturing the king, Ivorwulf brought-forth a ball of fire hovering in the air between his two hands.

"Now Amhar; die!" he said. The ball of fire spun toward Amhar and hit him mid-chest and Amhar's body burst into flames, the scream sending shivers of pleasure through Ivorwulf's body. He'dd finally completed his plan concocted over years. The Pendragons were dead. The only other two magicians in the land that had any hope of opposing him were turned into stone pillars. Soon he would help the faeries become fertile and re-instigate their magical numbers throughout the land. The knowledge that he would gain from them would be invaluable to aid him in maintaining his dictatorship. Now he could install himself as absolute ruler of everyone in the land and banish Christianity, that magic-inhibiting religion. Everything was happening exactly as he had imagined it. Ivorwulf was unbelievably happy with himself.

An incredible pain interrupted his rejoicing. It was a searing pain in his side. He looked down. A dagger had been plunged into his ribcage. Ivorwulf couldn't believe what he was seeing. He followed the hand holding the dagger in him and looked up straight into the face of King Amhar.

Amhar twisted the small dagger sending a crippling pain through Ivorwulf. He could not find the words to express what he wanted. He looked at Amhar in complete disbelief. Amhar gave Ivorwulf the answer to his unasked question.

"A final spell of beguilement from Merlin," Amhar smiled. Ivorwulf managed to turn his head to look at the stone pillar that had been Merlin. For just an instant he could see the smiling image of of Merlin's face there. Then it was gone. Too late he realised that everything that he had done to Amhar was just a simple illusion put into his mind. It was a simple spell that he had mastered whilst a child and yet it had fooled him completely. But how had Merlin cast it? He was a pillar of stone! Ivorwulf turned back to Amhar, who by this time had raised Excalibur up to the wicked Sorcerer's face. Paraphrasing Ivorwulf's earlier proclamation Amhar said quite smugly

"Now Ivorwulf; die!" Amhar thrust the sword through Ivorwulf's open mouth. It burst out the back of his head sending a splatter of blood across the ground. Amhar pulled Excalibur back sharply, and withdrew Excalibur's dagger simultaneously. Ivorwulf crumpled to the ground; dead.

Amhar looked up at the stone pillars that had been Merlin and Morgan. He could think of nothing else to say except

"Mine thanks," then turning back to what was left of the Knights of the Round Table he looked at them in the distance.

They were standing together watching him, their king, searching for direction, waiting for an order from him. Amhar knew at that moment exactly what he would do in order to give them the leadership that they needed. He knew what he would do for all of the people of Briton, regardless of their background, so that they could live without fear of being judged as something less than they deserved simply because of their national heritage. The disparate people of Briton could live as one. There would be a new future for Briton and Amhar knew exactly how to achieve it.

***

One month had passed since King Amhar had returned from the battle of Camlann to Caerleon Castle. He had issued a decree that was to be spread throughout the land not taking into account territories or borders. It would be carried forth to all of the peoples of Briton without regard of their perceived ethnic group.

"I King Amhar Pendragon of Briton renounce mine title and all lands and fortifications that were governed by mine father King Arthur. The Knights of the Round Table shall be disbanded and will no longer watch over the Castles that were symbols of mine kingly power. We shall retire to the land of Galloway and live out our lives learning and practicing the ways of the Christian religion. It is mine hope that by setting all of mine former subjects free from mine rule that ye will find a new way of life. One where ye may all live together in peace loving each other as people of Briton, one land for all of us living together as one people."

Gwenhwyvar found Amhar looking out the window of Arthur's study.

"Amhar everyone is waiting," she said as she walked into the room. He turned and smiled at his mother.

"Do ye think that I hath done the right thing?" It was a question that he had wanted to ask her ever since announcing his plans upon his return to Caerleon. The Queen had had plenty of time to ponder Amhar's unusual solution to the pact of Saxons that united to resist King Arthur and his expansionist plans.

"Amhar, Arthur wanted nothing more than for unity throughout the land. He fought many battles throughout his life to achieve that goal. If ye can achieve the same thing by renouncing the crown and making the people masters of their own destiny, how could I judge thee harshly with a clear conscience?" She pondered for a few moments and then added.

"Thine sublime plan to further the cause of Christianity in order to banish magic from the land is a masterful plan worthy of thine Father. There is no doubt in mine mind that if Merlin told ye that the days of magic were coming to a close then so be it."

She walked up to him and took both of his hands.

"The strange religion that they practice proclaims love and equality for all. The more of their message that spreads through the land the less people will be willing to bow to the overlords that remain. Ye hath planted the seeds of their demise as surely as if ye had battled each one individually and won." Amhar nodded in relief that his mother had seen the subtle nuances of his plan.

"Now come along, we should begin our journey to Pen Rhionydd."

She led him out of the castle to the main courtyard. The Knights were there, but without their usual chainmail and family standards. The ladies of court, now mostly widows, were there with their children. All of the preparations to abandon Caerleon were complete. The caravan was ready to embark upon their journey to resettle in Galloway.

Amhar took his mount at the head of the troop. He turned to Sir Pellus and nodded to him.

"Join us as soon as ye are able," he said. Sir Pellus held up Excalibur so that Amhar and indeed everyone could look upon it one more time. There was silence. The symbol of the King of Briton would be mysteriously returned from whence it came. Nobody other that Amhar, Sirs Pellus, Guaen and Garethe and Queen Gwenhwyvar knew where the resting place for Excalibur would be.

Sir Pellus jolted his horse into a cantor. Everyone watched as he passed them by and rode through the open gate of Caerleon. Amhar did not want to dwell upon the moment. He held up his hand and motioned forward.

"Onward to Galloway and our new home, Pen Rhionydd."

Epilogue: The Return of Excalibur to Matrona

Sir Pellus had been diligent. Nobody had followed him. He had gone quite a long way out of his way to ensure that he was not tailed by anyone whatsoever. Now he stood on the shore of Llyn Callyfyrth. The surface was amazingly serene. He looked at the perfect blade of Excalibur. It was the same serene and perfectly reflective surface. For a moment he thought that it was made of still water. But of course it could not be; it was a heavy sword. Beautifully honed and carved, but a sword nevertheless.

Pellus felt a sense of loss even though he had not yet carried out his instructions. This sword, pulled from the rock by King Arthur at the age of seventeen had served his father before him, King Uther. But King Amhar would not use it. Amhar was no longer king. So why continue to carry the symbol of that office? Pellus did not understand why it had to be thrown into this particular lake, but he was not about to disobey the final order given by King Amhar to him in private, before renouncing his crown and making is proclamation to the people of the entire country.

With a regretful sigh he twisted himself so that he could throw the sword as far out into the lake as he was able. It flew from his hand and plunged into the surface of the lake and froze there. The tip of the blade and barely broken the surface of the water. It sent ripples outwards. Pellus gaped in wonder at the sight of the sword resting upright on the surface of the lake.

Then water rose around it and formed a shape. The shape became a beautiful woman who was holding the sword with both of her hands. That is why it was not falling into the water of the lake. Sir Pellus could hardly believe his eyes. The woman looked at him and smiled nodding as if understanding why the sword was being returned to her. He did not know how but he was somehow absolutely sure that Excalibur was now resting in the hands of its true owner.

He managed a nod and smile in reply. He was mesmerised by her beauty. And as quickly as she had appeared she dissolved into the water, Excalibur too. And they were gone. There was not even a ripple on the surface now to show that they had ever been there, the woman and the sword. Sir Pellus was left wondering if he had imagined the entire thing.

After a while he mounted his waiting horse and began the long ride to join his friends, his family in Galloway. He looked back a few times to the lake. It remained perfectly still and beautiful. Looking forward he could feel the sense of expectation rise within him. A new way of living was being decreed across the land. Would it result in the unity that Kings Uther, Arthur and Amhar had all wanted and worked for? More than anything else in his life before, he hoped that it would.

The End

Connect with Aenghus Chisholme

Visit my website on www.aenghuschisholme.com[1]

Works by Aenghus Chisholme
Merlin the Sorcerer AD491

King Arthur is facing a war with the murderous Saxon Lord Aelle over the artisan land of Anderidae. Unknown to him magical forces have conspired with Aelle to ensure Arthur's defeat.

Guinevere the Queen AD494

Queen Gwenhwyvar and Sorceress Morgan Le Fay pursue the stolen Excalibur to a magical labyrinth where it is guarded by powerful Minotaur.

Sir Gawain and the Green Knight AD499

An animated corpse has Sir Guaen in its sights. How can you kill something that is already dead?

Arthur the King AD517

Caught in an untenable situation King Arthur is manoeuvred into a battle he cannot possibly win.

Murder on the Mary Celeste

One by one, the passengers and crew aboard the merchant ship Mary Celeste are being picked-off by an unseen assassin.

Jack the Ripper: The murder of Madam Athalia

A clever young detective thinks that he can outwit the most cunning killer in the history of London.

The Best Things in Life Begin with the Letter B

Consumerism can lead to happiness, providing you know exactly what it is that will make you happy. Enjoy a tour of the material and immaterial world of the exclusive and the everyday.

Commissioned works

---

1. http://www.aenghuschisholme.com

I am available to write something for you; fiction or non-fiction. Contact me through my website and tell me what you have in mind.